Diary of a Teenage Fairy Godmother

BOOK 1

Kathleen Baldwin
AND
Andrea Sisco

INK LION BOOKS

Illustrations by Kathleen Baldwin

The illustrations in this book are a primarily digital composites. Many royalty free stock images were purchased and used for these works of art. We would like to thank the brilliant stock artists and give them proper credit.

Image Credits:

Dedication

To Brett, my hero and soulmate, who always believed. To Frisco Professional Writers: Bill, Carole, Patience, Rae Dawn, Susan and Wayne. Thank you for meeting every Tuesday and critiquing this story until it sang like a butterfly. To Gretchen for your insights, your editing, and for primroses; to Nina for clarity and simplicity; and to Donna for joyful music and thematic water.

Thank you all for your unfailing encouragement and support. Friends like you are hard to find.

And to Andrea's granddaughters Caroline, Greer and Ali.
This story was written with you in mind.
We hope you enjoy it.
Love to you all.

Fairy Godmother Training Manual

Directive 1

A Fairy Godmother is a guardian and a warrior, not a giggling pixie in a pink tutu. It is no longer enough for a guardian to wave her wand and give a girl a new dress. This seldom solves the problem. A wise Fairy Godmother will carefully observe Cinderella's granddaughters, her offspring, and determine the girl's *needs*, rather than her *wants*.

– Beyond Ball Gowns: The Definitive Training Manual for
Today's Fairy Godmother
by Gryndelyn Myrddin
Great-granddaughter of Merlin
Headmistress, North American Fairy Academy

The Music of the Mission

Waiting.

Watching.

Lilliana Skye stood in the upper branches of a tall oak overlooking Lake Elm High and peered through the leaves. She listened closely to the strange music of human emotions as students shuffled through the front doors of the small Texas high school. Some of them emitted low, plodding oboe sounds with sad notes of doubt and aloneness. Others pulsated like wild offbeat snare drums.

Her first mission. She'd studied and prepared for this day her whole life. Soon, very soon, she would walk among the humans. Her own inner music soared up, whistling excitedly, flying out of harmony with the trees and wind. With a deep breath Lilliana calmed herself and tucked her training manual securely under her arm. Any minute now her orders would arrive.

She tugged down the short, uncomfortably tight skirt—a perfect disguise. A new dress may not solve any problems, but it sure was fun. Lilliana had duplicated the outfit, every last detail, from page thirty-eight of the latest *Teen Vogue*. She was totally prepared. Ready. Nothing to worry about. After all, these humans were just teenagers, like her. Well, except, none of them had a pair of five-foot-seven-inch wings sprouting out of their backs. Lilliana retracted hers.

Just then a bright red cardinal burst through the thick canopy of the old oak tree. He swooped down and dropped a small scroll into her hands.

"Thank you, Napoleon."

The feathered messenger landed on Lilliana's shoulder as she unrolled the parchment and read "School records altered. Proceed." Gryndelyn's official seal glowed on the bottom. As soon as Lilliana finished reading it, the message disintegrated into dandelion fluff and scattered on the breeze.

Suddenly, thunder shook the air. Except there wasn't a cloud in the sky.

Lilliana's attention snapped back to the school. The deep rumble blotted out the noise of the students. She searched for the source of the explosive roar. There! The loud, angry vibrations came from a girl in army boots and a camouflage T-shirt, the one who resembled a third world dictator stomping up the school steps.

Lilliana drew in a quick breath. She knew that girl. She'd memorized that profile, and she recognized the wild unruly hair, hair the color of deep red autumn leaves. It was Cinderella's offspring, Lilliana's C.O., the girl she was supposed to help. It was Jessica Harrison whose soul thundered as violent and black as a winter storm.

Yet, beneath Jess's throbbing drums of rage, Lilliana heard the unmistakable strains of anguish—taut strings of grief. Grief that resonated so sharply it hurt to listen.

INTRUDER ALERT

10:17 a.m.

For the third time that week, Jessica Harrison sat in Principal Jamison's office listening to him lecture about how he expected her to treat other students courteously and stop undermining his staff. Apparently, this time he thought Jess shouldn't have told her history teacher to *get her facts right or find another line of work*.

"Unacceptable behavior," Mr. Jamison complained. "Insensitive. You made poor Ms. Hargrove cry." Blah, blah, blah…

Jess growled low in her throat. It wasn't her fault Ms. Hargrove was menopausal and needed a refresher course on the events leading up to World War II.

Jamison sighed. "A little diplomacy, Jess, that's all I'm asking."

"Whatever," she conceded.

"Most girls in your situation would be depressed. Depression would be perfectly normal, but you…"

Depression? Didn't he know the black hole of depression yawned its mouth at her every morning, threatening to suck her into its dark abyss? Jess would never give in to it.

Never!

She would scratch everyone's eyes out if she had to, but she would stand out here in the land of the living and fight. Right here, right now, where she could do something. Change things. Protect the family she had left from the rotten people in this rotten world.

5

And if she couldn't protect them, she'd—

Jamison interrupted her thoughts, saying something that made her want to punch a hole in the universe. "I'd like you to meet with the school psychologist to discuss your anger issues."

"Issues?" Jess sputtered. What did he know about her *issues*? And what right did he have to bring them up?

He leaned forward with so much syrupy sympathy contorting his features that it made Jess want to puke. "After all—" He hesitated. "It's been almost a year since, uh, since your brother's unfortunate accident and—"

"Unfortunate accident!" It was all Jess could do not to hurl her backpack against the wall and shatter all of Jamison's neatly framed diplomas. Instead, she jumped to her feet. "Is that what you call it? Are you referring to the night Ryan decided to show off for his stupid girlfriend? The night he *accidentally* blew through a red light going a hundred and twenty miles an hour? The one where he lost control and cremated himself and her? You mean the *unfortunate accident* that has my parents walking around like numbed-up robots? That one? Really? Because you know what I call it? I call it the night my world exploded!"

Jess slammed her palm against his desk so hard the oak should've split. She clamped her lips together, letting the pain in her hand fuel her. "And if you think I want to talk about *that* with some second-rate school shrink, then you're the crazy one."

Jess stormed out of the principal's office. Let him suspend her. She didn't care. High school was a gigantic waste of time anyway. She was only a sophomore, but she'd taken the SAT early and scored higher than anyone in the senior class. Jamison could expel her right now for all she cared. She wasn't going to put up with him butting into her *issues*.

Jess shoved past a group of kids milling by the drinking fountain. Other students hustled out of the way as she stomped down the hallway.

Everyone at Lake Elm High knew her well enough to know

they'd better move. *Respectfully cautious*. That's what they were, and that was the way Jess wanted it.

But then she saw something that made the volcano churning inside her turn into an iceberg.

A ghost.

A ghost opening Ryan's locker.

Memories of that night slammed into Jess—police pounding at the door at two in the morning, red and blue lights churning across the dark lawn. Once again, as in countless nightmares, Jess felt the searing heat of flames. Flames she'd never actually seen. Flames that had consumed her brother. And now, standing at Ryan's locker was the girl who got him killed.

Cheryl.

Except Cheryl was dead, and there's no such thing as ghosts. There's a scientific explanation for everything. Action. Reaction. Cause and effect. *Physics*, that's what Jess believed in. Not ghosts.

So, why was one opening her dead brother's locker? A ghost who looked exactly like his dead girlfriend? *Same* skinny body. *Same* dark hair, pinned up loose and messy, half of it falling over her ears in the *same* stupid attempt to look sexy. It was Cheryl. Only…

It couldn't be. Jess marched over and yanked the interloper's arm. "What are you doing in my brother's locker?"

Just like Cheryl, the girl had dangerous green eyes. They widened. "Jess?" she gasped.

Jess jerked her hand back as if she'd been burned. "How do you know my name?"

Ghost girl caught the corner of her lip in her teeth and gnawed on it like someone hunting for a plausible lie. Jess closed the distance and bore down on her with all the diplomacy of an irate drill sergeant. "I *said* how do you know my name?"

The girl edged back and bumped into the locker. "I, um, I was sent…" Finally she blurted, "I'm here to help you."

Jamison's shrink? Jess stepped back and shook her head. No, it couldn't be. She was way too young. A student counselor? No, this girl looked clueless. So who was she? And why had Jamison sent her?

It didn't matter. "Tell Jamison to butt out."

"Jamison?" The girl blinked, pretending she didn't know the principal.

"Nice try," Jess snapped. "I don't care who you are or why you're here." She pushed the intruder aside and slammed Ryan's locker shut. "Stay out of my brother's locker!"

"But…" Cheryl's *clone* held up a newly printed schedule and pointed to a number in the upper left corner. "This is the locker they assigned me."

Jess scanned the schedule. Not only had the idiots in the office given away Ryan's locker, but half of the new girl's classes were the same as Jess's. Worst of all she'd be in Biology with—

Oh no.

This was not good—not good at all. Red-alert sirens screamed in Jess's head. "Go ask for a different locker," Jess shouted. "And stay away from my brother."

"Your brother? You mean his locker?"

Jess didn't wait around to explain. She elbowed her way through the crowd. Her combat boots thudded against the tile as she double-timed it down the hall to recruit backup.

Fairy Godmother Training Manual

Directive 2

Be tolerant of humans. Don't be alarmed if they exhibit strange or abrasive behaviors. You must endeavor to understand them. Adapt to your C.O.'s culture so that you may truly be of assistance.

—Gryndelyn Myrddin

Duet

"Wait!" Lilliana hurried after Jess.

The first day of her mission, the first hour, and she'd already messed up. Rushing to catch Jess, she dashed around a cluster of students. The hallway was packed. A crowd of football players were teasing each other, laughing and throwing things. She tried to squeeze past, but one of them stepped out and blocked her path. She couldn't see anything past the blue football jersey covering his broad chest.

"If I were you, I'd let Jess go," he said.

She was losing sight of her C.O. Lilliana pushed against the roadblock, but he didn't budge. Annoyed, she glanced up and listened. She expected his emotional music to sound like a typical conceited athlete, brassy trumpets and marching drums. But, no. He was cello to her violin.

Instantly, Lilliana's inner music tuned to his. She stopped trying to shove past him. Except her hands were still pressed against his muscled chest. She quickly withdrew them.

"Trust me," he said. "Give her time to cool down."

Trust him.

The timbre of his voice drew her eyes upward to the strong lines of his jaw and his mouth the color of summer plums. Lilliana blinked, unable to remember why she was running or who she was running after. Suddenly, she couldn't think about anything except his melting brown eyes and the wry smile on his lips. She scarcely remembered to breathe.

The music they made together intoxicated her. "Time?" she asked.

"Yeah," his smile broadened. "When my sister gets mad, it's best to give her some space so she'll—"

"Sister?" Her inner violin screeched to a halt. "Then you're…"

Light danced in his eyes. His cello strings rippled with infectious amusement. "Jess's brother, Jake."

"Of course." She connected his face to a photo in Jess's dossier. This was the other brother, the one between Jess and her oldest brother, who had died. Lilliana had dismissed Jake as unimportant. "Right. I mean I've seen your picture. It's just that, in person, I didn't expect…"

She didn't expect she'd want to rest her head against his chest and listen as his soul played music so rich and deep that it flowed through her like an achingly beautiful river.

Focus.

She had to focus on the mission. Lilliana swallowed hard and stepped back.

ATTACK FORMATION

.Jess charged down the crowded hallway past dozens of familiar faces. None of them mattered. She had to find the only two people in this whole dumb school that she could trust, the only two she could count on. Jess knew exactly where they'd be—huddled at Cai's locker. Cai and Maggie were reliable that way, predictable constants in Jess's ugly sea of change.

They were her friends, and not just because she'd known them since kindergarten. In a school where most of the girls only cared about what kind of mascara would stay on the longest or which boy was on the *Hot Ten List* that week, Cai and Maggie stood out. They had objectives. Goals.

Cai was going to be a famous reporter someday. She worked on the school paper, and her ability to uncover a story had already gotten some of her articles printed in the *Dallas Morning News*.

Maggie had an uncanny way with animals, and despite severe dyslexia she was studying her butt off so she could get through school and become a veterinarian.

Jess pulled out her cell phone to text them. Yeah, yeah, cell phone use was prohibited in school, but Jess had rigged the barrel of a ballpoint pen with a remote smart-microphone that converted voice to text.

"Urgent! Get to Bio ASAP. New girl is a Cheryl clone." Jess clicked send and rushed into the empty Biology room.

She headed straight for Mrs. Dawson's seating chart and frowned. There was only one seat open in the whole class—and

12

that one was at Jess's lab table. She groaned and raked her hands through her hair.

"What's wrong, Gadget?"

Jess jumped back from the teacher's lectern. Mark Winslow sauntered in.

"Nothing!" Her cheeks got hot, which meant her face was probably as red as her stupid hair. "Stop calling me Gadget," she said for the fiftieth time. Just because Mark was Jake's best friend didn't mean he had the right to use her brother's nickname for her.

"Okay, General." He gave her a lazy salute. "What's got you spitting hornets today?"

Before she could stop herself, the answer tumbled out. "There's a new girl coming, and I have to protect Jake."

"Protect him?" The corner of Mark's mouth quirked up, and his eyebrows arched so that he managed to look questioning and amused all at the same time.

"This isn't funny! She's just like *Cheryl*."

"Oh." His face immediately sobered.

She nodded, satisfied that he understood the seriousness. "I have to keep her away from him. But *I* don't want to sit with her either."

"Listen Jess, about Cheryl. I know you think the accident was her fault, but—"

"No!" Jess smacked her hand against the lectern. "I *know* it was." The sound echoed around the room. Jess'd had enough. She didn't want anyone else to bring up Ryan's *accident* today. "Either help me figure out this seating problem or leave me alone."

Mark sighed and turned his attention to Mrs. Dawson's seating chart. "Okay, how about this?" He grabbed the dry erase marker, rubbed out his own name and quickly scrawled it into the open slot beside Jess. "Think you could handle having me for a lab partner the rest of the semester?"

Jess swallowed. He'd do that? For her? She didn't dare look at Mark because telltale heat had rushed back into her cheeks.

13

"Yeah," she answered a little too breathlessly. "Except that leaves Jake without a partner. Worst case scenario. I don't want her sitting with him."

"Well, then we'll just move—"

Cai and Maggie rushed through the doorway.

"There's a new girl? Really?" Cai tossed her backpack onto a lab table. "What's she like?"

"Trouble."

"Why? What'd she do? What kind of trouble?" Typical Cai, firing too many questions all at once.

"I told you." Jess didn't have time for an inquisition. "She's exactly like Cheryl."

Cai considered. "How? Looks like her? Acts like her?"

"Both," Jess answered tersely.

Maggie tilted her head. White-blonde curls fell to one side like a lopsided halo as she zeroed in on Jess. Dyslexia made it difficult for Maggie to decipher letters, but when it came to people, she had a gift. Maggie could see straight through to the bones. Sometimes it was annoying. Like right now. Jess felt like a bug on a pin.

"What?" Jess demanded. She needed their help, and she needed it now.

Instead of pitching in, Maggie studied her more intently.

"You don't get it!" Jess tried to calmly explain as she smoothed her hand over the seating chart. "She was getting into Ryan's locker, and I just know this girl will dig her claws into Jake." She glared at them. "We HAVE to do something!"

Shouting never seemed to faze Cai. She could focus no matter what, and over the last year she'd developed a fairly bulletproof attitude toward Jess. "Okay. We get it. You're worried. What do you want us to do?"

That was better. *Cooperation.* Jess nodded. "We've got to position her as far away from Jake as possible."

Maggie perched on the corner of Mrs. Dawson's cluttered desk. "What makes you think Jake would fall for a girl like

Cheryl?"

"Because Ryan did." Jess didn't bother to look up from the seating chart.

"Except Jake isn't like Ryan." Maggie slid off the desk and headed down the aisle to her table. "So you can stop worrying."

Mark nudged Jess. "She's right."

"I'm *not* worrying. This is a preemptive strike."

Students meandered into the classroom, which meant time was running out. Jess lowered her voice. "I've got it. Maggie can be Jake's lab partner and Cai can sit with the new girl."

"No!" Maggie dropped her backpack and spun around. "I need Cai to read the assignments to me."

"She can catch you up after school."

"No." Cai shook her head. "You're forgetting Maggie handles all the dissecting and gross stuff." She shivered. "If I had to touch cow eyeballs or those ishy goat brains, I'd probably pass out."

She wouldn't. Cai was tougher than that, but Jess didn't have time to argue. "Fine!" she huffed. "We'll put the new girl with Everett Smythe."

Mark coughed as if he'd swallowed down the wrong pipe.

"You can't! That would be inhumane." Cai snatched the seating chart. "Seriously, Jess. Everett has a psychological block against oral hygiene—his breath is toxic. Really. The school should issue his lab partner one of those big yellow biohazard suits. Dawson only put Ashley B. with him because she knows Ashley's had so many sinus infections she can't smell a thing."

"Well, then who's going to sit with the new girl?" Jess grabbed the chart back.

"Lab stations, people! Now!" Mrs. Dawson bustled into the room clapping her hands to get their attention. "We have a full schedule today." She charged up to the lectern, her lab coattails flapping. "What are you four amoebas up to?"

Everyone but Jess and Mark scattered to their seats. "Helping," Jess asserted.

"Ri-i-ight." Dawson peered over the top of her bifocals, her voice dripping with skepticism. "If I need help, I'll ask for it." She shooed them away and plopped down a stack of handouts.

Jess stood her ground. "But there's a new girl, and I thought if—"

Mrs. Dawson interrupted her with a half-laugh half-snort. "You're not exactly the welcome committee type, Harrison. Now if you would kindly allow me to run my own classroom." She held out her hand, expecting Jess to hand over the seating chart.

Before Dawson took it away, Jess managed to smear her thumb across Mark's name so that the seat next to her remained open. If she had to give up sitting with Mark to save her brother, then that's what she'd do. She trudged to her lab station in the back of the room, scuffing her combat boots.

Not that sitting with Mark would've made any difference. He didn't think of her as anything other than *Gadget*, Jake's weird little sister. And why would he? She tugged on the cuffs of her camouflage jacket. Half the girls in school had a crush on him. She didn't stand a chance. Besides, Jess could do the social math. She wasn't girlfriend material.

Yet there he was sitting at her lab table giving her that lopsided grin that always made her stomach feel like she was parachuting out of a jet. She took a deep breath and slid in beside him. "You're off the hook. I erased your name."

He didn't move.

"You can go back to your old table."

Mark had an odd stubborn glint in his eyes. He crossed his arms. "And if I don't?"

"Come on. You have to!" Jess ordered, panic rising. "Jake's gonna be here any minute. If there's an empty seat at his table, you know that's where Cheryl's clone will end up." She grabbed Mark's arm. Her fingers slipped through the loose knit of his sweater and landed on rock hard muscles as she shoved. "Hurry!"

He didn't budge, not even when the warning bell rang.

Desperate, Jess let go. "Please."

Mark's rigid shoulders slumped. He shook his head and gathered his books. "You know, Genius Girl, sometimes you just don't have a clue."

Directive 3

Do not allow your personal feelings to interfere with your task. Cinderella's heirs often start out as ugly ducklings. However, they mature into swans and often end up holding positions of power and influence among mortals. Therefore, your mission is of vital importance to the future of both our realms.

– Gryndelyn Myrddin

Underground Jazz

Lilliana was so busy trying to clear the music in her head that she didn't quite catch what Jake was saying.

"What class do you have next?" he asked again.

"Biology." Lilliana showed him her schedule.

He glanced down the hall in the direction his sister had disappeared. "Me, too," he said quietly. "I'll show you the way."

As she walked beside him, Lilliana wondered how Jake and Jess could be so different. As brother and sister, they'd shared the same painful trauma, and yet Jake resonated with the calm strength of a deep lake, while Jess crackled with pent-up lightning.

Three guys stopped him in the hall, joking loudly, and glancing sidelong at Lilliana as they asked about the upcoming football game. She stood back and watched as he spoke with them. That's when she first detected his sorrow. It was a low, sad melody underpinning the warmth he felt toward his friends. How very strange, she thought, that she heard it now, in the midst of their rowdy camaraderie.

Curious, Lilliana drifted deeper into his inner music. Too deep. Images burst into her mind. Startling flashes of his dead brother. Worse! Jake had a premonition of his own death, secret visions of himself, dying, bloody, and pale. Fading away.

How could he think such things? He was here. Alive!

Then, with morbid clarity, she understood that his deep feelings toward his friends were because he accepted his own inevitable fate—death. This moment was all Jake Harrison felt certain of. He believed he was temporary.

Mortal.

Lilliana nearly forgot to breathe. In a scorching gasp, air rushed into her lungs. He was mortal. Fatally human. He *would* die. Of course he would. But not so young as he envisioned. Not so soon. Surely!

"Not on my watch," she vowed. The instant she said it, a powerful vibration whooshed through her, binding them. A fairy's vow. She'd scarcely moved her lips, and yet her words seemed to shake the air around them. Jake turned as if he'd felt it, too.

A rash promise. Could she really keep him from dying? But there was no taking it back now. A fairy's vow wove itself into the fabric of both their worlds.

Even so, Jake's pale, bloody visions remained. Lilliana backed away from him, trying to clear her head, desperate to escape his visions of death. Fairies didn't think of such things. They lived hundreds and hundreds of years. At least, most did. Her mother hadn't. She'd been only slightly older than Lilliana when she died.

Lilliana wanted to cover her ears and hide from the sound of her own dark truths spilling out. She needed to get away from Jake's music. It upset her far worse than Jess's angry drums ever could.

The bell rang, jangling her already frazzled senses. Lilliana turned and left.

"Wait up!" he called.

But she didn't. She strode swiftly down the hall and turned the corner, squeezing past clumps of gossiping students as she frantically hunted for her class. The room numbers turned into indecipherable blurs as she hurried past. Humans were so confusing. So temporary. As she fought to regain control of her tumbling heart, she got to the end of the hall and realized she must've missed the Biology room.

Dead end.

Jake caught up to her. "This way," he said quietly, as if he understood her inner turmoil, and gently led her back to their classroom.

To calm herself, Lilliana tried to block all the noise, especially Jake's soul sounds. She tried to blend them all together until the wild emotions became nothing more than background noise, like the buzzing and humming of a beehive. The moment they walked into Biology, the bell above the door rang so loudly it shattered her concentration.

She would never get used to school bells. As deafening as the bell was, it was nothing compared to the mind-shattering silent screech that blasted from Jess when she saw Lilliana standing in the doorway beside Jake.

STRATEGIC DEFENCE

Jake showed up just as the bell rang. So did Cheryl's clone. They stood in the doorway.

Together.

Jess wanted to scream so loud that everybody's toenails would shoot off—explode right through the ends of their shoes, like when people got hit by lightning. But she didn't. Instead she gritted her teeth and put a cork in it. Kids sitting near her table might've heard a low growl, but that's all. On the other hand, if this day got one inch worse, Jess figured her cork would most likely blow all the way to Jupiter.

"Nice of you to join us." Mrs. Dawson frowned at the two tardy students. Dawson's way of saying, *Don't ever be late again or I'll have your head on a spike.* "Listen up, everyone, we have a new girl. This is Lily Skye."

"Lilliana," The Clone corrected. "Lil-lē-yä'-na," she said again, emphasizing each vowel and slowly enunciating every syllable as if Mrs. Dawson needed a remedial course in name reading.

Jess snapped to attention. Nobody except Jess had ever dared correct Deadly Dawson. If your name was Suzie and Mrs. Dawson pronounced it Sacajawea most kids would've just said, "Thank you," and checked into changing their birth certificates.

Either the new girl had guts or she was just plain stupid. Jess opted for the stupid theory. Lilliana looked like a dumb model straight out of *Cosmo Girl* in her floofy skirt, ridiculous leggings, and those absurd spike-heeled boots, and *maybe* if Jake wasn't staring at Lil-lē-yä'-na like a lovesick groupie, then *maybe*, just *maybe*, Jess might have respected her. A tiny bit.

As it was, Jess felt an admittedly childish sense of satisfaction knowing that now Cheryl's clone would be permanently situated on Dawson's bad side.

"Very well, Miss Skye," Dawson said sarcastically. "Welcome to Lake Elm High. I suppose we need to find a seat for you." The pinched expression behind Dawson's thinly drawn lips meant she was sharpening her fangs, devising a proper payback. She pivoted in Everett Smythe's direction. "Do we have a volun—"

Hands shot into the air. Boy hands. Lots of boy hands.

Jess sighed and hoisted her palm to half-mast, resigned to the sacrifice she must make to protect her brother. If Dawson wanted to teach the new girl a lesson, she would seat her next to stinky Everett or put her with prickly Jess, the *Ultimate Unwelcome Committee*. No contest. She'd pick Jess. A perfect punishment.

Mrs. Dawson glanced around the room and zeroed in on Jess's uplifted hand. For a second or two, she looked perplexed. Then she glanced at Jake and Lilliana in the door, squinted at the seating chart, and the corner of her lip curled wickedly. "Hands down, people." She nodded to Jess. "Too bad you erased this, Miss Harrison. It was a good idea. Jake, what do you say we make you lab partners with Miss Skye?"

Jake's mouth bobbed open enthusiastically. But before he could say anything, Jess answered for him. "No!" she burst out.

The odd thing was, Lilliana did the same thing.

They turned to each other in surprise. Jess dropped back onto her stool wondering why The Clone would object to sitting with Jake? What could Lilliana possibly have against him? Everybody liked Jake. Maybe it was that warning Jess had given her.

A quick glimpse of Jake's face looking closed off and shut down gave Jess a twinge of guilt. A small pinchy sting of remorse. She shrugged it off. It was for his own good. He'd get over it. The alternative was unacceptable. He wouldn't survive the kind of damage a girl like that could do if she got her manicured hooks into him.

Deadly Dawson, having figured out how to make everyone suitably unhappy, wore a self-satisfied smirk as she directed her pencil point at Mark. "Winslow, think you can handle Miss Harrison, our resident firecracker, as your lab partner?"

Jess bristled. *Firecracker?* Teachers weren't allowed to do that, call names. But before Jess could think up a suitable response that wouldn't land her back in Jamison's office, Mark piped up.

"Dunno." He shook his head thoughtfully. "I left my asbestos gloves at home."

They all laughed, including Mrs. Dawson. It wasn't funny— not really. Not even when Jordan Dietz added something about keeping the fire extinguisher handy. *Ha ha.* Jess's cork felt dangerously close to popping off.

"All right, everyone, settle down." Dawson clapped her hands, bringing the class to order, and waved Mark forward. "Move your things to Jess's table. Oh, and Winslow, see if you can keep her from doing her other homework during my lecture."

Fairy Godmother Training Manual

Directive 4

Study your surroundings. Familiarize yourself with the flora and fauna in your C.O.'s environment. Acquaint yourself with the local trees, indigenous flowers, as well as vegetables. You never know when a beanstalk or a pumpkin might come in handy. Make allies with the fauna, especially smaller creatures: birds, toads, mice and the like. They will prove extremely useful in difficult situations.

– Gryndelyn Myrddin

Way Down Upon the Swampy River

Lilliana sat stone-like at the lab table. She struggled to close her mind to Jake's music, his scent, and something else about him that was almost electrical. The tiny hairs on her arm mutinously tickled up and leaned in his direction. She concentrated harder, but he sat only inches away, and his warmth radiated through the fabric of her sleeve. She could literally feel him breathing. Although, now that she considered it, his breathing pattern sounded odd, as if he was trying to hold his breath, almost as if he was as uncomfortable as she was. Curious, Lilliana risked opening her mind, just a tiny bit, for one quick peek.

Quiet.

Surprised, she glanced sideways at him. Jake sat as shuttered and locked away as she had meant to do. Muffled and faint, his music seemed to have receded deep into the earth. But when Lilliana hunted, she found it—a restless, pacing tune like an agitated wolf circling in his den.

Jake turned wary eyes to her.

Immediately she wished she hadn't been so rude and blurted out that she didn't want to sit with him. She wished she could take it back. As she stared at him, Jake's music changed timbre. It built, growing louder, more certain, washing over her with the force of a riptide that would surely sweep her away.

Lilliana struggled to refocus her attention. Ten years in fairy godmother school, top of her class, and still, nothing in her training had prepared her for this. She had a mission to fulfill. *Focus*!

What on earth was the teacher saying?

Mrs. Dawson clicked a PowerPoint slide onto a big screen in front of the class. "This is *Rana catesbeiana*," she announced in a voice that reminded Lilliana of a harried wasp queen. "Better known as the American bullfrog."

A photo popped up of a large frog squatting on a clump of muddy swamp debris. His vocal sac bulged, creating a giant bubble under his chin.

Lilliana relaxed a little. She liked frogs. She understood them. Of course, she didn't know this one personally, but obviously he was a large male from one of the southern frog clans. The brilliant yellow of his throat meant the photo had been taken in the spring while he was crooning for a mate. No doubt he was singing an amusing ditty about his phenomenal ability to snag three mosquitoes with a single slurp of his tongue. She sighed. At last, an ally.

Another slide flashed onto the screen.

Lilliana gasped and reeled back, scrambling away from the image so fast she nearly fell off her stool. Someone had cut a frog open, slit it stem to stern, peeled back the skin and pinned it out, exposing its entrails.

"You okay?" Jake whispered beside her ear, sending jolts of electricity zinging down to her already shocked toes. Lilliana shook her head, covered her eyes, and stifled a moan while Mrs. Dawson pointed out various body parts.

The lecture continued. Fortunately, the next slide was a simple line drawing of a frog's reproductive organs, and the next one diagramed the amphibian circulatory process. Lilliana's breathing almost returned to normal, except then Mrs. Dawson flipped on the main lights and said, "Go over these procedures with your lab partner for tomorrow's lab."

Procedures? Did that mean they expected her to…

"Read chapter thirty-two." Mrs. Dawson held up a stack of handouts. "And study these diagrams so you'll know exactly what to do in tomorrow's dissection. You're not just cutting open a frog, people. I expect surgical precision."

Lilliana covered her mouth to hold back her cry of dismay. Fairy godmother training had definitely *not* prepared her for this.

❦DEPLOY TROOPS

❦**D**espite Jess's efforts to save her brother, he was falling prey to the new girl's tactics. She watched The Clone manipulating Jake, winding him around her little finger like a piece of waxed dental floss. Subtle. Crafty. The girl had serious vamp skills. Jess wished she had installed a blast shield that would zoom up from the floor to block Lilliana from Jake.

Just look at the two of them. They stood way too close, almost nose to nose, and Lilliana wore a girly, flustered look guaranteed to unhinge any male. It looked like she was apologizing for something. Whatever it was, like a complete moron, Jake was falling for it.

Right about now, a blowgun armed with tranquilizer darts would come in handy. Jess wanted to shout at him *Don't be stupid!*

But Jake didn't turn. Instead Lilliana whipped around and gaped in Jess's direction. Her little-lost-girl face crumpled as if to say she was sorry. For a split second, Jess actually thought Lilliana might really mean it. Then she remembered who she was up against. A Cheryl clone. Apology not accepted!

Time to put a stop to this farce. Jess slid off her stool. She planned to go over and stomp on the new girl's touching performance, but Mark caught hold of her sleeve. "Hang on, Gadget. I wouldn't crash that party if I were you." He nodded in Jake's direction. "You'll just make it worse. You know, like Romeo and Juliet."

Jess groaned.

Lilliana and Jake were back at it, making cow eyes at one another. They stood so close Jake could probably taste Lilliana's words on his lips as she choked out, "I can't."

"Can't what?" Jake's voice caught awkwardly.

Yeah, *can't what?* Jess wondered. You can't turn my brother's heart inside out? Can't steal his sanity? Can't make him jump through burning hoops? Race his car at lethal speeds through red lights?

Lilliana inched away from Jake. Her gaze darted frantically over at Jess and then back to nearby objects until she finally grabbed hold of the frog diagrams. "Can't... um...can't do this to a frog."

"It's okay." Jake tried to close the distance between them, but she kept backing up. "You don't have to. I'll—"

Thankfully, the bell rang.

"I'm sorry." Lilliana grabbed her backpack, hugging it as if it were a life preserver, and edged past Jake, brushing so close that her wispy skirt snagged briefly on the rough fabric of his jeans. "I shouldn't. I can't."

Was she talking about cutting up frogs? Or messing with Jake's heart? Jess couldn't tell.

Lilliana hurried away, leaving him standing there looking like a shell-shocked soldier. "Wait!" Jake tossed his bag over his shoulder and bolted out the door after her.

Jess stomped her foot. She had to stop him.

"Leave him alone." Mark caught her arm. "He's a big boy."

Jess wrenched free. "Yeah, and big boys do really stupid stuff." She crammed her homework into her bag. "Because of girls." She slung her backpack over her shoulder. "Especially girls like her."

"Jess—"

She heard Mark's exasperated sigh as she marched off. She didn't care. He wasn't helping. She could tell he was going to give her a lecture, and she'd had more than enough lectures for one day.

What Jess needed now were allies.

"Wait up!" she called to Maggie and Cai.

They met up in the hall, forming a tight circle beside the drinking fountain. "We have to DO something!" Jess ordered. "She's already sinking her blood-sucking talons into him."

"You mean fangs," Maggie corrected.

Jess gritted her teeth, trying to hold down the panic rising in her gut. "I *meeean*, she's already hypnotized my brother and turned him into a brainless zombie."

Maggie shook her head. "Give Jake some credit. He's one of the smartest guys I know. He wouldn't fall for a girl like Cheryl."

"Yeah, well, don't look now, but witness for the prosecution says he just galloped after Cheryl's clone like a lovesick puppy." Jess pointed down the hall. "She's already turned him into a manipulatable pile of mush."

"Speaking of mush. What about you?" Cai asked cryptically.

Jess scrunched up her nose. "What?"

"Sitting with Mark Winslow?" Cai prompted. "Why aren't *you* melting into a puddle of happy goo? You've been crushing on him since forever."

Maggie leaned in excitedly. "Yeah, and he's gonna be your lab partner for the rest of the semester."

"Tune in, people!" Jess glared at them. "We're talking about my brother here. The *only* brother I have left! We have to do something about that, that, future accident."

"Like what?" Cai frowned. "Gag her, bag her, and stuff her in a supply closet?"

"Very funny." Jess twisted her features into a sarcastic glare so Cai would know exactly how well her little jest went over.

Maggie sighed. "Relax, Jess. Lilliana isn't like Cheryl. Actually, she seems kinda sad to me. Maybe she's had a really hard life." She paused as if she expected Jess to feel sorry for the new girl.

Jess torqued her mouth into an even more skeptical frown.

"Okay," Maggie shrugged. "I admit there's something unusual about her—something I can't quite figure out. And yeah, she has a strange accent. But so what? Maybe she's foreign. Maybe she's royalty or something."

"You've been watching Disney Channel again."

"No. I'm just admitting there's something a little different about her, but I still don't think she's like Cheryl," Maggie insisted. "Think about it. She's a new girl in a strange school with no friends. How would you feel if—"

"No more lectures!" Jess shifted her book bag and jammed her fists onto her hips. "Are you gonna help me or not?"

Neither one of them answered right away. Cai grabbed a couple of cashews out of a Ziploc bag and chewed nervously. "I don't know." She shook her head. "You saw Jake. He likes her, and he's as stubborn as you are. If you butt in, it could make him like her even more."

"Not if I'm careful. Listen, I saw her schedule. She has study hall next with you." Jess kicked the toe of her boot against Cai's shoe. "So, before class, run by Ms. Cartwright's office and tell her you'd like to write a story on Lilliana for the school paper, you know, a human interest piece introducing the new student. Then, Cartwright'll give you permission to do the interview during study hall. And then—" Jess stopped because Cai was already shaking her head.

"Uh-uh. Absolutely not. Nope." Cai waved stop-sign hands. "I see what you want. You want me to dig up something that'll make her look bad."

"No!" Jess backed up, indignant. "I just want intel. Data. Facts. I need to know who I'm dealing with here."

Maggie chuckled. "It's not like she's a spy or something, Jess."

Jess wheeled on her. "I wish she were. That would make things so much easier."

Cai swallowed another cashew. "Doesn't matter. I have a reputation to maintain. I don't do fluff pieces. No human-interest stories. Only hard-hitting news."

Jess bit her lip, glanced up, and counted the stained ceiling tiles in the hall in an attempt to keep her temper in check. "This is *Lake Elm*, Cai. How many hard-hitting stories are there?"

Cai's brows pinched together. "Well, two week ago, I broke the story about Kip Estler selling black-market test keys. And have you forgotten who got the inside scoop on the locker thefts a month ago?"

Maggie chimed in. "Yeah, and last semester she uncovered all that stuff about Mr. Orekson and the illegal bookie racket he was running during shop class."

"Yeah, yeah, okay. I get it. Diane Sawyer move over. You're a hard-hitting reporter, Cai. This assignment is beneath you. So I'm asking as a friend, do it as a favor to me?"

Cai dropped the rest of her cashews back into her Ziploc bag as if they'd suddenly lost flavor. "All right." She sighed heavily and nodded. "For you."

Good. Relieved, Jess got a quick drink from the water fountain and set off for AP Geometry. She could count on Cai to dig up *something* on Lilliana. Knowledge is power. She smiled for the first time that day.

Fairy Godmother Training Manual

Directive 5

Get to know the people in your Cinderella's life, her family, friends, and enemies. Study them well. Get close. Make friends with them, and in return they will provide you with valuable insights into your C.O.'s true nature.

—Gryndelyn Myrddin

Mademoiselle Butterfly

Lilliana hurried out of Biology with Jake chasing after her. She wove between students, hiding in the middle of the crowded hallway. Still, he followed. She glanced over her shoulder and ran smack into an enormous boy. At least, she assumed it was a boy, big as a grizzly and rumbling like a hungry rhino. She glimpsed a stained white T-shirt before whoever it was roughly shoved her into an alcove between the banks of lockers.

Lilliana stumbled like a wobbly top toward a glass door marked emergency exit. She caught her balance before smashing into the bar that would've set off every alarm in the building. On the other side of the door, the alluring sight of sunlight and trees beckoned to her.

She pressed her palms against the glass, wishing more than anything she were small enough to slip through the narrow gaps around the door and fly away to safety. No sooner had she wished it than she found herself suspended in the air, shrunken to the size of a ladybug.

Shocked at her sudden transformation, Lilliana quickly unfurled her wings and flapped like crazy toward the sliver of sky at the upper edge of the door. She was just about to fly through when Jake charged into the shallow alcove.

Startled, she squeaked—a tiny, nearly inaudible noise that he couldn't possibly have heard. And yet he turned in her direction as if he sensed her presence.

Lilliana flitted behind the uppermost hinge and watched him. Her tiny heart beat so loudly she was certain he must hear it thumping. Had he seen her change? She didn't think so, and yet he stood at the door scanning it and the grounds outside. His cello sounds raced wild and urgent, like a perplexed wolf chasing a scent.

She shouldn't be glad. She needed to stay away from him. He had some strange magnetic hold over her. He was a danger to her and to her mission. Terribly dangerous, but Lilliana couldn't help herself. She smiled. Foolish though it was, it felt wonderful to see him hungry to find her.

Jake turned away from the glass and strained up onto his toes, searching over the heads of the students parading past. Then his shoulders sagged, and he thumped his fist against the side of the lockers. "Where are you?" he demanded in a low growl.

Lilliana clung to the hinge. "Here," she murmured, knowing her words would never reach his ears. She wished she could soothe away the concern marring his beautiful face. Except Jake wasn't beautiful, not compared to the perfection she was used to among fairies and elves. His face had hard lines, too firm a jaw, hints of pain in his eyes. She leaned over further, nearly falling onto his shoulder. What made him so attractive?

A shock of dark brown hair fell across his eyes. Lilliana's fingers twitched with the desire to brush back those errant strands. Suddenly she felt herself growing larger. She panicked. "Stay small! Stay small!"

Jake's broad shoulders heaved with a frustrated sigh. He left. Abandoned her. Walked away to join the other students trudging toward their next class.

Lilliana watched him leave, and then she turned and half-heartedly winged her way through the doorjamb, heading for sunshine, tugging on her shrunken backpack as it snagged on the doorway's fuzzy weatherstripping.

Outside at last, she skimmed along the side of the building until she was safe from prying eyes. Uncertain exactly how she'd shrunk so quickly, she tried wishing she were big again. Immediately she was. Landing with a thud, she scraped her hand catching herself against the red brick school wall.

Overhead an observant trio of butterflies circled and looped until they floated directly in front of her. Naturally they would come. It was the smell of nectar on her. Butterflies couldn't resist it. Except Lilliana needed time alone, time to think, time to figure out what she should do.

But there was a saying among fairies, "If you are ever confused, talk to a butterfly." Having so few days to live, butterflies tended to be incurably philosophical. *Carpe diem* and all that.

So Lilliana consulted with her airy companions. "I shouldn't feel like this." She leaned against the brick wall, etching the dusty ground with the toe of her boot. "I have to stay away from him. But I can't," she confessed, unable to suppress the warmth flooding her cheeks. She put it in terms they'd understand. "Jake is like nectar." Saying it aloud made her heart speed up.

She listened to their faint melodic questions.

"No," she answered sadly. "I'm afraid it's impossible."

Petite choruses of *nothing is impossible* crescendoed on the breeze.

"He's my Cinderella's brother. It would never work."

They teased her with breezy songs pollinated with lovely possibilities.

"He's human. I can't!" Her loud response sent them fluttering backwards. It even startled her. But there it was. The truth. Jake was off limits not just because he was Jess's brother, or even because Jess had ordered her to stay away from him. It was because he was human.

She calmed herself, moderated her breathing, and disciplined her emotions and then assured them in an even tone, "It's against the rules. Forbidden."

A purple butterfly with orange spots somersaulted on an air current.

"Yes, of course. I'm absolutely certain." Lilliana fished out her manual, *Beyond Ball Gowns*, from the backpack and thumbed through it, desperately seeking validation. She knew the rule was in there. Everyone knew the rule: *Don't fall in love with a human.* Dangerous, shameful, blah, blah, blah.

Why wasn't it easy to find? It should've been written in big letters across every page.

The butterflies wheeled and twirled in graceful nosedives, laughing at her.

"Oh, I know you don't care about rules. It's different for us. We have to live with our mistakes for hundreds of years. If my mother had obeyed this rule, I might not have grown up alone." She fanned the pages of her book, growing increasingly frustrated. "You don't know what it's like." She slammed the manual shut and slumped against the wall. "Look at you. You have all your sisters. I'm *alone!*"

She realized she was speaking too loudly again and bowed her head, ashamed of her outburst, equally ashamed of her pathetic origins.

The trio instantly forgave her and landed on Lilliana's shoulders and hair, flapping their beautiful wings, humming mournfully and fanning her with comfort.

At last she sighed. "Thank you. Yes, I know. Death comes to us all." She grimaced at the platitude she'd heard quoted so often as a child, wishing it brought even a little solace, wishing it filled up the lonely places. But it didn't.

A blue butterfly danced in the air near her nose, singing of collecting nectar and finding a mate. Lilliana smiled. "You think love is worth the risk, don't you? I suppose for you it is." She, on the other hand, didn't have that freedom.

A sharp staccato whistle and the rapid descent of a familiar red cardinal interrupted her thoughts. The butterfly sisters whirled into hiding behind Lilliana, tucking away into the safety of her hair. "Leave them be, Napoleon."

A piccolo couldn't have trilled faster or louder as he fired questions at her, wanting to know what she was doing outside the school and if she had anything to report.

"No. I've run into a few problems. That's all."

She tried to wave him away, but he hopped onto the edge of *Beyond Ballgowns* and whistled even more insistently, demanding to know exactly *what* problems.

"Well, for starters, my Cinderella is not a sweet downtrodden waif who welcomes my help. On the contrary, she has the temperament of a mother badger and would rather tear me to shreds than hold a civil conversation. And her brother is, um, uh, well, let's just say he's an obstacle." She stopped, unwilling to say more. The last thing she needed was for her tutor, Gryndelyn, to hear she was making a major mistake on her very first mission. The council would reassign her for sure, probably to somewhere in the Saharan desert.

In an attempt to get rid of Napoleon and his prying, Lilliana flipped open her manual, forcing the little cardinal to flutter up into the air. She jabbed her finger at the text, unable to believe what she saw, a directive she'd forgotten. "Look at this. Instead of ordering me to avoid him, directive five says to make friends with him."

Friends.

She reread it. Clearly, the directive instructed her to become *familiar* with Jake. *Get close.* It opened the door to all those enticing possibilities the butterflies sang of, but in her heart, she knew the grave risk.

Other fairies might be able to resist an attraction like this, but not her. She'd barely been able to keep from flinging herself into his arms right there in class in front of everyone. Obviously, the directive hadn't taken into consideration certain genetic predispositions.

This intense attraction to a human had to be a family curse.

Most likely it was the humanity in her blood crying out for its own kind. Except she wasn't their kind! Nor was she completely fairy. Her shoulders drooped.

Halfling. Oh, yes, Lilliana knew exactly what she was.

She was Perian. An embarrassment to her race.

Not fully human.

Not completely fairy.

Fairies had taunted her with the names ever since she could remember. And yet could she not unfurl her wings and fly away with these butterflies? Yes!

Which only proved that, like her mother, she was too much fairy to fall in love with a human and survive. Then why, *why,* had she never felt this way about any of the elves that flirted with her? Why did this human make her heart pound like Thor's hammer?

The school bell rang, startling Napoleon. He soared skyward, a vanishing red dot. Time to go. Very well, Lilliana would go and do her duty. She declared as much to the remaining butterflies. "If I must make him a friend, then so be it."

She squared her shoulders and marched back to the school with her chin fixed at a noble angle, a sacrificial angle, a *Joan of Arc go-ahead-and-burn-me-at-the-stake* angle.

TELL ME NO LIES

Cai rushed into study hall. Tardy! If it had been anybody else, Coach Stanton would've hollered, "Drop and give me twenty." But there was more to Coach Stanton than his G.I. Joe haircut and the shiny whistle hanging around his neck.

Last year Cai had noticed that the players on Lake Elm's basketball team had unusually high grades, all Bs or better. She smelled a story. Were teachers giving the athletes a free pass? After interviewing several players, Cai followed a lead one of them gave her. She snuck into the gym and hid. That's when she saw Coach conducting after-practice tutorials. He worked through geometry formulas on the blackboard with Pete Gustafson, diagramed sentences with Javier Ramirez, and discussed American history with Alex Peterson.

Cai wrote the story and dubbed his tutoring program "Bs or Better" and sold the story to the *Lake Elm Courier*. The *Dallas Morning News* picked it up, and then channel 11 aired it on the nightly news. Coach Stanton became a local hero.

Cai handed him Mrs. Cartwright's memo. Coach slid his feet off the desk and caught the basketball he'd been spinning on one finger. He scanned the note. "Okay, Lois Lane." He pointed to Lilliana sitting at a table in the back of the room. "But keep the volume down."

Cai adjusted her glasses, mentally preparing a list of probing questions as she walked down the aisle. Even though this interview was a favor for Jess, Cai needed to turn it into something interesting. Her reputation depended on it. She had to find the *zing* factor. That's what good reporters did. Even Diane Sawyer did a human-interest story now and then, but she always found the *zing* factor. Maggie had said there was something unusual about Lilliana, and Maggie's radar never missed. So there was a story here. Cai just had to dig for it.

She set down her stuff and greeted Lilliana, carefully enunciating each syllable of her name exactly as Lilliana had in Biology. "I'd like to do a story on you for the school paper. Is it all right if I ask you a few questions?" Cai activated a tiny palm-size recorder and set it on the table. "You don't mind, do you?"

"Not at all." Lilliana smiled back. "As a matter of fact, I'd like to ask you a few questions, too. You're Jessica Harrison's best friend, aren't you?"

"Yea-ah," Cai answered warily, but then added with a chuckle, "But whatever you do, don't call her Jessica. She hates it. She thinks the name makes her sound like an airhead pop star."

"Got it." Lilliana jotted a note on a sheet of binder paper, except she used strange symbols.

Was it shorthand, Cai wondered? Or a foreign alphabet? She flipped open her own notepad and copied one of the symbols, planning to oogle it later. "You have an interesting accent. Where are you from?"

But before Lilliana could answer, Cai noticed something moving. "Wait. Hold still. There's something stuck in your hair." She reached for it. "A butterfly!"

"Don't touch her." Lilliana blocked Cai's hand. "It's harder for them to fly if you brush the powder off their wings."

Weird reaction, Cai thought. Butterfly or not, most girls would freak if they knew a bug was crawling in their hair.

Adding to the weirdness, Lilliana calmly said, "I'll take her outside after class." The butterfly flapped its wings slowly and steadily, apparently perfectly content to sit through class nesting in Lilliana's thick dark hair.

"Oka-ay." A hundred questions popped into Cai's head. She skipped over *how did it get there?* and settled on "Why's it in your hair?" Then she hit on a possible explanation. "Maybe it likes your perfume. You smell nice. What is that, tangerines?"

"Good guess." Lilliana looked impressed and wrote *smart* on her paper, this time in regular English, as if Cai couldn't read upside down. "I made it out of orange blossoms and gillyflowers."

"Gillyflowers?"

Lilliana tapped her cheek. "I think you call them carnations."

"You make your own perfume?" Cai asked, making a note for later. *I think you call them*? She must be foreign.

"Sure." Lilliana shrugged like it was no big deal—didn't everybody make their own perfume? Then she leaned forward and inhaled deeply. "I know a perfect scent for you, wildflower nectar and almond oil. I'll mix some up and bring it for you tomorrow. What about Jess? I could make a scent for her, too."

Cai shook her head. "Jess isn't exactly the perfume type." She pulled them back to the interview. "So tell me why your family moved to Lake Elm."

"They didn't." Lilliana scribbled more symbols. "She's not the perfume type, so what does Jess like?"

"Not much." Cai glanced at her, puzzled. Why did Lilliana keep bringing up Jess? Probably because of Jake. Cai pushed back to the topic. "So your family didn't move here?"

"No. My parents are dead."

Boom. Suddenly Cai's fluffy interview turned into an obituary. She glanced down at her notes and mumbled, "I'm sorry. That must be hard for you."

Lilliana shook her head. "No. I never really knew them. My mother died shortly after giving birth to me." She tapped her pencil against the paper. "There has to be *something* Jess likes?"

"Complicated stuff. Physics and Engineering." This was supposed to be Cai's interview. "Do you live with foster parents?"

"No." Lilliana shook her head. "Physics and engineering,

huh?" She perked up. "I could help her with that."

"I don't think so, not unless you're Einstein's long-lost granddaughter." Which gave Cai another idea. "You live with grandparents?"

Lilliana didn't answer. "Then, how would you suggest I win her confidence?"

"Win her confidence?" Cai set down her pencil, totally frustrated. She needed to regain control of this conversation. "Why all this interest in Jess?"

But her tactic backfired. Lilliana clammed up. Silence, not the comfortable kind, filled the space between them. The clock on the wall counted the seconds in slow metronome-like regularity. Dead end, tick. Dead end, tock.

Finally Lilliana spoke up. "I like you, Cai. You're smart."

"Me?" Cai laughed uncomfortably. "Not really. Well, I'm not an idiot or anything." Even though right then she felt like one.

"You're smart. I can tell because your soul music is so complex, layered, balanced."

What was she talking about? "My music? I'm not into soul."

Lilliana laughed and headed down another rabbit trail. "You're pretty, too. Why do you hide your beautiful eyes behind those glasses and heavy bangs? You should sweep your hair to the side. Here, let me show you." Lilliana gently tugged Cai's notebook out of her hands and sketched a hairstyle she insisted would flatter Cai's high Asian cheekbones. Then she drew in an eyebrow shape, suggesting Cai pluck hers into an arch. "To show off your eyes."

"Interesting." Cai smiled at the makeover drawings, impressed with Lilliana's artistic ideas. She carefully maintained a friendly mode as she edged back into the interview. "I'll try it. Thanks. But I'd really like to know more about you and why you came to Lake Elm."

Lilliana handed the notebook back and studied Cai for a minute. She leaned in and whispered conspiratorially, as if they'd been best friends since kindergarten. "I was sent here to help Jess."

She beamed as if she'd just handed Cai news worthy of a Pulitzer Prize.

But it wasn't Pulitzer material. It was a freaky weird statement. Cai shook her head. "Jess? What do you mean, *you were sent*?"

"Sent to help her. And since you're her best friend and you know so much about her, your input would be extremely helpful." Then she quoted a public service ad. "Don't you see? You could help me help her."

"What are you talking about? Help Jess, how?" Cai got too loud and Coach shushed her. She took a deep breath and leaned in, struggling to keep her voice low, "*Who* sent you?"

Lilliana clamped her lips together and sat back, making more strange symbols on her paper.

Cai squinted suspiciously at the new girl, trying to make sense of it, and then something clicked. She hit on a possibility. "A month ago Jess told me the navy's Weapons Development Team called to talk to her about the sonic cannon project she entered in the State Applied Science Fair. Are you here about that?"

Lilliana shook her head. "Nothing to do with that. I told you I'm supposed to watch over her."

Cai had a major story with plenty of *zing* factor unwinding right smack dab in front of her. Trouble was; the story had a choke hold on her best friend. "Watch Jess? You mean, like spy on her? Are you in one of those programs where they take kids and train them to be undercover operatives? I've heard about those, but I didn't think they actually existed."

Lilliana rolled her eyes. "I'm *not* a spy."

"But you *are* undercover."

Lilliana bit her lip, which was as good as a confession.

Oh, there was definitely a story here. Cai scribbled like mad on her notepad.

Lilliana slumped in her chair, brooding, tapping her pencil against her paper. "I need your help. I don't see any other way around it. I'll just have to tell you." She said the next bit almost to herself. "Maybe then you'll help me. It doesn't matter because you won't remember anyway."

Cai glanced covertly at the digital recorder. Still on. Oh, she'd remember, all right.

Lilliana took a deep breath, leaned forward, and whispered. "Yes. I am undercover." She sat back and added, "But not with the navy."

If she wasn't with the navy, was it the FBI? CIA? Homeland Security? Had Jess's computer hacking finally caught up to her? Cai's stomach did a flip-flop. Her best friend was in serious trouble. Suddenly the interview didn't matter. All that mattered was saving Jess.

"Who sent you?" Cai gripped the edge of the table hoping the answer wouldn't be as bad as she feared.

When Lilliana didn't answer, Cai leapt to the best-case scenario. "Are you trying to recruit her?" *Please let it be that.* "Did you come here to evaluate her for some government science program? It's true Jess is super smart, but she's not emotionally ready for—"

"No." Lilliana interrupted. "I'm not recruiting her. I'm not evaluating her. And I'm not watching her. Well, okay, I *am* watching her, but it's more like observing. I have to observe her if I'm going to help. That's where you come in."

"Me?" Cai shook her head. No way would she betray Jess's trust like that. "No way! The last thing Jess needs is a government agent snooping around and pressuring her."

"I told you I'm not from your government."

Sure. "If not our government, then whose?" That would explain the quirky accent. Cai frowned at the butterfly in Lilliana's hair, slowly waving its wings. It was probably a clever listening device telecasting their entire interview to an unmarked black van parked in front of the school.

This whole conversation was crazy, and she intended to put a stop to it right now. "Listen up." She leaned close, talking sternly to Lilliana and whomever else might be listening on the other end of that bug. "I don't know who you are or what you want with Jess. Because I'm her best friend, and I'm not going to betray her. And if you planned to get close to her on your own, you totally blew it. You may as well give up and go back to the Pentagon, or Prague, or wherever, because Jess hates you."

"Yeah, I got that. But why?" Lilliana riveted her full attention on Cai. She seemed unfazed by Cai's declaration as she asked, "What did I do wrong?"

Her directness disarmed Cai. "Jake," she blurted.

"Jake?" The spy, or whatever she was, blushed—a nice floral pink to go with her gillyflower perfume.

"Jess is afraid he likes you and—"

"He does?"

"Maybe. I don't know. What does it matter?" Cai blinked, trying to make sense of Lilliana's blushing question. "The point is, you're not the kind of girl Jess thinks is right for him."

"Why not?" It spilled out. But then Lilliana gathered her dignity and asked in a carefully moderated voice, "What's wrong with me?" She didn't sound defensive. She asked it matter-of-factly, her pencil poised to take notes.

Cai shook her head, unable to get her bearings. Flustered, she went with the only thing she could come up with. *The truth.* "You're too much like Cheryl."

The spy blinked. Totally clueless.

It wasn't nice to speak ill of the dead, so Cai phrased her explanation in the gentlest terms possible. "Cheryl is…" She stopped and corrected herself, "Cheryl *was* Jess's dead brother's girlfriend. Extremely pretty. But sadly, Cheryl was also a manipulative, social-climbing, *hey-look-at-me* type girl." Cai took a deep breath and told Lilliana about the accident.

Lilliana's perfect face pinched up. "But I'm not like that."

"Maybe not, but have you *seen* your clothes?" Cai tried to lighten the tension with a half-smile. "I mean, they're cute, but they practically scream *look at me*."

"I don't understand. I thought this outfit would have universal appeal. I found it on page thirty-eight of *Teen Vogue*." Lilliana glanced down at her ensemble.

Cai almost laughed. Apparently spy school didn't teach a course on *Clothes That Help Spies Blend In 101*. "See, that's exactly my point. *Teen Vogue* is the attention-grabber's bible."

Lilliana cringed.

Cai felt sorry for her. She really didn't seem to know. "Didn't you notice all the boys gawking at you? You're too A-list. Too beautiful. So naturally Jess thinks you're trouble. She's lost one brother, and she's not about to let something stupid happen to the brother she has left."

Lilliana studiously drew more symbols and set her pencil down. "Beautiful." She sighed heavily and shook her head, curling into herself. "How odd. Where I'm from I'm considered big and clumsy and dark." She twisted a wayward strand of her mahogany hair. "In my world it's *always* a contest over who's most beautiful, and I've never even been in the running."

That had to be a lie. Where on earth would she not be in the running? What government agency expected their people to be better looking than Lilliana? Cai frowned, pinching her thick eyebrows together, eyebrows she couldn't wait to get home and pluck. "In your world? What do you mean, in Budapest? Spy school? Interpol? Where?"

"The Forest." Lilliana propped her elbows on the table and rested her chin in her hands. Her features looked strained, almost sad. "And Jake—does he think I'm too *look-at-me-ish*?"

"I don't know." Cai was completely baffled. "The Forest? Is that code for someplace? Like MI-5 or Quantico?"

"No." Lilliana pressed her hand against her throat, glancing around the study hall as if she hoped to find a secret escape hatch. "The deep forest is a world hidden within your world."

"Uh-hum." Cai smirked. "I thought you spies were trained to

48

come up with a *good* cover story. This one is just plain bizarre."
She made a note in her steno pad to check out all references to *The Forest*.

"You're not going to help me, are you?"

"Betray Jess?" Cai shook her head. "What do you think?"

"This is not going well."

"No. It's quite possibly the worst interview in history."

Suddenly Lilliana waved her hand over the table, flinging sparkling dust into Cai's eyes and over her notepad.

"Hey! What's with the glitter?" Cai tried to brush it off her notes, but the powdery stuff stuck worse than glue.

Lilliana's eyes opened wide, and her perfect brows arched high. "You can see it?"

"Of course I can." For about the fifth time in this crazy interview, Cai wondered if the new girl had a screw loose. "You threw it all over everything. Look at this. It's even on my recorder." Frantically she dusted the recorder off with her sleeve, hoping the particles wouldn't get inside and ruin it.

The bell rang, blasting through the quiet room like a foghorn. Suddenly Cai felt dizzy. She held onto her chair.

Lilliana stood up to leave. "You should not be able to see *elingil*."

"*Elin* what?" Cai blinked, not sure what the new girl was jabbering about. She rubbed her forehead, unable to orient herself. It was as if someone had flashed one of those *Men-In-Black*-forget-what-you-saw lights in her eyes. If she hadn't known better, she'd have thought she bumped her head when the bell rang.

What had she and Lilliana been talking about?

Bits and pieces floated back. A vague uneasy feeling knotted her stomach, something about spies and Jess. Maybe her blood sugar was low. Cai reached into her bag to dig out a few cashews to tide her over until lunch. No, wait. She shook her head, still dazed. Where was she? Study hall. Lunch was next.

Fairy Godmother Training Manual

Directive 6

Count on the unexpected. Humans are unpredictable. Consequently, a mission rarely proceeds as planned. You will run into a snag now and then. When in doubt as to how to proceed, consult with your elders. The council is always ready to advise you. Your mission is of prime importance to us all.

—Gryndelyn Myrddin

Solo

Lilliana rushed out of study hall, a hailstorm raging inside her.

Cai had seen *elin-gíl*, star sparks, the essence of magic. Why? It was supposed to have blotted out her memory, but if she could see it, would it still have the same effect?

Things were not going well at all. Jess hated her. And apparently all of them, even Jake, thought she was craving attention. *Was she?*

Lilliana squeezed the fabric of her skirt, crumpling the organza in her fist. These clothes were conservative, *boring* by forest standards. She never dreamed mortals would be so difficult.

She needed a calm place to think, a place with water so she could contact Gryndelyn for advice. A nearby river. Or a brook. But where? How did these Texans survive without water flowing around them? It was so dry here. Her skin felt dusty and her soul thirsty.

Restroom.

Exactly what she needed. *Rest.* Lilliana pushed through the door, desperately seeking solitude. Except the small room wasn't restful at all. It blazed with harsh lights and luminous mirrors. Even the sound of her footsteps echoed noisily against thousands of small tiles.

Nor was she alone. A girl stood in front of a sink, preening in the mirror, and after fiddling with her hair she turned the faucet handle.

Water. Lilliana couldn't look away.

The girl ripped paper from the box on the wall, wiped her hands, and tossed the towel into a basket as she left.

Finally alone, Lilliana expelled the breath she'd been holding, took two long strides to the white basin, and rested her hands on the handles. In her world water flowed in abundance. Fairies always live near water's edge. But this wasn't the forest. She was here in their world now, Jess and Jake's. Sinks and faucets would have to do.

For a minute her pride stopped her. Two days ago she'd have laughed if anyone told her she'd be calling for help so soon. *Not her. She'd been on her own since she was a little girl. She didn't need help from anyone. Except she did.* She couldn't afford to mess this mission up, and as much as she hated to admit it, she needed advice.

Lilliana cranked the handle and water gushed out, clean and clear. She stopped up the sink with paper towels, filled the porcelain bowl to the brim, and turned off the tap. She sprinkled the pooled contents with *elin-gíl* and stirred her fingers through the frothy current. "Gryndelyn, I need to speak with you."

Nothing happened.

Lilliana squeezed her eyes shut. "Gryndelyn, please. I need your help."

At last crystalline features emerged in the center of the basin, a perfect nose formed in the swirling water, and high cheekbones materialized. Large entrancing eyes appeared, and a delicate mouth set in a grim line. The transparent lips moved. "What do you need?"

Gryndelyn's tone, as always, rippled like the quick notes of a saxophone, but today Lilliana detected the subtle shrillness. After ten years she knew her guardian's temperament. She stopped fidgeting and tackled the first issue.

"There's been a snag—"

"Already?" Gryndelyn's eyelids drooped, thinly veiling her boredom. "Have you forgotten this is tournament day? You do realize you've called me away from a winning hand of Surlkyn." With a gusty sigh, she added, "Would you deny me this one small pleasure?"

"No! No. Of course not. I'm sorry to have bothered you, but there's a problem." Lilliana stopped herself from chewing her bottom lip. It would only annoy Gryndelyn further. She straightened her shoulders and tried to appear as grown-up as possible. Competent. Not desperate. "One of the humans saw *elin-gil.*"

"Yes, and?"

"What I meant was—she could actually *see* it."

Gryndelyn chortled, three high sharp notes. "A few of them can. What of it? Surely, you didn't call me away for that? The manual explains all this in the appendices." Gryndelyn's features began to fade and descend back into the bowl.

"Wait!" Lilliana swirled her fingertips through the water to bring her back. "There's more."

"Study your manual."

"I have. I do. It's just that things are far more difficult than I expected. My C.O. hates me. She's much angrier than her dossier indicated, and—"

"Then you have work to do, don't you?" Gryndelyn's mouth pinched up briefly. "For pity's sake, *Lilly-anna*. Do your job." She exaggerated the human pronunciation of Lilliana's name, lending it an unmusical, nonfairy, flatness. "Of course." She paused. "If it's too difficult for you, I suppose you could just tuck your wings under your armpits and come crawling home. Is that what you want to do?"

Lilliana caught her lip between her teeth and shook her head. She was unable to speak for fear her voice would break and humiliate her further.

"Splendid. Then, perhaps you'll allow me to get back to my game." Gryndelyn's breathy notes were evenly moderated and ultra sweet. "I wouldn't want to lose this tournament because of you." In a flash, her face disappeared. Water sloshed over the rim, splashing Lilliana's skirt and leggings.

"Perfect!" Lilliana yanked a paper towel out of the box and wiped angrily at her soaked suede boots, stopping to blot her eyes, which betrayed her with burning tears. "Call Gryndelyn for advice on tournament day—*what a brilliant idea.* Oh, yes. Extremely helpful."

Her shoulders sagged, and she trailed her fingers wistfully through the remaining water. "I just don't know if I can do this."

The little pool stilled eerily, settling around her fingers in a glassy calm. She jerked her hand out. Then, as if the brown paper towels plugging the drain were leaking color, a fleshy tint swirled upward, slowly forming an ethereal face beneath the surface. Lilliana stepped back, wary of her uninvited guest until it spoke. "Be still my child. Answers will come."

The melodic words awakened memories: a face she couldn't quite remember, songs just beyond her grasp. "Who are you?" Lilliana edged closer to the basin, trying to make out the image.

The faint reflection wavered, shimmering with star sparks. "I am she who has always loved you and watched over you, even from afar."

Lilliana leaned closer.

"Do not give up on your Cinderella, Lilliana, love. Your mission is extremely important. You were specifically chosen for this task. You, and you alone, can reach Jess. The Council has foreseen it. You can understand her. She, like you, has suffered much loss. One brother is dead. Her parents, in their grief, have abandoned her. She needs you."

Memories seeped into Lilliana's mind. Soft arms. Rich forest smells. Laughter ringing like heavenly wind chimes.

She shook her head, forcing herself back to the present. "But

54

Jess hates me. She doesn't want my help. And she isn't a helpless Cinderella. Anything but! She doesn't need me. What she needs is a class on manners and maybe a straightjacket."

"No one said it would be easy, my dear. She's hardening her heart. You must prevent that. The Seers are troubled. Their visions tell us that if you don't help Jess, her anger will continue to grow until eventually she isolates herself even from her few remaining friends. Bitter and hateful, this brilliant young woman will use her genius for destruction rather than good. It will end in disaster for all of us."

"What have they seen?" Her imagination flashed to horrors and explosions. "You must tell me!"

"No. No, Lilliana. Don't dwell on dark possibilities. Focus on the good that you can bring about. Concentrate on your concern for Jess."

"This is too hard a task for my first mission. What if I fail?"

"You are our best hope. That's why you were chosen."

Trapped, Lilliana sighed. "But how do I help someone who can't even stand to be in the same room with me?"

"Oh, my dear, dear child, you're extremely resourceful. You always have been."

The voice was so lyrical, so calm, always on the verge of familiar laughter Lilliana could almost remember. "Who are you?"

Like the round full notes of an oboe, the woman's answer filled the room. "Look deep in your heart, Lilliana. You know me."

Every time the woman spoke her name, joy danced through Lilliana's soul. Suddenly, she remembered. *"Naneth?"* Lilliana whispered in wonder.

Water rippled over the image obscuring the face. "Yes, my little one. We've been long separated, but only by time and distance, not by love. Never by love." The apparition slowly faded.

"Grandmother!" Lilliana plunged her fingers in, stirring frantically, calling the image back. "Wait! Don't go." She had so many questions. Why hadn't her grandmother come before? Where was she? Would she come again? But the indistinct features, as dark and rich and nurturing as loam in the forest, disappeared. Lilliana clutched the porcelain basin, watching the water drain faster and faster through the makeshift plug until the last of it gurgled away.

Gone.

Alone again, Lilliana glanced up, intending to face herself squarely in the mirror, to buoy herself up to tackle her mission. Instead she saw Jess's friend, the blonde one, standing behind her, clutching the door of the metal stall.

Maggie!

Blanched. Mouth gaping. Eyes open wide with alarm. She'd heard everything.

Lilliana turned, ready to shower her with *elin-gíl*, but before she could, Maggie bolted out of the restroom.

LET THE SPY GAMES BEGIN

During fourth hour Mr. Davidson handed Jess a pink slip. It sentenced her to spend lunch, plus the whole entire boring afternoon *and* an hour after school, confined in ISIS, Inter-School-Isolated-Suspension. It was payback for mouthing off to Jamison that morning. The acronym ISIS was a lame attempt by the school to make punishment sound sophisticated and professional. It meant Jess had to serve detention sitting at a tiny desk inside a three-by-five plywood cubicle. Isolated.

Fine by her.

Her jailers confiscated Jess's cell phone but failed to turn it off and overlooked her remote microphone pen. She sent a quick text to Cai and Maggie. "Meet at my house tonight 6:30."

Before the bell rang at the start of fifth period, Jess had completed all the class assignments the ISIS monitor had brought her. Principal Jamison dropped by—*nice of him*—and assigned her an essay on the benefits of speaking respectfully to others.

Yawn. That took a whole fifteen minutes.

She dawdled for a while, interpreting the graffiti on her cubicle walls and contributing a few choice symbols of her own. The ISIS monitor strolled by, rapped on the cubicle wall, and reminded Jess, "You're *supposed* to be contemplating your behavior."

Yeah, well, they may as well have asked her to sort sand pebbles in the Sahara.

After Jess got tired of reading Bobby Ingstrom's graphically violent diatribe scrawled on the wall underneath the desk—*if they knew what it said they'd paint over it and lock Bobby up in a padded cell*—she decided to put the remaining hours to good use.

She pulled a pad of graph paper out from under her trigonometry book and turned to the section where she'd hidden schematic drawings for her sonic cannon. Hours later, she was busy figuring out how to recalibrate the frequency to a slightly less lethal setting when the ISIS monitor came by to parole her. "Didn't you hear the last bell, Jess? Afterschool detention is over."

Deep in a calculation, Jess waved the monitor away. "I'll leave when I'm good and ready."

"Jess, get out! Go home. They want to lock up the school."

At 6:08, she was home in her bedroom suite. To be precise, Jess sat in her kitchenette/computer room, trailing her fork through the contents of a *nutritious* TV dinner: greasy chicken strips, corn, mushy crinkle fries, and mac and cheese.

Carbed to the gills, she shoved away from the small table, spun her chair around, and rolled into the cockpit of her workstation. Time to get down to business. Flipping back her irritatingly frizzy hair, Jess stretched her fingers and then poised them on her ergonomic keyboard and master control panel. Not only did she have the best computer money could buy, she had a set of four security monitors mounted on the wall scanning via sixteen different cameras installed throughout the house and grounds.

She'd purchased the state-of-the-art security system with money her mom had given her to spend on her school wardrobe. Jess still remembered her mother's stricken expression when she explained that she didn't want Jimmy Choos or a Gucci handbag. It had been the high point of Jess's self-restraint when she hadn't added, "Besides, *hello-o*, we need a security system because you and Dad are *never* here!"

Like tonight.

She should have said it aloud. Heck, she had wanted to yell it, but she didn't. Jess understood—her mom and dad were just coping with Ryan's *accident* in their own way. Mom threw herself into charity work and Dad into his career. And Jake was busy with football.

Two small maps on the right corner of her wide screen indicated the location of her parents' GPS signals. A small blinking dot near Harwood and Ross meant her Mom was downtown at the Art Museum. Her Dad's GPS, which she'd planted in his laptop, was a stationary blip on a map of Osaka. Jess checked her watch, 9:09 a.m. Japan time. He'd be in a business meeting in Sumitomo Tower.

Ignoring a thirty-six-inch wall-mounted plasma TV silently broadcasting the world news, Jess's fingers tap-danced across the keyboard. A few minutes later she was digging into Lilliana's files. Files supposedly transferred from a high school in Chicago. At 6:33, movement on the porch made a red button on her security panel flash. The camera monitoring her parent's Gone-With-the-Wind style porch focused in on Cai and Maggie. Jess flipped on the intercom and was just about to tell them to come on up when she overheard them talking about her.

"…she said things about Jess. Awful things." Maggie sounded upset. "Do you think my dyslexia is making me hear voices and see things that aren't there? Am I going crazy?"

"Not you, Maggs." Jess zoomed in the camera and caught Cai shaking her head.

"No, but you *do* look kind of pale. If you had a fever or something, that could explain it." Cai put her hand against Maggie's forehead. "Nope, but don't worry. We'll figure this out. Whatever you do, don't say anything to Jess." Cai glanced furtively at the camera as she reached for the doorbell. "Shhh…she might hear us."

"Darned right I can hear you!" Jess shouted into the intercom. "Don't tell me *what?*"

They weren't allowed to keep secrets from her. They were supposed to be her friends! Her *only* friends. And friends didn't hide stuff from each other.

For a second Jess felt the greasy chicken fingers clawing their way back up her throat. She swallowed hard and slammed her hand down on the buzzer that electronically unlocked the front door. "Come up," she growled into the speaker.

Two minutes later her two best friends entered the room all fidgety and nervous, like a pair of conspirators.

"Hi!" Cai sounded too cheerful.

Secrets did that, they made people overly chirpy. Jess crossed her arms and stared at them. "Well? What is it? Tell me."

"Um…" Maggie couldn't lie worth beans. She'd never been able to. At the mere thought of not being honest, Maggie usually turned as red as Jess's silent alarm, and she was turning pink right now. "I was in the bathroom and—"

"It's nothing," Cai butted in. "Just some dumb girls in the bathroom saying rude things—you know how it is."

Jess knew exactly how it was. She knew nobody on campus would be nominating her for Miss Congeniality. "Uh-huh." Jess studied them, hoping that was really all there was to it. Except, they still looked jittery.

Maggie stared at the soggy remains of Jess's TV dinner. "You should've told us you were home alone. We would've brought a pizza or something. You shouldn't have to eat dinner all by yourself."

Jess shrugged. "What are you gonna do, come over every night?"

Neither of them answered, and if there was one thing that made Jess sicker to her stomach than secrets, it was pity. "It's okay. I'm not alone. Jake's here."

They seemed to relax a little bit. So Jess helped them along. "Yep, he's in his room studying Chapter Thirty-two, a bunch of boring diagrams about frog guts. All so he can impress *her*." She shook her head. "Pathetic."

"Oh, I don't know," Cai shot Jess a sideways smile. "Wouldn't you like to think Mark Winslow is home doing the same thing to impress you?"

Why did they have to go and bring up Mark? Jess grabbed a pencil and twisted it as if the stupid thing would unscrew. "Winslow knows where frog ovaries are without spending two hours studying a stupid diagram." She thumped the pencil eraser against the computer console. "Besides, he doesn't care about impressing me. He called me Gadget again. To him I'm just Jake's ugly little brainiac sister."

Maggie shifted uncomfortably. "That isn't true. He likes you."

"Uh-huh. Sure." Jess remembered how mad Mark sounded when he left Biology, when he'd told her she didn't have a clue.

She shrugged. So what? She didn't care. It didn't matter if anybody liked her. Not even Mark. Anyway, she didn't have time for him. She had to protect her brother. She turned to Cai. "What did you find out about The Clone?"

Cai dropped onto the sofa and sighed. "We talked the whole hour, but I didn't find out much of anything."

"Right. You? Diane Sawyer's protégée?" Jess tucked her army boots up under her chair and leaned forward. "I've seen you make the Inquisition look like child's play. Stop holding back!"

"I'm not. It's the weirdest thing. I can only remember bits and pieces. And listen." Cai pulled out her recorder, hit play, and held it up. "Nothing but garbled static. Useless fuzz." She clicked it off. "The whole interview sounds like that."

"What went wrong with your equipment?"

Cai shook her head. "Nothing. I don't understand it. I tested it later, and it worked fine."

Jess frowned. "You took notes, didn't you?"

Cai fished a steno pad out of her backpack and studiously flipped through the pages. "There isn't much here."

They all leaned closer to peek at Cai's doodles and cryptic shorthand. "What's that?" Maggie pointed to two stick figures drawn beside a row of consonants.

Cai hesitated, glancing nervously at Jess. "Lilliana's gone

through some sad stuff. Her mom and dad are dead."

Jess decided Maggie must have the flu. Something was wrong. Maggs didn't nod or say, "Oh, that's so sad," the way she normally would've. She just sat back, looking even paler than before.

"She probably lied." Jess crossed her arms and kicked one boot against the wheels of her chair.

Her two best friends gaped at her like she'd suddenly turned into Darth Vader. "Well, think about it. Does she look like a kid who lost her parents to you? If you ask me, she's pretty well dressed for a foster kid. And she doesn't act like an orphan either. Aren't orphans supposed to be all downcast, insecure, and stuff like that?"

Neither of them had an answer.

Jess asked Cai, "Did you find out anything else?"

Cai squinted at her notes. "There's something here about a *forest*." She shook her head. "But I can't quite make it out, it's faded. I must've tried to erase it. A weird symbol. Don't know what that means. Oh, here's something I *do* remember. She makes her own perfume, and she's going to make a special blend just for me. Almonds and wildflowers."

"Perfume?" Jess rolled her eyes.

Maggie didn't' say a word. She just crossed her arms tight across her chest.

Cai looked genuinely pleased. "She's bringing it tomorrow."

Jess hated to rain on Cai's parade, but her patience was stretched thinner than a dried-out rubber band on a wind-up airplane. "Did you find out anything *useful*? You know, pertinent?"

"Um...well..." Cai held up a sketch. "She showed me how to pluck my eyebrows to draw more attention to my eyes." She swept her bangs off her forehead and revealed newly plucked eyebrows.

Maggie glanced sideways at Cai's handiwork. "They look good."

"Unbelievable!" Jess smacked her hand against the arm of her chair. "Eyebrows? Perfume? What happened? Did that homemade perfume of hers asphyxiate you? Did it destroy your brain cells?"

Cai flipped her notepad shut, wounded.

"She conned you." Jess charged ahead, unable to hold back. "You! Cai Yung Stevenson, investigative reporter. She avoided telling you anything important. And what does that mean?" Jess frowned at them, waiting for them to draw the obvious conclusion. But they sat there, refusing to answer, like a couple of kids caught with half-finished homework.

Judging by their clamped-lip routine, they had both opted to remain silent until their lawyers arrived.

"Fine. I'll tell you what it means. It means she's hiding something."

"Look at this." Jess swiveled her chair back to her computer and flipped on a screen displaying a copy of Lilliana's school photo at the top of her transcripts. "Your poor little orphan girl falsified her school records."

"Are those her transcripts?" Cai jumped up and leaned over Jess's shoulder. "You hacked into the school computers again!"

"Hacked? No. That implies there was something to stop me. I didn't hack in. I simply opened a small back door and strolled in. Now, here's the interesting thing—a high school in Chicago supposedly sent her transcripts, right? But, get this, there's no record of a Lilliana Skye on their end. None. Nada. Zip."

"Which means you hacked the Chicago school's computers, too," mumbled Maggie.

Jess ignored her. "When I dug into their files, it turns out they never had a student named Lilliana Skye. And look at this." Jess scrolled down and highlighted the words *mother deceased* and the name beside it. "Her mother, the one she supposedly lost as a child—no birth records for her in the US. She never had a Social Security number. No property records. Never even had a telephone in her name. Nothing. I checked."

"Social Securi… you didn't go into government computers, did you? Tell me you didn't."

Jess shrugged.

Maggie groaned and wandered away into the connecting bedroom where she vanished into Jess's closet.

Cai actually sputtered and finally manage to shout, "Are you trying to get us all arrested?"

"You're overreacting." Jess tried to keep from smiling, but when Cai got upset, despite her Asian coloring her whole face turned as red as the little patches under her newly plucked eyebrows.

"I'm serious, Jess!" Cai jabbed her finger in the direction of the window. "Any minute now a Blackhawk helicopter is going to aim a spotlight in here and demand we come out with our hands up. The glass'll shatter as they throw in tear gas. I can see the headlines now: Promising Journalist, Cai Yung Stevenson, DEAD at Age 15, Killed During a SWAT Raid at Home of Notorious Computer Hacker Jessica Harrison."

"Very funny." Jess reached behind her, opened a kitchenette drawer, and tossed Cai a Hershey bar. "Relax. It's no big deal. Here. Chocolate will make you feel better."

"It is too a big deal," Cai grumbled. "And chocolate does not solve everything." She unwrapped it anyway. "You know what else? I keep having nightmares about you." She shook the chocolate bar threateningly at Jess. "Visons of *you* messed up with the government. Of people spying on you." She paused as if straining to remember something else. "There might be people watching you, Jess. There could be, you know."

"Stop worrying. I don't leave a trail." Jess glanced pointedly at the floor where Cai had inadvertently dropped a bit of foil from the candy bar.

Just then Maggie hurried out of the closet, smiling triumphantly. She held up a silky sapphire-blue blouse. "How come you never wear this? It would look amazing with your blue eyes and red hair. You can even wear it with those baggy carpenter pants you like. Then at least you'd be halfway there.

"Halfway to where?"

"To beautiful."

Jess flipped off the monitor that had been displaying Lilliana's school photo. "I don't *do* beautiful."

Maggie just stared at her for a minute. "Yeah, I forgot. How's that whole *Rambo-With-Breasts* thing working out for you?"

It shocked her. Maggie didn't usually resort to sarcasm, and she'd never said a mean thing in her life. Until now. Jess tried her hardest not to react. "Peachy. Thanks for asking."

"Then why'd you even buy this? Because it's beautiful, that's why. It certainly wasn't cheap." Maggie held up the still-attached price tag.

"My mother bought it."

That should've put an end to the debate. It didn't.

"Well, you need something pretty for tomorrow. So wear it."

"No." Jess didn't take orders from Maggie or anyone else. "There's no point."

"There *is* a point. You can't be a hermit forever. Mark Winslow likes you, and if you made a little effort—"

"Can we please get back to our problem with The Clone?" Jess ignored Maggie's sagging expression. "After careful analysis, I've decided we should follow Lilliana after school and find out where she lives. And then..." She paused, tapping the tips of her fingers together as she announced her strategy. "Then, we'll run surveillance."

Cai groaned.

"Haven't you heard a thing I said?" Maggie stamped her foot futilely against the plush carpet. "Mark Winslow is a great guy, Jess. One of the good ones."

"She's right. He's probably the only guy in the whole school smart enough for you." Cai shook the remaining candy bar at Jess, emphasizing her point. "You should've heard the poem he wrote in Creative Writing. Half the girls in class were actually sighing out loud when he read it."

"Sighing?" Jess arched one brow skeptically.

"You know what I mean. With his rock-star hair and those deep, brooding eyes, you aren't the only girl who has him on your radar."

Radar. *Clever.* Cai was using a military reference in an obvious attempt to pull Jess into their stupid discussion about Mark. "Newsflash. He wouldn't even notice if I did wear it. I told you before, to Winslow I'm just Jake's annoying little sister. Oh no, excuse me, his *clueless* little sister."

Cai and Maggs exchanged looks.

Light from the overhead fixture refracted off Maggie's white-blonde curls as if maybe God had ordained her as an angelic spokesman or something. "Don't you see? It's good that he's known you since you were little. He understands you. Just try to be friends with him, Jess. And don't take this the wrong way, but you *need* more friends. You really do."

Jess ignored them and pushed forward with her plan. "What I need is a triangulated reconnaissance team. I'll run point. That means you and Cai—"

"Us?" Cai coughed. She must've swallowed a lump of chocolate wrong because she rasped, "Us—follow her?" She started coughing again.

"No!" Maggie nearly shook her halo lose, vehemently declining. "We can't. I won't do it. I'm not the spy type. Huh-uh. Nope. Besides, I have to go home and feed the horses. My parents count on my help after school."

"Get one of your sisters to do it." Jess could barely remember how to adjust her vocal chords into a soft, persuasive tone, but she gave it a shot. "Come on, you guys. It'll be fun. A piece of cake. I'll wire you up with a mic and an earpiece . We'll all be in constant contact, and I'll walk you through the entire operation."

"I don't *do* sneaky." Maggie mimicked Jess, but then her tone softened. "Not even for you."

Jess glanced at the blue blouse Maggie was clutching. "What if I agree to wear that?"

Maggie blinked. Her resistance dropped several notches.

Jess took advantage and cranked up the negotiations. "Do this for me, and I'll wear that stupid shirt tomorrow."

Maggie fingered the soft blue fabric, her posture weakening, yielding—

"Whatever she's trying to make you do, Maggie, don't." Jake stood in the doorway, filling it with his broad shoulders, his feet planted wide like a gunfighter at high noon. "I'm warning you, Jess. Leave Lilliana alone."

She crossed her arms. "I'm not bothering her."

Maggie quietly laid the shirt on the bed.

"I mean it, Jess. I know you're up to something. Leave her alone. Or I swear I'll never drive you anywhere again."

"So what?" Jess blew off his threat. "It's not like I ever ask you to take me to the mall."

"The electronics store," he reminded her flatly.

"You wouldn't."

He didn't answer, but the stern expression on his face left no doubt of his sincerity.

It disgusted Jess. "A frilly skirt, homemade perfume, and suddenly you're drooling over her like a fifth grader on his first crush. Don't you get it? She's blinded you."

He frowned harder.

Against her nature, Jess begged him. "Listen to me, Jake. You don't know what you're up against. This girl, sh-she-she's…" Jess had never stuttered before, not in her whole life. She balled her fists in frustration. "She's trouble! Her story doesn't add up. There's something…" Jess glanced wildly at Cai and Maggie, hoping for backup, needing support, getting none. "Something's not right about her."

"I have to go home," Maggie whispered. She and Cai slipped out past Jake and hurried down the stairs.

Jake crossed his arms and leaned against the door. "I get it. You don't like her. She doesn't fit into one of your neat little categories. She's not a nerd. Not a jock. Not a—"

"Oh, she's in a category, all right!" Jess shouted. "The Cheryl category!"

He took a deep breath and shook his head. "Don't you get it, Jess? Ryan was the one who killed Cheryl. He was driving. That's the home truth. And it's obvious to everyone except you."

"Everyone else is an idiot!"

Jake turned to go, a mixture of pity and frustration on his face.

"Wait! Lilliana falsified her school records. She's hiding something. You can't trust her. You could get hurt."

"Leave it alone, Jess." Jake didn't believe her, Jess could tell. His jaw tensed, he looked ready to explode, but he didn't. He kept his voice low as he strode away. "I can take care of myself."

Fairy Godmother Training Manual

Directive 7

Record daily notes in the journal portion of this manual. Jot down observations and concerns you have about your Cinderella's offspring. Note any actions you take on her behalf, and analyze your progress.

—Gryndelyn Myrddin

Hitting the Right Notes

Lilliana loved sunset. Tangerine light reflected off the lake and bounced through the window, making her cave glow like polished amber.

"Hhmm. Analyze my progress." She sat at her writing table, tickling the feather of her quill against her chin, staring at the blank journal pages in Gryndelyn's Training Manual.

"Day one," she said aloud. "How shall I put this?" Day one was a complete and utter failure, a black fungus on the name of fairy godmothers everywhere. Weasel excrement.

Instead, she wrote:

JOURNAL
Day 1:

My C.O. presents a challenge. Conditions are much worse than her dossier suggests.

Jess is extremely hostile and full of suppressed pain. She speaks without considering anyone else's feelings and reacts explosively to the slightest provocation. Except for two very loyal, patient friends, she is completely antisocial. And not that it's important, but she dresses like a Foltharian swamp troll. Obviously, this is a personal choice, because Jess doesn't lack for wealth. So I can't help her in that regard. What she seems to need is…

What *did* Jess need?

Lilliana remembered all too well the agonizing sound of Jess's pain hidden beneath her loud, stormy music. What would soothe the girl?

Lilliana pulled the feather quill between her fingers as she contemplated her problem. The microscopic barbs reattached to each other making the pheasant feather appear whole and almost new. If only she could mend her charge as easily. Jessica Harrison was a complicated riddle, and Lilliana didn't have a clue how to help her. She sighed and poised the pen over the page.

I will try to become friends with Jess so I can figure out what she really needs. It won't be easy. She doesn't like me.

Scratch that. If this journal was going to be of any help at all, she needed to be brutally honest.

Jess hates me. A lot! Her friend told me I remind Jess of Cheryl, Jess's dead brother's girlfriend. Jess hated her because supposedly Cheryl was a manipulative, attention-grabbing, social climber. She blames Cheryl for Ryan's death. If Jess and her friends think I'm like that—

Lilliana dropped the pen and almost laughed. After all, it was funny, wasn't it? If Jess only knew. Except, Lilliana didn't laugh. That old kicked-in-the-stomach feeling of not belonging anywhere seized her for a second and squeezed hard. Ink spilled from the tip of her pen onto the paper.

(Splotch. Dot, dot, drip.)

She refilled the quill, tapped the excess into the ink bottle and tried to turn the splotch into a flower. But it looked more like a fat beetle, or maybe a tiny squat social climber with wings.

Jess's opinion seems to be based primarily on my appearance. It may help if I dress differently—much differently.

An idea blossomed in Lilliana's mind. Hope made her heart beat quicker. She had a plan. Smiling, she turned the page in her journal.

She felt certain that tomorrow she would be more successful, so certain that she penned an optimistic projection under tomorrow's entry.

JOURNAL
Day 2

Today will be much better than yesterday.

The next morning Lilliana walked down the hall confident in her new disguise. The uniform was perfect. No one could accuse her of trying to get attention in this. She smiled and smoothed out the navy blue sweater vest over a plain white cotton blouse and dull gray plaid skirt. She'd carefully copied the outfit from a solemn advertisement for St. Angelina's Preparatory Academy for Girls. Knee socks, loafers, she'd duplicated every sedate church-y detail. She'd even left her hair hanging loose, long and straight to her waist, understated, exactly like the girls in the photo. Surely these clothes would convince Jess that Lilliana wasn't trying to be popular.

She sorted through all the noises in the crowd, listening for a familiar voice. Amidst all the chattering, clattering, and locker slamming, she pinpointed Cai talking to Maggie. She couldn't see them yet; they were too far away, but she focused on their voices and their music.

Cai said, "Have you seen all the froofy skirts like the one Lilliana had on yesterday? Different colors but same style. I counted twelve before I even got to my locker this morning."

"They must've noticed the way the boys were staring at her yesterday." Maggie sounded distracted, preoccupied.

Cai clucked her tongue. "It's just plain weird—that's what it is. This is Lake Elm. They had to drive all the way to Dallas to buy those skirts."

Maggie sighed. Her soul music sounded guarded and troubled.

"And then there's you, Maggs. Camouflage? Really? I feel like I've stumbled into the *Twilight Zone* or something. And if all that isn't weird enough, Jess actually wore the blue silk blouse."

Maggie shut her locker. "I know she did. That's why I've got this on. I have to play superspy after school. I promised."

Lilliana was close enough to see them now. Both girls seemed surprised to find her standing in the hall behind them. She felt bad when Maggie's expression quickly changed to alarm. Lilliana needed to sprinkle her with *elin-gíl* so Maggie would forget everything she'd seen yesterday in the bathroom. She smiled, hoping to put them at ease, and handed Cai a vial of golden liquid. "It's the perfume I promised you."

They stared at the tiny bottle uncertainly.

"Wildflowers and almond oil," she assured them.

Cai uncapped it and sniffed the contents. "Oooh, it's heavenly." She dabbed some on her wrists and her inner music sounded like dozens of tiny bells ringing with delight. She held out her wrist to Maggie. "Smell this. It's amazing."

While they were distracted, Lilliana lightly dusted Maggie with *elin-gíl*. But something went wrong.

Maggie whirled around. "What did you do?"

Speechless, Lilliana gaped at her. Maggie's face and hair glittered with star sparks. She ought to be feeling soothed and peaceful. Instead, her eyes flashed, wary and alert.

Cai brushed some of the *elin-gíl* off Maggie's shoulder and frowned at Lilliana. "Did you throw glitter powder again?"

"No, I..." Only Lilliana couldn't very well explain, so she conceded to the partial truth. "Yes. Sorry."

"Listen, sparkly stuff was fun in grade school. But we've outgrown it. So cut it out." Cai's tone held an edge of irritation.

Strange that both girls could see *elin-gíl*. Even stranger that it hadn't caused Maggie to forget everything she'd seen yesterday. Her guarded expression meant she still remembered. But Lilliana noticed Maggie's music did sound slightly calmer, a little bit more tranquil. Perhaps it hadn't been entirely ineffective.

Maggie wiped some of the glittery particles from her cheek and inspected her sparkling fingertips. "What is it?"

A perceptive question. She could just answer "glitter," but that wouldn't be the truth. How could Lilliana explain star sparks? She recalled the rhyme fairies memorized as toddlers to teach them about what *elin-gíl* was. "Spinning fire, whirring sound, building-blocks of the world around." But even that simplistic rhyme would not be explanation enough.

She shrugged and diverted their attention with a question to Cai, "What do you think of this outfit? No more *Teen Vogue* girl, right?" She smiled broadly, waiting for her critic to approve.

Cai hesitated. "Well, yeah, it's better..." Clearly, Cai did not approve.

Failed again. Lilliana's hopes took a nosedive.

"You're right, it isn't as *Teen Vogue*." Cai took a deep breath before delivering the bad news. "But it's, um, well, still attracting a lot of attention."

Lilliana suppressed her thudding drums of disappointment. "Oh."

Maggie, much more relaxed now, smiled sympathetically and whispered in Lilliana's ear. "See that group of boys across the hall? The ones staring at you as if you're the first girl they've laid eyes on since they hit puberty?" She tugged the sleeve of Lilliana's white cotton blouse. "It's this innocent schoolgirl look. It turns some guys into hormone-driven idiots." She hooked her arm around Lilliana's and led her toward the Biology classroom.

Cai scolded the boys across the hall, "Stop staring, Peterson. You're drooling on your shoes."

As they neared the classroom, a caustic stench burned Lilliana's nostrils. She put on the brakes. "What's that smell?"

Cai just wrinkled her nose.

"Formaldehyde," Maggie answered casually, as if the odor of solvent and death was nothing more than a minor everyday annoyance. Lilliana kept walking, a decision she regretted.

TACTICAL ERROR

Jess got to Biology early to hide out. She hated wearing the stupid silky shirt. She felt like blueberry Jell-O, all shivery and artificial and ridiculous. She fidgeted with the forceps, rattled the scalpel around in the metal tray, and tightened the loose knob on the Bunsen burner. All the while she ignored Kermit the Frog staked out spread eagle on her dissection tray.

Mark showed up early, too, just like yesterday, not that she was logging his arrival times or anything. When he saw her, his eyebrows lifted and he grinned.

Great! He was laughing at her. Jess reminded herself she didn't care. She absolutely did not care if he thought she looked stupid. She really didn't. The fact that she suddenly felt nauseous was because of the formaldehyde or gas leaking from their Bunsen burner.

Mark brushed his fingers against the sapphire silk on Jess's arm. "What's with the new clothes, Army Girl? You running for prom queen or something?"

"*Something,*" Jess responded tartly, wishing Maggie had never found this dumb shirt in the back of her closet.

He laughed. "Have I ever told you how cute you are when you're mad?"

"I'm not mad." She wasn't mad. She didn't care what he thought. And she knew for a fact she wasn't cute.

The corner of his mouth quirked up.

Jess dearly wanted to wipe that mocking grin off his face, but before she could say anything, the warning bell rang, and the rest of the class poured in. Maggie and Lilliana came through the door arm in arm like old friends. They didn't get very far before The Clone took one look at all the frogs splayed out on the lab tables and let loose with a startled half scream, half gasp.

An obvious ploy for attention, Jess thought. Except the yelp sounded real, not quite as fake as Cheryl would've done. Plus, Lilliana turned white, seriously white. The Clone was going to pass out over a few dead frogs.

Jake rushed into the room, shoved past the crowd, took one look at Lilliana's ashen face, and hustled her over to a stool at their lab table. "Are you gonna faint?" He hovered around her like a lovesick paramedic.

She didn't seem to hear Jake at all. Lilliana fixated on the frog skewered on her dissection tray. A teardrop the size of Texas trekked down her cheek. Then, she made a completely *duh* observation. "He'll never sing again." Her face twisted with grief over *Rana catesbeiana* as if she was mourning a friend at a funeral.

Jess rolled her eyes. This wasn't a funeral; it was an autopsy.

"Pick up your scalpels." Dawson's voice boomed over the chatter. "As you can see, I've prepped your specimens, so we'll have time to get everything done today. Get started." She bustled down the center aisle muttering, "Never enough time to finish these labs."

Jess cringed as her brother, softhearted mush brain that he was, brushed the tear from Lilliana's cheek and gently turned her face away. "Don't watch," he whispered. "I'll do it." He even double-checked to make sure The Clone wasn't looking before he pressed the tip of his knife against their frog's midsection.

Jess didn't know where Jake expected Miss Priss to look because everyone in class was cutting into their frogs. Maggie, who would make a first rate vet someday, had already slit hers open and was probing the abdominal cavity.

Lilliana covered her mouth, stifling another gasp.

"It'll all be over soon." Cai advised. "Close your eyes." Her own were squeezed into narrow wincing slits.

"Good grief!" Now The Clone even had Cai fussing over her. "Pull yourself together," Jess muttered. At least Cheryl wouldn't have started boo-hooing over a bunch of pickled frogs. And she wouldn't have started eulogizing them either! Which is exactly what Lilliana did next.

"No more hopping," she mourned. "No more leaping. No more singing." Her eyes looked wild and panicky as she implored the students near her. "You've heard them, haven't you? Their funny songs?" She swung her frantic gaze around the classroom. "Hasn't anyone heard them sing?"

"Lilliana, it's okay." Jake turned to her. "Stay calm. We've all heard them." He held a scalpel in one hand and a pair of tweezers in the other, but Jess could tell he wanted to put his arms around Lilliana and comfort her.

"Hello-o. Ding-dong, anybody home. They're dead," Jess reminded her, loudly. "Dead! Their singin' days are over."

"Shut up, Jess." Jake glared at her.

She ignored her brother and used the forceps to lift their specimen's abdominal muscles while Mark made an incision. "Besides that, nobody's gonna miss a bunch of noisy croaking."

"C'mon, Jess." Mark nudged her while they worked. "Haven't you ever listened to frogs singing on a summer night? There's something kind of cool about it."

Lilliana's head drooped and her eyelids fluttered like she'd fallen into some weird trance. In a singsong voice she said, "I love their music. Ballads about hunting flies. Odes to long pink tongues. Lullabies to unsuspecting mosquitoes."

"Less talk!" Dawson clapped her hands. "More dissecting."

Lilliana seemed deaf to Dawson's order. She droned on. "Serenades to plump lovers."

Somebody grunted, probably tired of listening to Lilliana's lecture on lily pad musicians. Then Jess heard another muted groan. Or was it a croak?

It happened again. Definitely a croak.

One of these frogs wasn't quite as dead as Jess had thought. Except the other students were bent calmly over their trays. No one shouted, "Oops, my frog is still alive." Lilliana's blabber about frog songs must've stimulated Jess's imagination, that's all.

But she heard it again, clearer this time. "Croak. Ribbit. Thrummm-rumm."

Oh, there was definitely a bullfrog loose in the classroom.

"Did you hear that?" Cai looked like she was about to climb up on top of her stool.

Everett Smythe jerked back from his tray with his eyes bugged out. "What the heck was that!?"

Nancy Kowalski yelled, "Mrs. Dawson, I heard something. A frog! I heard a frog."

"Nonsense." Dawson marched toward Nancy.

Trent called from the across the room. "I heard it, too."

"Brumm-ba-rumm."

Panicking, the entire class checked under their lab tables. Jess checked, too. There wasn't anything under hers.

"Ooong-ga-roomm."

She spun around. Nothing behind her, but it sounded like a loose guitar string twanging in the corner. "Thrumm-ra-rumm." It was answered by a croak near Dawson's desk.

This was a trick. It _had_ to be a trick.

Every time a frog croaked, Nancy Kowalski squealed.

Low bellows increased, mingling with Nancy's high-pitched squawking, rising into a chaotic chorus. Mrs. Dawson clapped her hands, thundering over all the noise. "Nancy, stop screaming! This is just a childish prank."

Nancy choked back her next blubber, but the croaking got louder.

"All right. Very funny." Dawson roared. "Whoever is doing this, turn off your MP3 player this instant!"

She was right. It had to be a player of some kind, maybe several, hooked into a multidirectional sound system. Jess scanned her classmates. Who, besides her, could've rigged anything that sophisticated? Maybe Lance Davis—he'd installed a set of woofers in his car that could deafen an entire neighborhood when he cranked them up.

Except *nobody* turned *anything* off.

Nobody even moved.

"I mean it!" Dawson shouted, her fury escalating. "We don't have time for this fooli—"

Everett Smyth screamed at the top of his lungs.

He pointed at the chalkboard ledge and stuttered so badly nobody could tell what he was saying. Lisa Carson stood beside him. In quavering gasps she choked out, "G-g-gho..ost. Ghost frog!"

"I've had enough of this!" Dawson stomped in their direction growling like a grizzly bear. "Whoever you are, turn off the frog noises! If you don't, I swear I'll have you suspended for the rest of your life."

Ashley B. screamed and ran for the door.

Dawson clapped, demanding order. "Ashley, get back to your lab station."

Jordan Dietz swore and pointed to the top of the supply drawers. "Look!"

Jake dropped his surgical instruments in the tray and put his arm around Lilliana, holding her protectively to his side.

Everyone was losing it. Jess had to do something.

"Everybody relax," she ordered.

They didn't listen. They panicked like a herd of spooked cattle.

She waved her hands to get their attention. "It's okay. This is just a hoax! There's no such thing as—"

That's when Dawson screeched—"OhmiGod!"—and turned a shade of white usually reserved for bed linen. Not teachers. A silver-gray vaporous frog leapt from the supply cabinet and landed on the lab table right beside her.

Jess stared at the ghost frog. Uncanny. It didn't look like a hologram. At least, not a simple one. For one fleeting second she entertained the idea that it might be real. But no. It couldn't be. It had to be a hoax. A trick! But who? Who else knew how to hook up a hologram projector?

"Whoa!" Mark leaned closer to the hologram, blinking. "Awesome."

Another frog appeared on Jake's desk. And another one. Suddenly there were ghost frogs everywhere, croaking like crazy.

That's when Mrs. Dawson, shaking like a crazy woman, messed up royally. She shamed her postgraduate degrees.

Worse.

She betrayed scientists everywhere. Deadly Dawson sprinted out of the classroom, shrieking. And most of the class stampeded after her.

"Wait! Come back!" Jess shouted after them. "There's no such thing as ghosts!" She whirled around, holding out her arms, blocking her brother and her friends, barring them from leaving. "You—you're behind this." She stabbed a finger at Lilliana. "How'd you do it? Hidden speakers? Holograms? Anything to get attention, right?"

Jake pushed Jess away. "Lay off."

She needed backup. "Cai, help me out here." She pointed. "Check up there. There's got to be a projector above the cabinets."

But Cai didn't move. Her face looked almost as white as the ghost frog squatting on top of her Biology notes, crooning to her like a hoarse Willie Nelson.

Maggie leaned closer to study it. She ran her hand through the air around the frog to cut off a projection. "Jess, you better come look at this. I think they might be real."

Mark slowly poked his finger at the hologram. It jumped as if in response. "Whoa! Incredible. A real ghost."

"Oh, sure," Jess mocked. "I see dead amphibians. Film at ten."

Except her heart started to bang against her chest, and she suddenly felt like she might puke.

What about Ryan? Was her brother some flimsy wisp of gray somewhere just beyond Jess's reach?

No. No. No. She edged away from Maggie and Cai's table. *Dead is dead. There is no such thing as ghosts.* She repeated the mantra in her head.

Jake tugged Lilliana away from their lab table. "C'mon. We should get out of here."

"No!" Jess stomped her foot. "It's fake! A show. It has to be. She's doing this." Jess snatched a half-dissected frog out of the tray and thrust it toward Lilliana, waggling it. "See this!" The innards dangled out of its opened cavity. "This is real! This is death! Mangled guts. Empty carcass. Deal with it."

Lilliana blinked. The blank stare left her face. She blinked again as if she was emerging from a dumb stupor.

The croaking stopped.

The ghost frogs vanished.

"It *was* you! How'd you do it? Mass hypnosis? It doesn't matter. I don't care. You had no right. Death isn't a joke! It isn't funny! Death is…it's…" Jess was so angry she couldn't speak. Couldn't think. She flung the mangled frog at Lilliana. "It's ugly!"

Jake tried to pull Lilliana out of the way, but the frog hit her square in the chest. Formaldehyde splattered everywhere, making them all wince. The frog slid down her sweater vest, leaving a moist, icky trail.

Lilliana started to shake, but not because she was going to faint. No. Jess knew that look. Lilliana was mad. Jess backed up, admitting to herself she may have gone a little too far, throwing the frog and all. But at least she'd proven who was behind the supposed ghosts.

Lilliana scooped up the mangled frog from the floor and laid it carefully on the table, never taking her eyes off Jess. "How could you do that to him? Desecrate him like that?" She kept walking toward Jess. "You have no respect."

"Run." Maggie whispered loudly and shoved Cai toward the aisle. "Run!" Maggs was dragging Cai to the door. "Wait." Cai refused to go and kept turning back to watch.

"You." Lilliana didn't shout, but for some reason the dissecting instruments rattled in their pans. "You need—"

"What?" Jess wasn't afraid. She stood behind her lab table with her arms crossed, ready for anything The Clone might throw at her.

"A lesson in manners!"

It all happened so fast. Sparks flew out of Lilliana's fingertips straight at Jess. A fireball ignited above the Bunsen burner. Flash. The explosion felt like a giant fist punched all the air out of the room. Jess was vaguely aware of flying backward before her world went black.

She awoke to the sound of smoke alarms and Jake shouting her name. "Jess! Jess, wake up!"

Stunned, she puzzled over the fact that it was raining in the lab. No, she realized, those were the fire sprinklers.

Mark was sprawled out against the supply cabinet, coming to, rubbing his head. He crawled over to her. "You okay?" He shouted over the fire alarm.

She nodded, and they both struggled to their feet. No sign of Lilliana, but Cai and Maggie stared at Jess as if, this time, she was the ghost.

She glanced down at her shirt and understood why. Char marks zigzagged across the blue silk. A sprinkler directly overhead was thoroughly dousing her, plastering the shirt to her chest. She pulled a lock of hair forward. Totally frizzled. The ends of her hair were burnt. The singed-off ends were steaming. She must look like someone who'd just escaped hell.

Water ran in rivulets over Mark's cheeks as he grabbed Jess by the shoulders. "Are you sure you're okay?" He took one look at her soaking wet shirt and slipped his hoodie off. She thought he winked as he eased it over her head. "Not the best day to leave your army gear at home, was it, Gadget?"

Jake shouted to them over the noise of the sprinklers and alarm, "We better get you to the nurse."

She shivered under the spray of cold water and nodded. Mark must've been in shock, too, because he held Jess tight, like he really cared. She was definitely in shock, because she let him. Not only that, she thought it felt incredibly good.

Fairy Godmother Training Manual

Directive 8

Moderate your emotions.

There is nothing worse than a Fairy Godmother out of control. Let us never forget the embarrassing truth behind the disappearance of Atlantis. And then there was that little volcanic incident at Mount St. Helens a few years back…

—Gryndelyn Myrddin

Requiem

Lilliana trudged home after school, nearly blind with frustration and numb with guilt. How could everything have gone so wrong?

**JOURNAL
Day 2**

~~Today will be much better than yesterday.~~

I didn't mean to do it. Honestly!

[Splotch.]

[Tear stain.]

I don't understand what caused the explosion. I threw *elin-gíl* to shake her up, not to—

Lilliana shuddered. She'd nearly blown up her C.O.
And the school.
And Jake.

Her heart tumbled painfully. She was as big a menace to the world as Jess. Lilliana sat on a rock at the edge of the lake, staring into the murky water, speculating on various ways to escape the planet's atmosphere and fly away into the dark clutches of space where she couldn't hurt anyone else.

Meanwhile, a school of minnows tried to cheer her up by playing kissing games with her toes as she swished her feet back and forth. She dropped her training manual on the grass beside the rock and leaned on her elbows, ignoring the fish. She couldn't bear to write any more in the journal. What was the point?

The truth stunk worse than formaldehyde. Today had been a total disaster. Never mind that it had all been an accident—she'd almost barbecued Jess.

She would never forget the look of horror on Jake's face when he saw what she'd done to his sister. He would never forgive her. And Jess certainly wouldn't. Lilliana sighed and whispered to her reflection. "She'll probably declare all-out war."

Ironically, Lilliana thought she'd finally glimpsed the real problem, the secret lurking behind Jess's angry façade. The ghost frogs had been an embarrassing blunder, a foolish loss of control on Lilliana's part. But Jess's reaction to them provided a valuable clue.

What Lilliana didn't know was how, *in the name of all that was magic*, was she supposed to help a frightened girl make peace with death? A peace Lilliana had never been able to find for herself.

She sighed and kicked her foot, sending a spray of droplets sparkling across the lake, jewels capturing the golden fire of the afternoon sun.

How, exactly, does one make peace with something that destroys their happiness with such a ruthless scythe? Lilliana shivered and hugged herself against a sudden chill.

CRECONNAISSANCE

Cold wind tousled what was left of Jess's scorched hair. She and Cai hunkered down in a makeshift bunker atop a grassy knoll overlooking the lake and Lilliana's trailer. It hadn't been easy to track Lilliana here. She had disappeared after the explosion, probably hiding out so she wouldn't get in trouble. Then, out of the blue, she'd shown up in fifth period, sitting in World Geography looking all meek and innocent, just as if she wasn't responsible for blowing up half the school.

Jess was right about The Clone. She was trouble, every bit as bad as Cheryl or *worse*.

Fake ghosts.

Explosions.

At this rate, Jake wasn't the only one in danger. At least Cheryl hadn't jeopardized the lives of everyone in the whole school. Just Ryan.

Jess's stomach tightened with a familiar sick feeling. The same gut punch that always hit her when she thought of Ryan, followed by the screaming question that always followed, no matter how much she tried to silence it. Why? Why? Why? Jess hated that stupid question because she knew exactly *why*. Because girls like Lilliana and Cheryl didn't care about anybody but themselves, that was *why*.

Except there'd been a moment in Geography when Lilliana glanced over her shoulder at Jess and a guilty flush had reddened Lilliana's cheeks. A brief break in character, as if The Clone actually felt bad about all the damage she'd done.

More smoke and mirrors.

Girls like Lilliana didn't care if they hurt other people. So she'd turned red. So what? It didn't prove anything. It didn't mean she was sorry. It didn't even mean she was embarrassed.

After school, Jess, Cai, and Maggie used a triangulated surveillance technique to follow Lilliana here to the lake. Now Jess and Cai were lying on their bellies at the top of the hill, watching, while Maggie did the close work. She'd insisted that she be the one who snooped in the trailer. Which was weird, because Maggie hated spying. Maybe she'd noticed that Jess was still a little wobbly on her feet.

Or maybe it was something else?

Maggs seemed awfully secretive lately. Whatever the reason, she was down there hiding in the brush, closing in on their target. They'd seen Lilliana leave the trailer, and now Maggie was getting ready to sneak in.

Jess pressed the Talk button and whispered. "Do you copy?"

Static crackled as Maggie responded. "Yes. I hear you. Stop checking, or Lilliana's gonna hear you, too."

Jess wanted to be down there in the danger zone. She ignored Maggie's garbled plea and tried out their code names. "Red Dagger to Yellow Rider. What's your position?"

Yellow Rider wasn't as enthusiastic about the code names. "Shut up, Jess. You know where I am. Out," Maggie snapped.

"Do you have a visual on the perp?" Jess quizzed her surly operative.

Maggie didn't answer.

Cai was staring, but not downhill at the lake or at Lilliana's trailer. She was staring at Jess.

"What?" Jess asked, annoyed.

"It's just so weird seeing you without any eyebrows. And your hair is—"

"Sticking out every which way. Yeah, I know. So what?"

"Did you try to brush it?"

"Couldn't. The ends melted into sizzled knots. Fried hair." Jess pulled out a pair of high powered binoculars.

"You know who you look like?"

Jess took a deep breath, trying to remain patient with this line of questioning. It didn't matter *who* she looked like. The problem was *what* she looked like, and the answer to that was *crap*. She shrugged.

"Queen Elizabeth." Cai said, sounding pleased with her declaration. "You know, the first Elizabeth, the one with the red hair and no eyelashes—"

"Knew the old gal personally, did you?" Jess handed the binoculars to Cai. "Could we please get back to business? Check for movement down there."

Cai took the field glasses but, unfortunately, she kept talking. "I hope the nurse called your mom to warn her about what happened. Because she's going to throw a fit when she sees you looking like that."

"You just said I looked like Queen Elizabeth. If anything, it's an improvement."

"Jess, your mom will freak."

"Yeah, yeah, The nurse left a message." Jess didn't add that it would probably be days before her mom even noticed. Jess plucked a blade of grass and used it to point down the slope. "Look down there behind those trees. See if that's Maggie moving in. She should've checked in by now." Jess reached for the Talk button on her headset.

"Wait." Cai grabbed Jess's arm. "Give her time. It's only been a couple of minutes." She abandoned the binoculars and gawked at Jess again.

"Would you stop staring at me?"

"You still look pale." Cai leaned in and whispered as if she was worried someone might overhear them out here in the middle of nowhere. "Did it scare you? The blast, I mean."

"Not really." Jess hedged, unable to meet Cai's worried gaze.

Instead, she grabbed the binoculars and adjusted them into focus. "Besides, from what I hear, I'm doing better than Dawson."

"Yeah," Cai said. "Did you hear? She slipped running down the hall. Paramedics loaded her onto a gurney and wheeled her past everybody while we were standing outside. Poor Mrs. Dawson, she was hysterical." Cai shook her head. "Too bad you were stuck in the nurse's office. They evacuated everyone from Hall B. Policemen and firemen were everywhere. Mr. Jacobsen got on the loud speaker and said a minor gas leak caused the explosion. And get this, he said the gas fumes caused hallucinations. Nothing to be alarmed about. Yadda-yadda-yadda."

"That's a possible explanation."

Cai shook her head. "No. I saw those ghost frogs. You saw them. They were real."

"No such thing as ghosts."

Cai sighed. "I know what I saw."

"Illusions." Jess adjusted the binoculars and scanned the area beyond the trailer. "Lilliana's behind it somehow. That's why we're here. It's why we followed her."

And it was time to get on with the mission. Jess pressed the Talk button. "Red Dagger to Yellow Rider, we're a go. The perimeter looks clear. See if you can get inside the trailer."

Maggie's voice buzzed excitedly in response. "Jess, you won't believe—"

Jess jammed her thumb impatiently against the button. "Yeah, yeah, we've all seen junk trailers on the lake. Get inside. We need proof she set up that spook show this morning. Look for video equipment. Mirrors. Speakers. Wires—"

"No, listen." Maggie's urgent whispers sizzled with speaker static. "It's not what it seems. You've *never* seen a trailer like this."

A shadow, too small to be a cloud but big enough to be a problem, moved across Cai and Jess. Jess twisted around and stared up at…

"Jake!" She flipped off her headset, jumped up, and tried to hide the binoculars behind her back.

"I told you to leave Lilliana alone." His voice was low and growly.

Jess swallowed. Her brother didn't get mad easily. But when he did... "Um, so how'd you find us?"

"You aren't the only one who knows how to use a tracking device." He reached down and ripped a small sticky patch off the side of Jess's carpenter jeans, turned it over and showed her the miniature transmitter.

She snatched it away from him. "You stole this out of my equipment closet."

"Had to keep track of you somehow." Jake looked as stern as their dad. "What are you doing out here?"

"Nothing." The heavy binoculars twitched in her hand.

Jake nodded toward the lake. "That's where she lives, isn't it?" He meant Lilliana. There was no mistaking the lovesick twang in his voice or the way he hesitated on each word and avoided saying her name.

Jess didn't answer.

Suspicion slid across his features. "Where's the third musketeer? Where's Maggie?"

Fairy Godmother Training Manual

Directive 9

Pay strict heed to the laws governing your magic.

Turn to Appendix 13A for a comprehensive list of Forbidden Magical Acts. In many situations, you ought to rely on your wits rather than your wand.

—Gryndelyn Myrddin

Sing a New Song

Lilliana tuned her inner music to the rhythmic sound of the lake softly lapping against the rock as she sat and searched through her manual. She ran her finger down the list in Appendix 13A of magical acts she wasn't allowed to do. "No love spells, mind alteration, personality modification, or time reversal..." She stopped on item 9.

> *9. DO NOT revive the dead. Repeat: do not*
> *attempt to bring anyone back from the dead.*
> *Dire consequences!*

She scanned the rest of the page and chewed her bottom lip. Fine. No reviving. Except it didn't say anything about ghosts. Lilliana was considering an idea that might help Jess, arranging for a short meeting between her and her dead brother's ghost. But Rule 9 threw some doubt on the legality of her plan.

"Summoning a ghost isn't the same as actually reviving the dead," she said aloud.

Or was it? She debated the uncertainty with herself. After all, she'd made frog ghosts appear this morning and no one had come and hauled her off to the fiery dungeons for it.

At least, not yet.

Napoleon flew over her shoulder and landed on the page. His tiny toenails ticked against the crisp paper as he waddled across the list, pecked at Rule 9, and squawked. The cardinal's shrill warnings hurt Lilliana's eardrums. She shooed him off her manual.

"Hmm. I wonder if it makes a difference that they were frog ghosts, rather than human." Lilliana sighed and tapped her finger against the page. Napoleon ignored her and limped across the grass as if she'd wounded him when she'd brushed him away.

"I suppose there's only one way to find out for certain. I'll have to ask Gryndelyn."

Lilliana began to stir the lake to summon Gryndelyn. Napoleon fluttered up to her shoulder and huddled behind her hair. A whirlpool formed, boiling with energy, rising, spraying them as it swirled upward and towered over them.

Gryndelyn's beautiful image appeared with glassy perfection, albeit brown glass, as Texas lakes tended to be muddier than the crystalline ponds of the north. Sun shone through her wings and turned them to a fiery bronze. Rather than relaxed and folded back, her wings were peaked and spread wide, which meant she was definitely not in a good mood.

Gryndelyn's soul music always leaned toward clarinets and saxophones. Today, however, she sounded particularly trumpet-like.

"Uh-oh." Lilliana murmured.

Napoleon streaked into the sky. Lilliana envied the little bird as she stood atop her rock perch and tried not to feel like an insect in front of her guardian.

"What is it now, Lilliana? I was teaching a class."

"I have a question." Lilliana's mouth went dry. She tried in vain to swallow. "I checked the manual, and the appendices, but—"

"Is this going to be a daily occurrence, snatching me away from important matters to answer your silly questions? Isn't it enough that the entire school is gossiping about your stunt with frog ghosts this morning?"

"Oh," Lilliana sighed. "You heard about that." She couldn't

look up, knowing the disapproval she'd see on her mentor's face.

"Of course I heard. *Everyone*'s heard. Did you think you could keep something like that a secret?" Her glassy wings vaulted into sharp points. "You're my ward. My apprentice. Do you have any idea what your disgraceful behavior is doing to my reputation? To say nothing of the other repercussions. Not more than an hour ago a first-year was showing off—copying you. The silly child tried to summon a rabbit ghost, short-circuited her entire nervous system. It'll be months before the foolish twit recovers enough to move her arms, and as to whether she'll ever speak again..." Gryndelyn shrugged. "Debatable."

"Oh, I'm so sorry. The frogs were an accident. I didn't even realize until it was too late."

"An accident? It's hard to believe you're the—" Gryndelyn clamped her lips tight, and in an unexplainable shift of mood, her wing tips rounded slightly. "Very well. What's your question?"

Lilliana's chest felt as if she were trapped beneath the large rock instead of standing on top of it. She dared not ask about summoning a human ghost. Not now. Clearly, such things were not done. And yet, how else could she help Jess? She held the manual out in front of her as a shield, a defense. "The rules say it's forbidden to revive the dead. But I couldn't find any mention of ghosts."

Gryndelyn crossed her arms, and the lake around her began to bubble.

"I didn't intend to make the frog ghosts appear, but..." Lilliana glanced sideways at her teacher and rushed into the question, "Is it permissible to conjure human ghosts in the same way?"

"Permissible?"

"For the benefit my C.O?"

"Have you completely lost your mind?"

SHE WHO RUNS AWAY LIVES
TO SPY ANOTHER DAY

Maggie's headset went silent. No more reassuring static hum.

So much for being in constant communication, she thought. Although, it was probably just as well. If Jess kept demanding an update every fifteen seconds, Lilliana was bound to overhear. Maggie crouched behind a stand of spindly river birches, hoping her camouflage shirt blended with the sumac and hackberry bushes.

After the explosion in Biology, she knew Lilliana could be dangerous when pushed. She also knew she wouldn't find speaker wires or cameras inside Lilliana's trailer. This was no ordinary girl. The incident in the bathroom proved that. And no matter what Jess thought, Maggie knew those frog ghosts were real.

Jess had her reasons for this mission.

Maggie had hers.

Well, not reasons so much as questions. *Big questions*. And those questions were getting bigger by the second.

At first, Lilliana's dilapidated trailer looked ordinary—faded turquoise and white paint, dark murky windows, and rusted aluminum skirting. Then Maggie blinked. She only closed her eyes against the wind for a second. The trailer transformed into haze—a million fuzzy pixels swimming apart, evaporating into a giant blur.

Maggie didn't know what had happened. For a minute she thought maybe her dyslexia had gone haywire. She squeezed her eyes shut. When she reopened them again, her vision wavered, flickered, and then snapped into focus the way a television spurts back on after a cable outage.

Except Lilliana's trailer had disappeared—changed.

Maggie was used to seeing things wrong, Ds that should be Bs, 8s that should be 3s. Over the years she'd learned how to blot out the confusion and force herself to concentrate so she could see what was really there. She called it *seeing-true*. This time, seeing-true made her whistle softly through her teeth.

"Whoa." She pushed aside a clump of hackberry to get better look.

In place of the trailer was a cave-like hut carved into the side of a cliff beside the lake. The doorway was braced by winding roots framing a small wooden door. It looked like a cottage from a fairytale. Wild onions grew among the grasses on the roof. Round purple blossoms on slender stalks, they bobbed comically on the breeze. Early blooming bluebonnets and brilliant red Indian paintbrush grew thick as carpet around the base of the little hill house.

The flowers were lovely.

But there were also deadly-looking clumps of pale mushrooms. Slick with sulfuric yellow ooze, the mushrooms bulged like poisonous guardians along the path to the door. Quartz crystals lodged in the earthen cliff walls refracted sunbeams and cast weird shadows in front of the cottage. If Maggie didn't focus hard, the cave shimmered back into the original image of a rusty old trailer.

Yet, even though she squinted as hard as she could, it seemed as if phantom coyotes skulked in the tangled garden, warding her off. Lilliana's cave appeared both idyllic and frightening, a storybook cottage and horror-show cavern all at the same time.

She left her hiding place to find out which it was.

Maggie had a personal prime directive in life: there would be nothing secret from her, neither in heaven nor earth. She would have the truth. Not blindness. Never that. Dyslexia did its best to fool her, but she was determined to see-true. No matter the cost.

Toads sprang away from the path as she approached the door.

In the wild gardens on her left and right, she heard the unmistakable sound of slithering. Maggie ignored it. She ignored the shadows slinking toward her. She also ignored the unsteady scampering of her own pulse.

She knocked on the thick wooden door. Her soft thump sounded cottony and dull, barely audible. But in response, fat roots shifted in the clay and stones of the wall, unwinding like knobby mechanical arms, pointing with hairy fingers in her direction. She jiggled the handle, willing to face Lilliana's anger rather than stand out here and get strangled by roots.

The heavy door slowly swung open.

"Hello?" she whispered into the dim interior. A faint echo answered her. Maggie stepped farther inside. What she saw took her breath away.

Crystals on the exterior wall, the same ones that had cast dread outside, refracted soft rainbows on the interior. She walked deeper into the cave on a thick moss carpet. The iridescent pattern on the far walls rippled as a breeze blew in from the door.

Maggie shivered. Then she noticed the earthen wall was covered with thousands of sleeping brown moths. Exquisite peacock circles on their wings shimmered like a thousand watchful eyes. The moths hummed faintly in their sleep, harmonizing with the low soothing song of a flute. A small brook accompanied them as it trickled through the center of the cavern. Maggie stepped over the stream, searching for the source of the melody.

Lilliana's schoolbooks looked out of place stacked atop a stone table. As did a teen fashion magazine, folded open, with photos circled and notes scribbled in the margins. But it explained a lot.

Brightly colored veils, purple, green and several shades of blue gossamer, hung from the ceiling, waving like pennants adorning a royal courtyard. There was a bed of leaves and bright feathers nestled against the far wall with a blanket of creamy silk draped over the end.

Maggie found where the music came from, an enormous hand-hewn aboriginal-style flute hanging on the wall. She guessed the air in the cave must waft through the long oddly curved cylinder exactly right to make it play such gentle breathy notes.

"Lovely," she murmured and ran her fingers over the smooth wood, admiring the swirling grain and polished knots.

Two knots winked open. Wooden eyes glared straight at her. "Don't touch me."

Maggie stumbled back. Her foot splashed into the brook. She fell and landed in an awkward heap on the opposite bank.

"Manners, child. Manners!" the flute snapped. "Get your dirty shoes out of the life stream." Its wooden eyes rolled toward the ceiling in disgust, and a slit that served as a mouth pursed.

Maggie jerked her foot out of the creek. "I…I fell."

"I can see that." The flute snorted, sounding like Maggie's dad when he blew his nose.

Moth wings on the wall ruffled in response.

"Now look what you've done. You've woken them up."

Maggie glanced around the quivering walls in desperation. "Sing them back to sleep."

"I don't take orders from you." The flute puckered up and made a popping noise. "I'm here on loan from the Elf King himself."

A ferret dashed out from shadows behind the door. It scurried along the wall, jumped over the brook, and leapt into Maggie's lap. The furry little bandit stood on its hind legs, stretched its long body up to her chin, and chittered loudly. Maggie would've sworn the ferret pointed to the door. She tried to pet it, but as soon as she laid her hand on his beige coat the little fellow nattered at her even more. In a bristly huff, he scampered off her lap, bounded over to the flute, and repeated his agitated chatter.

The flute blew an arrogant toot. "Yes, she's a human. What did you think?" He listened to the ferret's excited squeaking and answered, "Well, don't look at me. You're the one who let her in."

"You understand what he's saying?" Maggie stood up and

crossed the creek to the flute.

"Naturally." His brow puckered up haughtily, as if Maggie smelled a bit foul. "I am an arm of the oldest tree in the Elf King's forest, fluent in hundreds of languages, perhaps thousands. How do you think I know yours, human? I've been watching your kind for several millennia."

Maggie hugged herself, trying to rub away the damp coolness on her arms. "Lilliana is an elf?"

"Heavens, no." The flute chortled.

Before he could say anything more, the ferret scurried up Maggie's leg, hissing, his tail spiked out like an angry puffer fish. He sprang onto her shoulder and thumped his nose against the side of her head.

"He wants you to leave."

"I got that."

A bright red cardinal zipped into the room whistling frantically. In wild flashes of scarlet, it flapped a tight circle around them, chirping madly and dive-bombing Maggie.

"Oh good gracious, Gryndelyn herself is here. You'd better go." The flute's tone went up several notches. "Now, child! You must go. Hurry."

"Okay, but you didn't answer me about Lilliana. Is she—"

The kamikaze cardinal shrieked and made another pecking-pass at her.

"Hey!" Maggie scooped the quaking ferret into her arms to shield it from the attacking cardinal. She was rewarded with an ungrateful nip on her finger. The ferret leapt down.

"Go!" boomed the flute. "Run!"

The cardinal's ear-piercing squawks left no doubt that he agreed. Bristling, the ferret yipped and rammed his little head against her ankle. Moths fluttered away from the wall, and darkened the room as they formed a whirling brown cloud.

"Run!" The flute hooted.

Maggie did.

She ran out of the cavern into blinding sunlight with an insane cardinal, a mad ferret, and a mob of moths chasing after her. She dashed for the lake, thinking she could dive in to escape her pursuers.

But when Maggie neared the shore she skidded to a dead stop. The ferret crashed into her legs, squeaked, and slunk into the underbrush. The cardinal stopped whistling, did a jet-propelled U-turn and disappeared. The moths shrouded her in fog but quickly streamed away.

She'd seen something in the lake. Something far more frightening than a swarm of angry moths. A towering column of water, sculpted into a terrifyingly beautiful goddess. She had fierce pointed wings like Nike, the Greek goddess of battle.

The goddess was shouting at Lilliana. "Alär hiswe mar!"

The strange words made Maggie tremble with a weakness that spread cold all the way to her bones. Then the glimmering goddess pointed in her direction and screeched, "Now see what you've done."

Lilliana turned and gasped. "Maggie!"

The lady in the lake twirled around and shattered into a million droplets that rained into the sloshing waves.

Maggie wanted to run. She wanted to tear out of there and never look back. But her legs felt like wobbly brittle sticks. Even if she could move, surely her bones would splinter. She took one feeble step backward and started to turn around.

"Maggie, wait!" Lilliana sprouted wings and whooshed overhead, cutting off Maggie's retreat.

She flew. Real wings! Lovely wings. Not like the goddess's. Hers were beautiful, bright shades of blue, green, and purple like the gossamer hanging in her cave. Soft, flowing wings, like... like a... "You're a—"

Jake sprinted up the path and startled them both.

Lilliana spun around.

He fell to his knees, and two words rushed out. "An Angel!"

102

Fairy Godmother Training Manual

Directive 10

Magic is no longer in vogue with humans. They prefer explainable phenomenon, quantifiable miracles. Science is the current fashion. Consequently, we must operate incognito. However, on rare occasions it may become necessary to reveal yourself. Do so with the utmost caution.

WARNING: Revealing your true identity can be somewhat upsetting to your C.O. if not handled with the utmost care. Use caution and sound judgment. We have documented cases of humans who were unable to cope, and despite profuse applications of elin-gíl, they were eventually hauled away, slobbering, in straightjackets.

—Gryndelyn Myrddin

Singing the Blues

That evening Lilliana sat at her desk doodling in her journal, staring at her misbegotten entries from earlier in the long tumultuous day, uncertain how to record everything that had happened.

JOURNAL
Day 2

~~Today will be much better than yesterday~~

I didn't mean to do it. Honestly!

[Splotch.]

[Tear stain.]

I don't understand what caused the explosion. I threw *elin-gíl* to shake some sense into her, not to— [slurred ending. Followed by a frustrated squiggle]

Lilliana brushed the soft quill feathers against her cheek and doodled a stick figure of an angel.

"ANGEL"

That's what he called me. An Angel.

No one has ever looked at me like that, with such utter adoration. When he fell to his knees and stared up at me—oh, I wished with all my heart that I really was an angel.

Okay. I admit it. I may have been wishing a little too hard to be a real angel. My wings *might* have been a little more radiant than normal. And maybe a teensy-weensy golden halo sprang up.

And I don't know for certain. But I'm pretty sure there was a general white glow.

I couldn't help it.

Really.

Fine. I'll be completely honest. I couldn't resist. And then I touched Jake. You know, like a saint-blessing-a-sinner sort of thing. All I did was rest my hand against his cheek. It made him happy.

And it made me happy. I've wanted to do that since the first time I saw him.

It wasn't until he closed his eyes and pressed his lips into my palm that I realized I had carried things a bit too far.

Jake's kiss still lingered. Lilliana traced the center of her palm with her quill feather.

She remembered exactly how it had felt. Like heaven. He was the angel, not her. The mere touch of his lips had transported her to a place of goodness and warmth. He'd felt it, too. She saw it in his upward gaze. She'd shivered, weakening with the urge to have his lips on hers.

No longer the supplicant, Jake had sensed the power he held over her. Surprise and heat had quickened his features. The eagerness in his face melted Lilliana's resolve. She'd nearly collapsed to her knees, had nearly forsaken everything and fallen into his arms. He reached for her, pulsing with joy, his face as radiant as a real angel's.

Too bad he would never remember.

Lilliana pressed her quill against the page and scratched the next words so hard, the nib broke slightly.

Jess charged up the path with all the grace of a wild boar.

Lilliana drew a line through the harsh words and started again.

Jess ran up behind Jake and surprised us.

She totally ruined the mood, that's what she did.

Obviously, Jess has recovered from the explosion—except for her hair. (Note: must do something about her hair.) She shouted profanity at me. Things like: "What the hell ARE you?"

And that was her least foul curse. What if I'd been a real angel? She'd be in very deep trouble.

The whole mess turned ugly. Shouting. Confusion. I've never had to use so much *elin-gíl* in my life. I'm exhausted.

Elin-gíl still doesn't work very well on Maggie. Fortunately, it did calm her down, but I still had to promise

I'd explain everything tomorrow night at Jess's house. That should be…

Awkward?

A nightmare?

Lilliana sighed, set down her quill, and shut the book.

She brushed her fingertips against the side of Flute's cheek. "Would you play the theme from *Romeo and Juliet* for me?"

Flute frowned. "Are you sure that's wise, my dear?"

"I'm not feeling very wise tonight. Would you please play it anyway?"

She thanked the fireflies for their service and set them free from the lamp on her desk. It was getting late. She scooped up her ferret and snuggled with him in her bed.

Flute grudgingly played her request, but he muted the dramatic passages and turned the ill-fated lovers' theme into a bittersweet lullaby.

As Lilliana hummed and stroked Tik-Tik's silky fur, she couldn't stop remembering the way Jake had looked at her. Sadly, she also remembered the moment *elin-gíl* washed the passion from his features. It made her stomach feel like a stone tumbling into a dark, endless well.

Of course, the star-sparks made him forget. He's only human, she reminded herself. He should forget. Must forget. But when Jake stood up, dusted himself off, and walked away as if nothing had happened, as if he wasn't carrying away her heart in his cold indifferent pocket, her heart had broken.

"Never mind," she crooned to Tik-Tik. It was just as well. He's human, off-limits, dangerous, forbidden. It was good that he forgot her weakness for his lips. Good that he would not remember how his touch had melted her resistance. Good that he would never know how easily she could've fallen into his arms.

Tik-Tik nuzzled Lilliana's cheek and coiled up next to her. Lilliana pulled the silk sheet over her shoulders and tried to sleep.

It was useless until a firefly-sized hope blinked into her weary mind.

Maybe the *elin-gíl* would wear off. Maybe tomorrow he would remember.

IMPENDING INVASION

School on Thursday seemed dull in comparison to the *Industrial Light & Magic* show from the day before. But Jess didn't mind. On the upside, she didn't run into Lilliana all day. On the downside, Jess, along with half the student body, sat packed in the gym most of the day watching movies while cleaning crews and workmen mucked out the water and made repairs to the damage in Hall B. There was an upside to that, too. No homework.

Cleanup must've gone miraculously well, because at three o'clock Jacobsen announced classes in Hall B would resume the next day. A collective moan went up in the gym.

After school, Jess sat at her computer console scrolling through county property records, searching for who owned the lake property where Lilliana had camped her trailer. Cai paced the floor in Jess's war room, munching nervously on a bag of potato chips.

"Calm down, Cai. She's not coming."

"Maggie thinks she will." Cai wadded up the chip bag, tossed it into the wastebasket.

"Yeah, well, Maggs isn't *always* right."

"She usually is," Cai argued and brushed the salt off her fingers. "You know what's bugging me? I can't remember what happened at the lake yesterday. Can you?"

"Sure." Jess scanned the property records, hoping Cai wouldn't quiz her too closely. Truth be told, the details were all a bit fuzzy.

"What, exactly, do you remember?"

Inwardly Jess groaned, outwardly she just shrugged. "Jake tracked us to the bluff overlooking Lilliana's trailer, got mad because we were spying, dragged us out of there, and drove us home. End of story."

Cai mulled that over for a minute. "Except you've left out a few things. I distinctly remember running down a dirt road toward the lake. Running fast, like there was something wrong. There was something shiny in the water. After that, all I remember is Maggie looking scared. Bright lights. Colors. Then, I don't know." She threw up her hands. "It's like I'm trying to remember something through a thick fog."

"Uh-huh." Jess kept scrolling through the records. She remembered lights, too. Probably more of Lilliana's techno hocus-pocus, but she had no intention of acknowledging it.

Cai wouldn't let it go. "When I got home, I was dusty and sweaty. That's proof."

"Of what?"

"That we ran." Cai frowned and fidgeted with the stack of papers on the corner of Jess's console. "I guess it doesn't really prove anything. But something's hinky. I can tell."

"You're right about that." Jess smacked the desk with her hand and spun to face Cai. "I just found out she's a squatter, illegally camped. A corporation based out of Chicago owns that parcel where she's parked her trailer."

"That doesn't prove anything. She's from Chicago; maybe it's her family's company."

"Not a chance. If they're rich enough to own lake property, why would they make her live in that old piece-of-junk trailer?"

Cai looked skeptical. "She may live in an old trailer, but she obviously has money. Didn't you see what she had on today?"

"No. Didn't see her. I was stuck in the lower bleachers, squished between Bobby Townsend and Amy Reed."

"Well, her clothes looked expensive. Probably designer." Cai swept the lines of a dress with her hand. "A gauzy white dress with a bluish metal belt."

"Bluish metal?" Jess rolled her eyes.

"Iridescent, you know, like blue butterfly wings, and she had a gold band in her hair. With all that white, she looked kind of like an—" Cai froze. Her mouth dropped open as if she remembered something important.

"Looked like what?" Jess demanded.

"An angel," she muttered.

"Prefect disguise for a devil." Jess waved the issue away. "Anyway, who cares?"

"Everyone but you." Cai shook herself free from whatever vision she'd been having, opened the fridge, and poured a glass of chocolate milk. "Haven't you noticed? Monday, Lilliana wore that frilly skirt and leggings. Tuesday at least twelve girls showed up in leggings and poofy skirts. You saw her parochial school uniform yesterday, right? Well, today, anybody'd think Lake Elm had converted overnight into a Catholic school. From where I sat in the bleachers, I counted sixteen girls in plaid skirts with blue blazers. You just wait until tomorrow. It'll be white angel dresses with shiny belts."

"Lemmings." Jess inhaled deeply. It disturbed her that one girl could change Lake Elm High so easily.

The doorbell rang. Jess's gaze flew to the front door monitor. She stared in disbelief at the image on the screen. The Clone. "Speak of the devil."

Cai swallowed milk with a loud gulp. "You said she wouldn't come."

Jess would've laid odds on it. And yet, there was Lilliana. Standing on Jess's front porch. Invading Jess's private territory.

Cai nudged her. "Are you gonna let her in?"

Jess crossed her arms tight. "I don't know. This was Maggie's idea, not mine."

"Well, Maggie's not here."

The bell rang a second time.

Fairy Godmother Training Manual

Directive 11

Patience is not a virtue—it's a weapon.

We who find ourselves in service to mortals must learn to use patience to our advantage. Observe. Watch the humans carefully. Tolerate their foibles. Make allies of your C.O.'s friends, but above all, wait. Wait for the perfect moment to spring your plan.

—Gryndelyn Myrddin

March of the Mountain Fairy

Virtue or weapon, Lilliana had never cultivated patience as a child. She disliked waiting. Waiting was not fun. Truth was, she *hated* waiting.

As for having a plan to spring…

Evidently, she wasn't much good at planning either. More to the point, she didn't like the idea of springing a trap on anyone, especially not on a girl like Jess, a girl who needed Lilliana's help. Building trust seemed more important than building a trap.

Lilliana just wasn't the patient, plotting, planning type. Although she admitted to herself that she *had* concocted one small plan today. She'd worn clothes specifically chosen in the hope they would trigger Jake's memory of her posing as an angel. A foolish lovesick angel.

That had proved a dismal failure.

Planning and trapping skills—zero.

Now what? How could she make Jess understand the whole Fairy Godmother thing? She should be patient. Wait. Plan.

Lizard fuzz!

There was only one way to handle this.

* * *

Lilliana rang Jess's doorbell again, this time more forcefully. They were in there. She could hear the low rumble of Jess's rage, Cai's rippling curiosity, and—

Jake. He opened the door. "Lilliana?" His voice sounded husky and uncertain, as if he wasn't quite sure whether he was awake or dreaming.

Another fairy might've thought of something light and clever to say, but Lilliana imprisoned her tongue behind tightly pressed lips. Silence felt safer than speaking. What was this strange inexplicable attraction she felt? One look at him and she wanted so much more than the exchange of mere words.

Kissing. That's what she wanted. She wanted to kiss him as much as she wanted to breathe, and that definitely would not be safe.

Lilliana stepped into the doorway, unable to stop herself from searching his face, his eyes, his mouth, watching for any nuance of expression that might betray whether he remembered seeing her at the lake with her wings extended. Did he remember kissing her palm? Did he remember turning her heart into a witless, frantic bird?

He didn't.

The struggle and confusion on his features and his inner music made that abundantly clear. But he stared at her intently and drifted closer, dangerously close. She could feel his essence calling her, taste the delicious scents flowing between them. She marveled at the way their music intertwined so effortlessly. He reached toward the gold circlet in her hair as if it were a magnet, pulling his hand, triggering a forgotten emotion, sliding him toward a memory.

"Jake!" Jess shouted from the top of the grand staircase.

Jake blinked. His hand dropped away. Enchantment changed to hyperconfusion.

"Lilliana. Up here," Jess barked an order, not an invitation.

Turning red, Jake raked his fingers through his hair. "Oh, I get it. You came to see my sister."

Lilliana nodded. Her hopes slid away and shattered on the white marble floor.

Just then Maggie bounded onto the front porch and smiled. "Oh, good. I didn't miss anything." She slipped between them into the entry.

"Didn't miss what?" Jake shut the door.

Maggie's eyes opened big, and she mouthed, "Oops."

Lilliana covered for her. "I told Maggie I'd come and explain everything they saw at the lake."

"Explain what?" He shook his head as if he was trying to clear out cobwebs.

Lilliana caught the corner of her lip before answering. "You don't remember." It wasn't a question. It was a simple statement of fact. The plain truth. So, why did it hurt her stomach to say it? She and Maggie hurried up to Jess's room.

Jake ran up the stairs after her. "Wait!"

"Whoa." Jess held up her hand, barring him from her room. "This is private. Girls only."

A DIPLOMATIC SOLUTION

Jess shut the door of her inner sanctum. The torn-up look on Jake's face made her furious. It had only been a few days, and The Clone was already doing a tap dance on his heart. But then, that's what clone's do. Destroy people. Jess planned to put a stop to that. She sat down in her high-back computer chair and mustered up the dignity of a military judge presiding over a court-martial.

"Maggie, you called this meeting. Let's get on with it." If Jess had owned a gavel, she would've pounded it three times and warned, "You have sixty seconds to present your case."

"Okay." Maggs sat on the couch and rubbed her palms against her jeans the way she always did when she got nervous. "Well, yesterday when—"

Lilliana stopped her. She stepped into the center of the room like she was about to address the court. "I promised I'd come and explain everything that happened at the lake and why I've been watching—"

"Watching." Cai sat up straight, as if the word jolted her. "That's it! I remember now. The interview. You're a spy!"

Cai had gone completely bonkers. Jess wondered if the chocolate milk had been in the fridge too long. Maybe it had fermented or something.

"You know, like from the CIA or something..." Cai continued to assert her whacko theory, with decreasing volume, until her voice practically faded out with "...sent here to watch Jess."

Jess leaned back and squinted sideways at her best friend.

"You're losing it."

"That's what she told me." Cai turned back to Lilliana. "You did. And I recorded it. But then you spilled glitter all over and messed up my player, and—"

"I'm not a spy," Lilliana interrupted calmly. "And I'm really sorry about your recorder."

"But I distinctly remember, you said—"

"Yes, I told you I was sent here to watch over Jess. That part is true."

"Sure." Jess snorted. "Okay, I'll bite. Who sent you to 'watch over' me?" She caught herself using air quotes. Jess hated air quotes. She never used them. She must be more rattled than she wanted to admit.

Jess stood up and jammed her hands into her pockets. She went into her tough street-fighter mode, getting up in Lilliana's face. "If you're my babysitter, who sent you, huh? NSA? Scientific American? My mother?" The Clone didn't budge, so Jess kept pushing. "Homeland Security? The local library. Who?"

Lilliana smiled and, cool as a vanilla yogurt smoothie, she said, "I'm your Fairy Godmother."

Jess choked.

Really choked. Her throat strangled up in a snorted laugh that couldn't make up its mind. It ended up choking her good. She tried to swallow, bent over, hiccupped, sucked air, half laughed, coughed, and choked again.

Maggie hurried to the sink and filled a glass. "Try this." She patted Jess's back.

After several sloppy gulps of water, Jess's throat finally cleared. "You're my *what*?" she rasped.

The corner of Lilliana's mouth tipped up in a triumphant smile. "Fairy Godmother."

"That's what I thought you said." Jess dropped into her chair, shook her head, and laughed. "Gotta hand it to you, that's creative."

"It's the truth."

"Okaaay. I don't read much fiction, but aren't fairies supposed to be like two inches tall?" Jess squeezed the air between her thumb and index finger, held it up to one eye, and compared it to Lilliana. "Wow! I guess you're the star player on the fairyland basketball team, huh?"

Lilliana didn't say anything

Jess tapped her foot, unable to wait for a comeback. "Oh, I know—maybe you're a *giant* fairy? *King Kong* of Fairyville. Paul Bunyan's little fairy sister. Goliath—"

"Enough." Lilliana raised one finger into the air between them. "For your information, most fairies are as tall as humans. I am not a giant. Well, okay, I'm a little bit taller than most, but only by a few inches. You're thinking of pixies." She mimicked Jess's pinch-fingered measurement. "Small fairy servants. Think of them like worker bees to the queen, except way more temperamental. Ever since what's-his-name wrote *Peter Pan*, you humans have confused pixies with—"

"J. M. Barrie," Cai blurted, wide-eyed.

Lilliana and Jess stared at her. "What?" they asked at the same time.

"He wrote *Peter Pan*," Cai explained, as if this factoid was somehow important.

Jess turned her attention back to Lilliana. "Oh, sure. We humans have it all wrong. And I suppose the pointy ears are just a myth started by—"

Lilliana swooped back her thick hair.

Jess's breath caught in her throat.

Maggs jumped up and stared at Lilliana's very pointed ears.

Jess crossed her arms. "They could've been surgically done, or it could be a deformity."

"Pretty phenomenal deformity," Maggie muttered, the vet in her unable to keep still. "Can I touch them?" She hesitantly traced the graceful arch of one of Lilliana's ears. "Can you hear better than humans?"

Lilliana shrugged.

"Maggs! Don't tell me you're buying any of this?"

When Maggie didn't answer, Jess kicked the wheels of her chair. "C'mon! She has weird ears—so what? Cai?"

Cai shook her head and glanced at the floor. "I thought all that stuff was make believe, but—"

"Thought? For pity's sake, guys! It IS make believe." Jess waved her hand at Lilliana, wondering why her friends were missing the obvious. "A *fairy*? Really?"

"I dunno, Jess." Maggie faced Jess. "I saw some weird things at the lake and in her cave—"

"Trailer," Jess corrected

"Cave," Maggie insisted. "A talking flute. The walls were carpeted with moths. A berserk ferret and a cardinal attacked me for no reason. What else could explain—"

"There's always an explanation!" Jess paced and enunciated each word slowly and distinctly so they would get the point. "Because, there's … no … such … thing … as … magic!"

They didn't get it. Maggie and Cai still stared at Lilliana as if she were Santa Claus and they were five years old.

"Ignorance…" Jess mumbled and pointed angrily at Lilliana. "Fine. Let's play it your way. If you're my Fairy Godmother—prove it!" She dared her. "Do something magic. Don't I get three wishes or something?"

"That's a genie," Cai corrected.

Jess rolled her eyes, leaned closer to Lilliana. "What's wrong, magic girl? Cat got your wand?"

Lilliana's jaw flexed, and she lifted her chin, all haughty and imperious. "I don't need a wand."

"No?" Jess smirked. "What'd ya do, sing a song? *Bibbity Boppity Boo*?"

"Hardly."

They faced off. High noon at the OK corral.

"Careful," Cai pleaded. "Remember the explosion."

Careful was for weenies. Jess was in full-metal-jacket mode. "So, do it!"

"Very well," Lilliana said, way too calm. "You want magic, I'll give you magic. I've wanted to do something about your hair since the first day I met you."

Jess flinched, unable to stop her disloyal hand from flying up to her matted frizz. "There's nothing wrong with my hair."

Cai chuckled. Jess shot her a missiles-at-the-ready glare.

Maggie clicked her tongue against her teeth. "Admit it, Jess. You've never bothered with your hair much, and ever since the explosion you haven't tried at all."

"The explosion is her fault." Jess turned back to Lilliana and found herself face-to-face with a cloud of tiny glowing hummingbirds whirling in the air. Except, these hummingbirds had tiny faces and jeweled hands.

"*These* are pixies." Lilliana fixed Jess with defiant smile. "The best in the business."

The bright pink and yellow swarm reacted to Lilliana's proclamation by twirling and squealing in high-pitched giggles.

"It's true. You are the very best Hair Pixies anywhere." Lilliana flattered the tiny creatures, speaking in a high melodic pitch. She almost sang when she spoke to them. "I would not have called any other clan for so difficult a task as this."

With preening sighs and coos of satisfaction, the pixies spiraled into a fluttering ribbon and streamed around Lilliana's head.

"No, my dears. Not my hair today. But thank you." She pointed at Jess. "Hers."

The cloud of pixies arrested midair and turned. For a moment, the only sound was the whirring of wings. Jess took a step back. Then, like tinkling glass bells, the pixies erupted into fits of teeny-tiny laughter. In a mad rush they zipped around Jess's head, attacking her hair like crazed hornets.

"Stop!" Jess shouted and waved her hand. "Get them away!"

"I'd hold very, *very,* still if I were you." Lilliana's voice held a note of menace.

"Hey! Let go." Jess swatted at one of the pixies tugging on her hair. "Ouch!" One of them stung her. Blood dripped from her finger.

"Careful." Lilliana issued a tardy warning. "They're armed with razors. How else did you expect them to cut your hair?"

"I don't!" Jess clutched her wounded finger and tried to dodge the swarm. Hordes of buzzing beauticians descended on her, lifting out sections of her hair and slicing away Jess's damaged locks with amazing speed.

"No such thing as magic." Jess mumbled as a red curl floated down her nose and drifted to the floor. "There's an explanation for this," she insisted, and dodged behind her workstation, trying in vain to flee the miniature mob. "Call them off."

Just then, two pixies repelled down Jess's forehead, hanging onto curls that framed her face. With miniscule flashing blades, they shaved away some of the strands. As they bounced down her nose, she scrunched it, afraid she might sneeze.

"Hold still." Lilliana warned.

Jess froze. Pixies wielding shiny razors tiptoed across her cheek, pulling stubborn matted locks with them, hacking away at her hair like swordsmen in battle. One by one the bumblebee-sized barbers finished jousting with her hair and fluttered back to Lilliana's shoulder, where they hovered and twittered in annoyingly high voices.

"Yes," Lilliana agreed with whatever they were saying. "Charming. Very nice work. No, she's not always this grumpy." The corner of Lilliana's mouth twitched. "Say thank you, Jess."

Jess glared at the army of pixies and their ruthless dictator.

"Thank you, ladies." Lilliana inclined her head to the pixies, who sang back a quick two-note acknowledgement and disappeared in a glittery swirl.

"Wait!" Cai roused herself out of her stunned stupor and called to the vanishing hairdressers. "Can you do that for me?" But the room remained buzzless.

Lilliana smiled. "You have beautiful hair, Cai. We'll talk later. First..." She tilted her head toward her victim. "What do you think?"

"Wow." Maggie circled Jess. "I never realized before just how amazingly pretty you are."

"You have to see this." Cai grabbed Jess's hand and dragged her to the dresser in her bedroom. "Look!" She squared Jess's shoulders in front of the mirror.

Curls waved artfully around her face. Her features actually looked delicate, almost fine. No more soldier. In some ways she looked almost as fairy-like as Lilliana. The short cut drew attention to her blue eyes. She *did* look pretty. Jess whispered to her stunned reflection, "There's got to be an explanation."

"There is." Lilliana stood behind her, smiling into the mirror. "I'm your Fairy Godmother."

Directive 12

Humans are stubborn creatures. This is not merely my opinion. It is a conclusion arrived at after centuries of study.

Not only that, they readily confess their stubbornness. (Generally, this confession is in reference to an acquaintance rather than themselves.) Humans have a saying: "You can lead a horse to water, but you cannot make him drink." This, of course, refers to their own obstinate behavior. A thirsty horse would never behave so irrationally.

Thus, reasoning with a human may prove frustrating for a novice. Study the Chart of Manipulative Techniques & Strategies in Appendix 23C. There you will find a useful list of diversionary tactics and motivational devices.

– Gryndelyn Myrddin

Climb Every Mountain

Several of the tactics from the *Manipulative Techniques & Strategies* chart probably would have worked better than what Lilliana chose to do. But she couldn't bring herself to use that awful list.

Schemes and tricks were too demeaning. Humans deserved more respect. She didn't feel that way simply because she was a Halfling. Lilliana liked things straightforward. She preferred an honest, direct approach to life. Besides, deception gave her a stomachache.

Unfortunately, her straightforward approach often met with obstacles. Today's obstacle was Jess's gorilla-sized stubborn streak.

TACTICAL EVASION

"This doesn't prove a thing," Jess argued at her own perfectly framed features reflected in the mirror. She couldn't bear to look at the stranger wearing her face a moment longer. She spun around and glared at Lilliana. "I don't know what you are, or how you did this, but I'll figure it out." She pointed back at the direction of the offending face in the mirror. "That's not me. I don't look like that."

"You do now," Maggie said softly and backed away.

"No! This is another one of her tricks. She used hypnosis. Mass hysteria. *Something*." Jess slowly peeked over her shoulder at the mirror and groaned when her transformed image peered back. She squeezed her eyes shut and mussed up her hair. When she reopened them, her curls had fallen back into perfect pixyish order. "I can't look like this. It's too...too..."

"Pretty?" Cai offered.

"Fragile," Maggie mumbled under her breath.

Jess stomped away from the mirror and paced between the two rooms. "How did you do it?" She paused in front of Lilliana, but didn't wait for the answer before stalking off again, muttering. She realized she was stuck in an infinite loop between her war room and bedroom. Finally, she stopped.

In a calm, reasoned voice she presented her argument. "Let's pretend, for a moment, that you are telling the truth. Why me?"

Lilliana caught her lip between her teeth and backed up.

Yeah, that had her. Jess pressed her advantage. "Why not Cai?" She pointed like a game show hostess offering Lilliana the prize behind door number two. "She was orphaned in Korea. Or why not

Maggie? There isn't a stray animal within fifty miles she hasn't tried to help. They're the ones who need a Fairy Godmother. Not me. I can take care of myself." Jess narrowed her focus, watching Lilliana's face for a microburst of truth. "Why me?"

Lilliana's gaze flitted around the room, fleeing Jess's scrutiny. "I don't know."

"Oh, there's a reason. I can see it your eyes."

"Of course there's a reason. They assigned me to your case."

"They?" Jess pounced. "They who?"

"The Council."

"Council? Like City Council?"

Lilliana shrugged. "The Fairy Council. They give an assignment to each graduate."

"So, you just graduated?" Jess crossed her arms, planted her feet wide, and laughed. "You're not even a full-fledged Fairy Godmother?"

"Of course I am. You don't understand. Fairy Godmothers are born, not made. But…" She shifted uncomfortably. "We do have to go to school."

"This story just keeps getting better and better." Jess shook her head. "You still haven't answered the question. Why me?"

Maggie butted in and whispered to Lilliana, "Tell her the truth."

Lilliana gave Maggie a futile warning look to hush up.

"Yeah, tell me the truth," Jess demanded.

Lilliana debated silently and finally blurted, "You're a descendant of Cinderella—that's why."

"Good one." Jess snorted and applauded—a dull sarcastic clap.

"You're a direct descendant on your mother's side. The fifty-sixth generation. There was also a crossover line in the fourteenth century from your father's side. Your lineage indicates—"

"You don't mean Cinderella was real?" Cai's mouth pursed in disbelief.

"Finally, some healthy skepticism," said Jess.

"No. I meant you should tell her the other thing," Maggie urged Lilliana. "If she knew, she might change how she—"

Lilliana shushed her.

Jess wheeled on Maggs. "What other thing?"

Lilliana waved her arms and shouted, "Don't say anything!"

"It's okay. She should know." Maggie frowned and looked worried. Frightened even.

Whatever Maggs was hiding, Jess wanted to know and she wanted to know now. "What other thing?"

"I overheard her in the bathroom." Maggie glanced at jess and then at Lilliana, hesitating.

"Tell me!"

Maggie turned away, mumbling nonsense. "There was a talking face in the bathroom sink."

"A talking face?" Jess closed both eyes tight and tried to hold onto the tiny thread of patience she had left. "It's just *Wizard of Oz* stuff, Maggs. Smoke and mirrors. Behind the magic curtain there's just a teenage con artist from Chicago."

"No. She didn't know I was there." Maggie's white-blonde curls shook frantically. "Listen to me, Jess. This is important. I saw it. A face in the water. It told Lilliana she had to keep you from hardening your heart or else you'd get angrier and angrier until someday you'd blow up half the world…or something."

Jess stared at Maggie. And so did everyone else. No one moved. No one made a sound. Or even blinked.

Maggie's face compressed in anguish. "That came out all wrong." She put her arm around Jess. "I'm sorry! Really sorry. I shouldn't have said it like that."

"You believed her." Jess shook her head and pushed away from her best friend. "You've known me all my life, and still you believed her. You actually thought I'd be capable of something as horrible as that." Jess was stunned. "That's why you've been so weird lately."

Maggie flushed, and the fact that she couldn't meet Jess's gaze confirmed it.

"Can't you see? I'm not the problem." Jess jabbed a finger through the air at Lilliana. "She's the one who blows things up! Not me."

"Are you so sure, Jess?" Lilliana dropped onto the couch beside Cai. "I still don't understand why the lab exploded. It's true, I threw *elin-gíl* at you, but…" She curled forward and pressed her face into her hands, shaking her head. "I only meant to rattle you up a bit. I didn't expect the explosion. It's not the way *elin-gíl* works. You must've had something to do with it. Unless the principal was right, and there really was a gas leak." Her hopeful expression died when she glanced up at Jess.

Jess wasn't angry. She was boiling. Boiling and churning like a typhoon. And yet, somehow she managed to keep her voice from shaking. "For someone who's supposed to keep me from getting angry, you're not doing a very good job. Maybe they shouldn't have sent an incompetent trainee."

Lilliana jumped up, fists balled. "I graduated top of my class. And, I'm the *only* one," —she poked Jess's shoulder—"the *ONLY* one the Seers said could deal with you. I can see why. You're so pigheaded you don't even recognize a good thing when it's standing right in front of you."

Jess shoved her away.

Lilliana took a quick jagged breath. "You know what I think? I think they should've sent someone with a giant horsewhip. You're nothing but a spoiled baby. Look at you! You have everything I've ever wanted. A home. Friends. A family!"

"*Family,*" Jess growled and crossed her arms tight. "Right. Let me tell you how that works. One day they're all smiling and laughing. Next thing you know a policeman wakes you up in the middle of the night to say there's been an accident." Jess kicked the corner of the couch. The thud made the same muffled sound as a funeral drum.

"Family." She said it like a curse word. "My mom can't

stomach being in the house. Too many memories." Jess caught her lip between her teeth and looked up at the ceiling, blinking. "And my dad...have you seen him? I haven't. Last I heard he was in Japan sweet-talking investors."

Lilliana stepped back, biting her lip. In a much softer voice she said, "You have Jake."

"Yeah, that's right. And now you want to take him away, too." Jess leveled cold fury at Lilliana.

Lilliana met Jess's icy disgust with unexpected compassion. "You don't have to worry about your brother and me." With a deep sigh her shoulders sagged, and she backed away. "No matter how much I like him, it can't happen." She sat down and pulled her knees up, hugging them, speaking more to herself than the others. "Fairies are not allowed to fall in love with humans. It's forbidden."

"Why?" Cai asked.

"For good reason—we can't mate with humans. Well, we can, but it doesn't end well." She looked up at Jess, her face twisted with pain. "I should know. It's why my mother died." She buried her face in her knees. "She died giving birth to me."

Jess sank into her desk chair, studying Lilliana's strange ears, the line of her face, the translucence of her skin. She seemed human enough, and yet, not. "If your mother fell in love with a human, then you're—"

"Yes. Half human." Lilliana's shoulders slumped. "So, you see, your brother is safe from me. I would never want my child to grow up without a mother."

Jess leaned back, considering a realm of possibilities that seemed utterly absurd. No, it was outright impossible.

"If only you would realize how lucky you are." Lilliana's voice turned soft and conciliatory. "Your parents may be distant, but, at least sometimes they're here. Seeing them sometimes is better than never seeing them. And Jake, he's..." Her soothing voice shook slightly. She took a deep breath. "You're lucky to have him." She

129

smiled at Maggie and Cai. "Plus, you have two friends who love you."

Jess stared at the carpet, trying her best not to let Lilliana's hypnotic words confuse her. She'd never considered herself lucky. Not with all the crap that had happened. Except, maybe she was.

Lilliana leaned forward, straining to get a response from Jess. "The only family I've ever known was a long time ago, my grandmother."

"The woman in the bathroom sink." Maggie squeezed onto the couch beside her. "The nice one."

Lilliana nodded.

"And the other lady, the mean one, who's she?"

"Gryndelyn isn't really mean, just stern. She's my guardian, my mentor. After my grandmother left, the council sent me to live at the school. Gryndelyn is headmistress there."

"How come don't you live with your grandmother?" Maggie asked.

Good question. Jess stretched out her legs and crossed them at the ankles. "Yeah, why don't you toddle off to Chicago and live with her?"

"She isn't in Chicago." Lilliana pulled a tattered photo out of her pocket. "I think she lives in Texas."

"Another nice neat coincidence," Jess mumbled under her breath.

Lilliana held out the photo for Cai and Maggie. "This is my grandmother, but look in the background of the photo. There's the name of a business painted on the glass in the window. It says Dreston Bea—. I don't know what Bea is, but Dreston has to be the name of a town."

They nodded.

"I checked. Only two towns in the whole world have that name. One is in England. The other is right here in Texas, across the lake, only twenty miles away." She leaned back against the sofa. "Even though it's so close, I wouldn't begin to know how to find her once I got there. All I have is this." She let it flutter into her lap. "And it was taken a long time ago. She could be on the other side of the world by now."

"Jess could find her!" Maggie suddenly bubbled with energy. "She can find anybody! You could, couldn't you, Jess?"

The question hung in the air for a moment. Jess shrugged but glanced sideways at the faded black-and-white photo. "That picture's really old."

Lilliana smoothed her fingers over the creased corner and stared longingly at the two women in the tattered photo. "You're right. It's not much to go on, probably impossible."

"I didn't say that." Jess took a closer look at the photo. "The girl beside your grandmother looks just like you. Is she—"

"My mother." Lilliana confirmed with a deep sigh.

"Then, I'm sorry, but your grandma can't be still alive." Jess shook her head. "She's already old in this photo, and it looks like it was taken back in the sixties. Do the math. Your grandmother would be more than a hundred."

"You don't understand." Lilliana shook her head. "Fairies don't age the same as humans. She's still alive. I know she is. She has to be."

"Then, how old are you?" Maggie interrupted. "Sixty or something?"

Jess rolled her eyes, held up the photo, and pointed to the girl. "It doesn't take a calculator. Her mother looks about thirteen. That means, *fairy* or human, Lilliana couldn't possibly be more than forty."

Maggie studied Lilliana's face, probably checking for wrinkles.

Lilliana laughed. "Don't be silly. I'm only fifteen. But my grandmother—I don't even know. Two, maybe three hundred."

Jess studied the photo for a long time. "I'm not saying I believe any of this fairy nonsense, but what if I helped you find her? Do you think *Granny* here," she flicked the snapshot, "would let you live with her?"

"I don't know," Lilliana hedged, her guard up. "She might. Why?"

"And you'd move in with her, right?"

"If she'd let me."

"Good. Then I'll do it. I'll find her."

"Why?" Cai cocked her head.

"I love a mystery."

Cai pursed her lips skeptically.

Jess opened her arms in an effort to appear genial. "All of us will help. Won't we?"

Maggie aimed a skeptical expression at Jess. "Why are you being so cooperative all of a sudden?"

"She has an ulterior motive," Cai said. "If Lilliana moves in with her grandmother, she'll be further away from Jake."

Lilliana sighed. "I told you, your brother is safe from me. He and I cannot be together—it's forbidden."

"Yeah, yeah, Tinkerbell, I get it. Humans are off limits for you *fairies*." Jess waved her hand through the air dismissing the feeble argument. "Last time I checked, forbidden love was a major turn-on. Or don't you fairies read *Romeo and Juliet*? Besides," She handed the photo back to Lilliana. "These two women don't look like fairies to me. Either way, if you move in with your grandma, my problem is solved."

"You really are a pain in the neck." Lilliana looked like she'd had enough. She headed for the door, but stopped beside the workstation. "You don't get it. Even if I move in with my grandmother, I'm still your Fairy Godmother. Whether you believe it or not, you're stuck with me."

"Oh, that's right." Jess snapped her fingers. "I'm your as-signment. You're supposed to make Jess happy. Well, it would make me extremely happy if you moved away."

Maggie quietly suggested, "Show her your wings, Lilliana."

"Excellent idea." Jess whirled around to grin at Cai and Maggie, who were sitting on the couch. "Ooops! I guess she left her wings back at the trailer. Anybody have some wire and tissue paper she could borrow?"

Jess's sarcasm faded when saw the look on Maggie's face. Her eyes were transfixed on something just beyond Jess's shoulder. Cai's mouth dropped open.

Jess swallowed hard and slowly pivoted.

Wings arced elegantly from Lilliana's back, catching the incandescent light and glittering like jeweled silk. A rainbow of emerald greens, deep blues, turquoise and azure, sapphire and purple. They nearly touched the ceiling, waving slowly, boldly, making Jess's lavish bedroom suite look petty and small.

Jess wobbled. She grabbed hold of the chair to steady herself, but didn't say a word. All she could do was stare.

The door flew open and Jake burst into the room.

"I remember!"

Fairy Godmother Training Manual

Directive 13

Control the situation at all times. Think ahead. Never let your C.O. out maneuver you. Remember, you are a Fairy, a higher being. Do not fall prey to your human's petty whims.

A successful Fairy Godmother employs well-thought-out tactical strategies to coax her C.O. into the optimum circumstances for maximizing her potential. This is much like playing a masterful game of chess.

—Gryndelyn Myrddin

Whistle in the Dark

Lilliana slammed the manual shut. Honestly, she was beginning to think Gryndelyn didn't like humans very much at all.

This was all a chess game for Gryndelyn.

She groaned, remembering all too well her mentor's failed attempts to teach her how to play the game. If it all came down to chess, Lilliana may as well quit her mission tonight.

Directive 13 throbbed in her head. Petty whims? Jess's brother had died. There was nothing petty about that. Tactical diversions? Lilliana didn't have any tactics, much less diversions. Coax Jess into optimum circumstances? Where? What? Maybe Gryndelyn expected her to hogtie Jess and drag her off to Happyville.

If her mentor would try to appreciate humans a little more, if she understood how interesting they were or how amazingly brave and forthright, maybe she would give Lilliana more useful advice.

Stars peppered the night sky, tiny pinpricks of fire holding their own against the enormous black heavens. She sighed. Some humans were truly wonderful.

Flute stopped playing the sonata she'd requested and cleared his throat, meaning she should stop staring out the window and get on with her lessons and then into bed. Lilliana sighed and opened her manual to the journal pages.

The blank lines stared back at her with unblinking soberness.

What should she write?

How could she excuse tonight's behavior?

How could she explain the way she'd felt when Jake burst into

135

Jess's room?

He remembered. He'd been so deliciously desperate to see her. And when he found her with her wings unfurled...his face...

That look!

Remembering it still made her foolish heart pump faster. Still made her cheeks hot.

She glanced at her reflection in the window and pressed her palm over the warmth rising on her face. "I mustn't," she whispered.

"Too late, I should guess." Flute's nasal comment sounded haughty and disapproving.

"Too late for what?" Lilliana tried to sound innocent, confused.

"Oh, come now, my dear. Did you think I wouldn't notice all the melancholy songs you've had me playing? *Romeo and Juliet. Moonlight Sonata.* All a bunch of romantic folderol," he grumbled. "Music to accompany you as you gaze out of the window." He blew a long, scornful, low note. "And sigh."

What could a hollow old stick know of her breaking heart? "You couldn't possibly understand." She climbed down from the window and strode as regally as possible back to her desk. "And since you mentioned the sonata, I'd like to hear it again, if you don't mind."

"Well, I do mind. And if you ask me—"

"Just play it." She sat down, dipped her quill, and poised it over the empty page.

Flute snorted off-key, pretending he was tuning up, but she knew better. Finally, he launched into Beethoven's romantic masterpiece, playing the slow rippling cadence a trifle too fast.

It didn't matter.

Lilliana elegantly penned the date, putting a swirl at the end with a little spray of dots. To avoid the truth a little longer, she drew in the margins. But finally she abandoned her curlicue flower sketches and doodles of butterflies with heart-shaped wings. With a deep breath she confessed all.

JOURNAL
Day 3

I couldn't bring myself to throw *elin-gíl* at him. Not tonight. I couldn't make Jake forget again. Not when he looked at me like that. He deserves more from me than a muddled memory. They all do.

Besides, repeated doses of *elin-gíl* could pose a health risk. Who knows what the long-term effects might be? I can't find anything about it in the manual, nor in the appendices or in any of the kajillion irksome tables or charts.

And I most certainly will *not* ask Gryndelyn.

The truth is—I panicked. There's no other way to say it. They all stared at me like I was a muskrat painted pink. Jake was about to say something.

I know, I know, I should've made him forget. I didn't. I ran. Well, I didn't run, not exactly. I backed up. Stumbled. When I bumped into the wall, he lunged to help me keep my balance.

That's when I really panicked.

He held onto me—to keep me from falling—and of course, that's the only reason he was holding me like that. But while his arms were around me, I felt a frantic throbbing in my veins. I was afraid I'd do something stupid, like kiss him.

It's true. I almost did. His mouth was right next to mine. So close.

There are forces at work here I don't understand. I felt like I had to kiss him or my blood was going to pump so hard I might faint. Either way, I'd be in big trouble. So, I closed my eyes and pictured myself here, at home, safe from his too-beautiful lips.

And Poof!

Here I was.

Alone.

Lilliana quit writing, left off the rest. It was too humiliating.

She'd come home and found herself, despite the company of Tik-Tik, Flute, and a thousand softly snoring moths, terribly, horribly, inexorably alone. Alone and wishing for what could never be.

While a very grumpy flute serenaded her limping heart, she stared out of the window at clouds hanging over the lake in silvery moonlit strands. Time wove slowly on night's loom, dotting the black sky with pinpricks of starlight.

Far, far away, beyond the ferret's mindless chatter, beyond Beethoven's sympathetic strains, she heard a train whistle, a distant shriek, a plaintive cry. That lone whistle seemed the one true song of her heart. And across the plains, barely stirring the dark lake, came the faint howling echo of loneliness.

CREPORTER ON THE SCENE

"The story of the century and Cai witnessed the whole thing firsthand. But if she reported that she'd seen a real live fairy, complete with amazing wings, standing in Jess Harrison's bedroom in Lake Elm, Texas, Cai would be laughed out of journalism forever. It wouldn't matter that several people could corroborate her story. No one would believe it. At least the fact that Maggie and Jess also saw it meant Cai wasn't going crazy.

Jake was there, too. He had even held Lilliana in his arms after she stumbled. Cai wondered what the wings felt like. Softer than gossamer, she guessed. Jake didn't let go of Lilliana, and neither of them seemed to care that they had an audience. It was like the big mushy moment in the movies when the violin music turns mellow and slow, and everyone absolutely knows the guy is going to kiss the girl.

Cai was just about to look away, to give them some privacy, when poof! Lilliana vanished.

Jake's arms, which had been full of moist-lipped fairy, collapsed around empty air. He whipped around, scanning the room, but it was equally empty except for Cai, Maggie, and Jess. Empty, and somehow darker, as if the incandescent lamps in the room only emitted a dull gray light. In the flickering dimness, Jake sagged against the wall.

He didn't shout, "Where'd she go?" He didn't demand to know, "What happened?" He didn't even ask, "What is she?" Jake just slumped against the wall, the duskiness in the room creeping over him, its smoky fingers closing around his sadness.

"Don't!" Jess spat into the mournful silence. "Forget her. She's a...I know it seems impossible, but she's a...a fairy." She winced and muttered under her breath. "I can't believe I said that." Jess grabbed Jake's shoulder and shook him. "Fairies can't BE with humans."

He looked up at his sister as if waiting for her to understand his pain. When she didn't, he shrugged her hand off his shoulder. "It doesn't matter." He glanced a few feet past Jess to where he and Lilliana had stood together as if he could still see her there, glittering wings and all. "I don't care."

"Good!" Jess crossed her arms over her chest with finality, satisfied with his answer.

Cai and Maggie exchanged glances. Jess had definitely misunderstood. Was she blind? Jake cared, all right. It was 100 percent obvious. Cai knew by the way he stood up, straightened his shoulders, and walked out of the room like a soldier willing to die for a noble cause. It didn't matter if he could never BE with her in that way—Jake didn't care what price he had to pay. Fairy, human, or angel, he loved Lilliana Skye.

Someday, Cai sighed, she hoped a man would feel like that about her.

Fairy Godmother Training Manual

Directive 14

A Fairy must protect her dignity at all times. Never stoop to unbecoming human standards of behavior. As higher beings, it is our duty to set an example of proper conduct.

– Gryndelyn Myrddin

Giving Up Is So Very Hard To Do

Lilliana groaned and flipped past the directives. Gryndelyn's manual was becoming a first-class, top-of-the-line aggravation. And Lilliana was already aggravated enough, thank you very much.

No doodles today. She aimed her quill at a blank journal page and poured out her frustration.

JOURNAL
Day 4

Today I got sent to the principal's office.

Punished! Me! And for what? For my clothes. Can you believe it? Humans are obsessed with their wardrobes.

Although getting sent to the office was probably a good thing because it separated me and Jake. As soon as I walked into Biology, he rushed over to me. I got so nervous I couldn't breathe.

A gasping fairy is not a pretty sight. Really. Gryndelyn

would've called it "unbecoming." I kept trying to catch some air, stretching my neck up higher and higher. Any minute my feet were going to leave the floor, and I'd be sucking air and floating all the way to the ceiling.

Jake stood really close, and even though I was bobbing up and down like a helium balloon, he leaned down and whispered in my ear. "Why did you disappear?"

How was I supposed to answer that? Because you make me so nervous I can hardly breathe? Or last night I was afraid if I didn't kiss you I'd explode into a million billion pieces?

Luckily he didn't wait for me to answer. He said, "You don't need to hide what you are from me. I will always—"

Mrs. Dawson interrupted. "You can't come to class like that!" She slapped a pink slip of paper into my hand and pointed at the door. "Inappropriate dress. Go to the office."

She ruined everything. Now I would never know what Jake was going to say. Ever since the frog incident, Dawson has seemed irritated with me. I think she blames me for the explosion. You'd think a nice rest in the hospital would've improved her mood. It didn't.

When I asked her, "What office?" I thought Mrs. Dawson was going to hit me over the head with her ruler.

Evidently, breaking the school dress code is a grievous error and must be punished by the school's supreme authority, the principal, and he has a special room for administering this discipline. Principal Jamison is a very busy person. A row of students sat outside his office waiting. Their inner music did not sound at all happy.

I admit it. I had given up trying to fit in.

This morning I decided to just be comfortable and wear

what I normally wear in the forest. Nobody said anything about it until Mrs. Dawson got so upset, not unless you count the boys in the hall, but they always whistled and said rude things.

Fortunately, Mr. Jamison wasn't nearly as mean as Mrs. Dawson. He read Rule Fourteen aloud to me. It says that both of my shoulders must be covered by a strap that is at least 2 inches wide. The strap on my right shoulder was too skinny. There wasn't a strap on the other side. Because I was a new student, he said he would "cut me some slack." From the lost and found box, he dug out a dusty white button-up men's shirt for me to wear.

Then he measured the length of my skirt. (The hem is supposed to reach past the end of my fingertips.) Anyone knows that leaves do not grow in perfectly straight lines. Neither do magnolia petals, and no matter how tightly you weave them, they won't lay flat. So, naturally, my leafy petal skirt had a jagged hem. At least in some places it was up to code. So, he let it go this time with a suggestion that in the future my skirts should be made of actual fabric, not stuff I find along the creek.

I tried to explain that my spider-spun sandals weren't flip-flops, but he just shook his head, handed me a pair of clean tube socks and a pair of old boots from the box. I could see why someone left those things behind—they were smelly, hard, and bumpy inside.

By the time Mr. Jamison was through reforming me, Biology was over. I spent the rest of the day clunking around school in big ugly boots and a man's shirt.

I only saw Jake for a few minutes between classes in the afternoon. I don't know why he grinned at me like that. How could he think this outfit was better? That's what he said, "Better." As if it was a big relief to see me dressed like a grungy old troll.

It wasn't funny. And I didn't like being laughed at. Under no circumstance were these ratty old clothes "adorable." But I did like the way Jake patted my arm when he said it.

Anyway, one good thing happened today. In study hall, Cai handed me a note from Jess. It said she'd found some information about my grandmother. Saturday they'll pick me up and we'll all go to Dreston. They're going to help me find Naneth.

Tomorrow!

I can't wait.

EXPEDITION INTO ENEMY

TERRITORY

"**W**hy'd you bring this car?" Jess adjusted her aviator sunglasses and crossed her arms. "I feel stupid in it, and you look like a chauffeur." She sat pinned between Jake and Mark in the front seat of their dad's Lincoln Town Car. They were on their way to pick up everyone else. "And Dad's gonna ground you for life when he finds out you took it."

"No, he won't. This trip was your idea, and my Camry wouldn't hold all six of us." Jake shrugged. "Besides, I only agreed to drive so I could keep an eye on you."

Actually, he didn't look like a chauffeur. Jess just said that to throw Jake off his game. He sat behind the wheel wearing his favorite shirt, the dark blue one with *Ski Breckinridge* scrawled across his chest. She knew exactly why he was willing to drive them to Dreston. "You're doing this so you can see *her.*"

Jake frowned at the road. "Okay. Fine. That, too. But I can tell you're up to something, Jess. Whatever it is, you better not be making trouble for her."

Trouble for her? The Super Clone? The more Jess thought about what had happened in her room, the more flustered she felt. The whole Fairy Godmother thing was totally crazy. Not to mention impossible.

Yet Jess had a new pixie haircut that said differently. She figured there were only two possible explanations. One, Lilliana was a regular girl with some super deluxe techno/hypnotic skills, or two, Jess would have to rethink her whole view of the universe because there really was such a thing as a Fairy Godmother.

In either case, Lilliana was every bit as dangerous as Cheryl had been.

What was more, Jess didn't want a Fairy Godmother.

She didn't *need* a Fairy Godmother.

She *needed* Lilliana to stay away from Jake. Whether Jess's Fairy Godmother was using magic or employing Cheryl's technique of wrapping men around her little finger before destroying them, she was turning Jake into a love-blind robot just like Ryan was before he...

"I'm not making trouble for her," Jess said. She knew who the real troublemaker was. "I can't. She's supposedly a Fairy Godmother, remember? You know, as in, *MAGIC*, a superior being, invincible, trouble-proof."

"She has feelings, and I don't want you hurting them," Jake warned in a low voice.

"You said her mother died, right? So, that means she isn't invincible." Mark glanced sideways at her. "Anyway, I know you, Jess. You wouldn't hurt anybody. Not really." He said it like he actually believed it, and then he casually draped his arm around Jess's shoulder as if they'd been boyfriend and girlfriend for years.

Jess had a dizzying hormonal response to Mark's arm around her. She tried to convince herself it was just chemicals firing in her brain without permission. But dang, chemicals should not feel that good or that exhilarating, and above all they should not make her want to snuggle in for more.

But she did anyway. As she settled against Mark, Jess felt a twinge of something else. Guilt? Except she didn't need to feel guilty about today's mission. Her plan was simple, straightforward, foolproof. Nobody would get hurt. They would locate Lilliana's long lost grandmother and convince her that Lilliana needed to move in with her in Dreston. That would put Super Clone in a different school, which may as well be a different solar system.

Out of sight, out of mind.

Ergo, Jake would be safe.

Life would return to normal. Flawless logic. Simple but effective.

Jess took a deep breath to dispel her pointless guilt. "Your hoodie still smells like smoke." It was the same sweatshirt Mark had lent her after the explosion.

He grinned lopsidedly and lifted one eyebrow as if he knew something she didn't. "That's funny," he said quietly and tugged her a little closer. "I think it still smells like you."

Jake pulled the car up to the curb in front of Maggie's house and honked. Cai had slept over at Maggs's, so both girls hurried out and piled in. Jess noticed a camera hanging around Cai's neck. "Planning on documenting phenomena?" she teased.

Cai grinned and patted her camera. "The never-before-photographed variety."

"Good luck." Maggs chuckled as she slid into the backseat and buckled up. "She'll just throw glitter and erase it."

Cai shrugged. "Maybe. But it's worth a try."

A mile later they turned onto the bumpy dirt road, dodging potholes as they drove toward the lake. Dust billowed up in their wake, coating the black car with a fine limestone powder. Jake slowed and pointed toward Lilliana's trailer. Or cave. Whatever it was. "There she is."

Lilliana sat near the road on a big rock, hugging her knees, looking very unfairy-like in jeans and a T-shirt. Well, except for the bright red cardinal perched on one knee. Jake slowed the car down so much they could've crept up on their hands and knees faster. His face contorted back and forth like a guy who couldn't make up his mind whether to smile like a moonstruck idiot or clamp his lips into a straight, unknowable line. He settled on the latter and shifted the car into park.

Mark opened his door, and pulled Jess out with him. The minute they stepped out, the cardinal zoomed up and swooped at the Town Car, chirruping like a fire alarm, and then rocketed across the lake.

"What's his problem?" Jess muttered, but then she noticed Mark was letting The Clone slide in next to Jake. "Hold on a minute," she protested.

Mark blocked her, teasing her with a seductive expression. "There's no room for all four of us in the front. Let Cai take shotgun so you and I can sit in the back." It was a ploy. She knew it was. But before she could protest further, he had maneuvered her into the back seat. Jess muttered that she must be as manipulatable as her brother. Putty. It must be a Harrison family failing.

Jake looked ridiculously pleased about Lilliana climbing in beside him. He and Mark must've worked out that little dance step beforehand.

Mark reached over the seat and extended his hand to Lilliana in a *hello-welcome-to-earth* formal greeting. "Hi. So you're Jess's Fairy Godmother."

Lilliana dropped his hand like a hot potato. Her eyes opened wider than an airplane hangar as she turned to Jess. "You told him?!"

Jess crossed her arms defiantly. "That a problem?"

"Relax." Mark tapped the seat beside Lilliana's shoulder. "I figured there was something weird going on when the ghost frogs showed up. Only I never would've guessed the Fairy Godmother thing. If anybody but Jess had told me, I wouldn't have believed it." Mark shook his head. "Wow! A fairy. Too cool."

Lilliana shook her head and frowned at Jess. "You shouldn't have told anyone. It's against the rules. We're not allowed to—"

"Hey, no worries." Mark leaned up. "Your secret's safe with me. But I've got like a million questions. Jess told me about your wings. Maybe later, you would show them—"

"No more questions." Jake broke through Mark's inquisition. "We need to get going. I have to get the car back before Mom gets home tonight."

Her face still pinched with worry, Lilliana settled into place next to Jake. He pulled the center seatbelt out and leaned across her. "Have to buckle this," he murmured, fumbling with the clip. "So you're safe," he explained. But as he clicked it into place, he jerked his hand back as if he'd been burned. "Those are flowers!" Red crept up his cheeks.

What Jess had mistaken for a multicolored T-shirt turned out to be rose petals laced together. Bits of torn blossoms fluttered from Jake's fingers and filled the car with the smell of roses. "The buckle knocked off some of the petals. I..." Jake stared at the fragile petals and then at Lilliana. "Sorry." He swallowed hard, put the car in gear, and drove off, clutching the wheel as if he wished it was her he was holding.

The rich flower fragrance in the air couldn't be making this trip any easier for him. And it didn't help that Nickelback's old love song, "Far Away," came on the radio, drowning him in knee-deep romantic sap. When, in a heartbroken, gravelly voice, the lead singer wailed on about how he kept dreamin' he'd be with the girl he loved, Jake blushed. One hundred and seventy pounds of football-toughened warrior and he blushed like a little girl.

Jess wanted to smack her brother on the back of his head. Instead, she issued a loud order. "Change the station."

It surprised her that without a word of protest Jake tossed her the stereo remote. She flipped from station to station. There were too many wrong songs, songs about love lost, love missed, love found. She ran through the entire XM range and then started in on FM.

"Pick something, Jess," Cai urged. "You're giving me a headache."

Jess kept on flipping until, finally, she found a heavy-metal station. Reception wasn't too good out in the middle of nowhere, so the loud angry chords wafted in and out between static. That was okay. At least it wasn't some dumb song that would make her brother go all mushy between the ears.

Lilliana sat quietly, except her shoulders kept jumping up, like she was shocked every time the shrieking guitars and drums blared back on. And she kept glancing sideways, checking out Jake when she thought he wouldn't notice.

Oh, but he noticed, all right.

The radio station dropped out again, filling the car with a static roar. Except this time it sounded weird and distant, as if they were picking up a garbled broadcast from another planet. It gradually changed, sounding closer, more gravelly, like someone on a ham radio was trying to contact them.

"What is that?" Jess leaned up and grabbed the back of the seat. In almost understandable patterns, the ghostly voice moved in and out of reception. She stared at the green LCD numbers identifying the station. It hadn't changed.

The crackly static gathered strength until it became clearer, and distinct syllables formed. "Lil... pshhh... lee...psh... na." Whoever it was, she didn't sound happy. "Lilliana!"

Jess's superinvincible Fairy Godmother stiffened up like a scared third-grader sitting in front of the principal.

"You are in violation of at least six different directives," the voice announced.

"Directives?" Jake asked.

Lilliana didn't answer. Her hand trembled as it flew up to cover her mouth.

Trouble. It meant trouble. Jess held her breath.

"Who is that?" Jake's tone was businesslike and as commanding as their dad's.

"Where are you going?" the radio demanded in a harsh staccato. "Answer me!"

Maggie leaned up and peeked at Lilliana. "That's Gryndelyn, isn't it?"

Lilliana barely nodded.

"Of course it's me, you ninny. Now, answer my question."

"I...we're...it's Saturday," Lilliana stammered, and then blurted, "I'm off duty."

"You're never off duty. You don't get days off." Irritation dripped from Gryndelyn's words like battery acid. "Now, where, *exactly*, do you think you're going?"

"You don't have to tell her anything," Jake growled.

"She's my guardian," Lilliana whispered as if that explained everything.

"Stay out of this, *human*," the radio blurted.

Jake gripped the wheel, as if squeezing it tighter gave him control over the situation. "Turn off the radio, Jess," he ordered.

"Don't be insolent, boy."

Jake didn't wait for Jess. He pushed the volume knob to off. But the speakers kept buzzing, and the phantom in the radio kept bullying Lilliana.

"I'm losing patience," Gryndelyn warned.

Jess aimed the remote and pressed the power button. "It won't shut down."

Jake pressed the button on the steering column. When that didn't work, he shoved his palm against the knob on the stereo, harder this time. And again. While he gaped at the unresponsive radio, their front tire skidded onto the gravel embankment.

"Jake!" Jess yelled.

He jerked the wheel to the left, overcorrected and veered across the double line. Then he swerved back into his lane. Good thing there wasn't any traffic, just miles of wheat fields.

"Do something!" Jess grabbed Lilliana's shoulder and shook her.

Lilliana nodded and hesitantly smoothed her hands over the wood-trimmed dash the way a normal person would pet an angry puppy to calm it down. "Gryndelyn." Her voice shook. "Don't be mad. Please." Steadier, she began to sound almost cheerful. "These are my friends. Everything is okay. They've offered to help me find my grandmother, and—"

"No!" Static exploded. "Turn around this instant! Go back. Do your job."

Bitten, Lilliana jerked her hand away.

"For once, Lilliana, do as you're told." Calmer, more instructive tones hissed through the speakers. "You've been given *Directives* and orders for a reason. Your elders know what's best. Obey."

"But I am following orders." Lilliana pleaded with the phantom in the radio. "My C.O. is right here with me. I'm watching over her. I promise. We're almost to Dreston, and if my grandmother is still there—"

"No!" The radio howled. "Absolutely not. Turn around! Go back. Do as I say, you foolish Halfling—"

"Enough." Jake punched the Scan button. The radio jumped to festive Hispanic music. Peppy accordions and guitars didn't play long before they were interrupted by a bulletin from beyond.

"Don't do that again, human!" Gryndelyn was panting hard, as though she had to jog through the airwaves to get to the new station.

He hit it again, and the radio skipped forward to a local weather report. Despite the forecast promising sunshine, Jess predicted they were all in for a storm.

"I'm warning you!" The speakers screeched. Obviously the banshee didn't understand men. And she had definitely underestimated Jess's brother.

He pushed scan again. This time it skipped to a classical station. Cellos. Violins. Woodwinds. Very soothing.

Gryndelyn interrupted the classical music and bellowed with demonic fury, "That's it!"

The radio went dead.

"How come there's never a ghostbuster around when you need one?" Jess muttered.

After a moment of unexpected silence, Jess remembered the radio was actually *supposed* to be off. Jake must've had the same thought because he cautiously pressed the power button. Sure enough, the sound of cellos and violins drifted out of the speakers, still sawing their tranquil melody.

"Uh-oh," whispered Lilliana as if the peaceful chamber music signified impending doom.

Jess hung over the seat. "Why? What's wrong?"

"Don't worry." Jake reached for Lilliana's hand and cupped it inside his. "It's over. She's gone."

That's when the first tire blew out.

Directive 15

Report to your mentor at regular intervals. The success of your mission may depend upon her valuable counsel. She will warn you away from potential disasters and guide you toward successful outcomes with your C.O.

– Gryndelyn Myrddin

Heavy Metal

They skidded wildly across the road. In a earsplitting chorus, fear exploded from the occupants of the doomed vehicle. Their screams blasted through the car, louder than ten radios.

"I can't turn! She's not letting me steer." Jake wrestled with the steering wheel, fighting to keep the car from flying off the shoulder and plunging down the embankment.

Gryndelyn was mad, but surely not so mad she would hurt innocent bystanders.

Not humans.

Not a C.O.

Not one of the offspring.

She wouldn't. Would she?

Lilliana gripped the seat and held her breath. She couldn't think. Couldn't move. She'd broken the rules. This was her punishment.

A loud bang. Suddenly they veered in the opposite direction.

"The other tire." Jake swore through gritted teeth and grappled for control. He slammed both feet on the brake pedal.

The car screeched, sliding sideways onto the gravel shoulder. They spun in a dizzying, rock-spitting circle. Their speed slowed. Just when it seemed they would come to a rest, the car rolled down the incline. With a sickening crunch it thudded to a full stop, nose down at the bottom of a drainage ditch.

"No!" Jake slammed his fists against the steering wheel as if that short fervent denial might make the whole accident nothing more than a bad dream. He quickly turned to Lilliana. "You hurt?"

Then he checked everyone in the backseat. "Anyone hurt? Jess? Maggie?"

"I'm all right." But Jess's voice shook, very un-Jess-like.

He stared straight ahead at the grassy embankment and the crumpled front end. "I can't believe your *guardian* did this."

Lilliana swallowed hard, fighting the suffocating tightness in her throat.

Instead of scolding her, Jake leaned close, turning worried eyes on hers as he unlatched her seat belt. "Are you sure you're okay?" His normally calm cello-like inner music sounded off-key and ragged with worry.

It would've been easier if he had shouted at her. She shook her head. "No, I'm not okay. This is all my fault." She bit her lip to keep her fears from spilling out, but it tore out of her throat in a painful gasp. "You could've *died* because of me."

"I'm fine," he reassured her. "We're all okay."

It wasn't enough. As Jake took charge, doublechecking on the others, Lilliana mentally traced the line of his jaw, frantically memorizing every detail of his face, his dark eyelashes, the soft plum of his lips, the slight cleft in his chin. She couldn't help it. Fear had painted a different portrait of him, horribly vivid, painfully familiar. She couldn't stop seeing him lying tangled in twisted metal wreckage, pale, unspeaking, bloody.

Lifeless.

Suddenly, she needed to vomit.

FORCE FIELD

Jess unbuckled her seat belt. "I'm fine," she answered her brother for the third time, banishing the unsteadiness from her voice.

"Me, too," Maggie confirmed.

Mark tried to open his door, but it jammed against the grassy side of the embankment, leaving him and Jess only a narrow slit to wriggle through.

As soon as Jake opened his door, Lilliana scrambled past him. She bolted toward a clump of grass and brush at the edge of the field, dropped to all fours, her shoulders heaveing He ran after her. "You're hurt."

"No!" Lilliana's face contorted with tears. "Stay back."

But he didn't.

Out came the glitter. She raised her hand at him like a stop sign. Jake stumbled backward. He caught his balance and tried to rush to her again, but smacked into something transparent but solid.

Jess and Cai went to investigate. They groped the invisible wall like a pair of mimes.

"It must be a force field," Cai said.

"No. Too sticky." Jess poked her finger at the surface. It felt like thick gelatin.

"Please, don't come any closer." Lilliana turned such a pathetic expression on Jake that even Jess felt sorry for her.

"Come on. She doesn't want you to see her doing that." Jess tried to pull him away.

Jake stubbornly thumped the invisible barrier with his fist. "No. She needs help."

"I'll take care of her." Jess managed to get in between him and the Jell-O-like wall. "Go see if you can get Dad's car out of the ditch."

Jess had an idea she'd be able to pass through Lilliana's barricade. When Jake finally stepped back, Jess turned and eased her hand into the gelatin. It felt moist and suctiony. Without any more hesitation, Jess walked straight through the force field as if it didn't exist.

"Hey! How did you...?" Jake rammed into the wall full blast. Then he leaned his shoulder into it, but it held firm.

Jess waved him away. "Go. You're just making things worse." She ignored his baffled expression and marched over to Lilliana. Jess hated playing nurse. It wasn't her thing. Even so, she gathered up Lilliana's dark hair and held it back while her Fairy Godmother retched into the undergrowth. Finally, Lilliana stopped heaving up glittery puffballs.

Jess let go of her hair, stood back, and studied her pale, trembling Godmother. "So," she said, feeling oddly compassionate. "Fairies puke, too." It wasn't a question.

Lilliana confirmed Jess's diagnosis with a micronod of her head and downcast eyes, giving Jess a pretty good clue why Lilliana had the sick stomach.

"Doesn't feel too good, does it, almost losing someone you care about?" Jess would never forget how sick she'd felt the night policemen told them Ryan had been in a fatal crash.

Lilliana didn't answer. She slanted a distrustful glance up at Jess, but her shoulders stopped shaking. She plucked a leaf from a maple sapling and wiped her mouth with it.

The clump of grass where she'd thrown up was no longer just grass. It teemed with brand new patches of primroses, pink blossoms springing up and bursting open like microwave popcorn. Because...

Face it...

Lilliana was exactly who she said she was.

A fairy.

Lilliana slowly got to her feet. She and Jess stood face-to-face, appraising each other, neither saying a word. Jess wasn't exactly sure what was causing the bouncy happy feeling inside her. She felt like laughing, which was pretty weird considering absolutely everything was going wrong. Crazy. Whacko. Wrong.

There shouldn't be any such thing as a fairy. Jess's father's car shouldn't be sitting at the bottom of an embankment. She shouldn't be pleased that somewhere in the universe someone had decided she needed a Fairy Godmother. Most of all she should not be pleased that maybe, just maybe, Lilliana really, truly, actually cared about Jake.

Or maybe she *should* be pleased about that.

"You really do care about him, don't you?"

"That's your question?" Lilliana's brow pinched together studiously. "A hundred things you could ask of me, and that's your question?"

Jess nodded.

"You already know the answer."

Jess liked how Lilliana kept her gaze level and steady. Moxie. Her F.G. had guts. "Yeah, I guess I do."

A ruckus at the barrier caught Jess's attention. Cai, still intently thumping on the barrier, attempted to plunge her hand through but only succeeded in jamming her fingers. "Yowch."

"Oh, hold on. I'll take it down." Lilliana flicked her hand in Cai's direction, sending a cloud of glitter floating toward the wall. It shimmered in the sunshine and stuck briefly to the barrier. Then the whole wall exploded into a fine sparkling mist.

Jake and Mark were trying to shove the Lincoln up out of the drainage ditch while Maggie drove. "Put it back in reverse. Turn the wheel," Jake shouted to Maggie. "Other way. Left. Left!" The engine revved, trying to back out without front tires. The guys muscled the car uphill onto the shoulder. "That's it, Maggs. Brake."

"Better go help." Jess headed in their direction.

After they secured the parking brake, everybody gathered around the front end and stared at the broken headlight and crunched right fender. The two front tires were totally destroyed.

"Sorry, man." Mark shook his head and slapped Jake on the back. "I hate to say it, but your dad *is* gonna ground you for the next two decades, man."

"Nah," Jake offered with wry optimism. "He's just gonna kill me."

Mark stooped down to check out the two shredded front tires. "Only one spare. We'll have to call a tow truck."

"Maybe." Jess rapped her knuckles against the hood without looking at any one in particular. "So, how does this Fairy Godmother gig work?" She tilted her head in Lilliana's direction. "It's not like the genie deal with three wishes, right?"

"Oh." Lilliana brightened. "You want me to fix it."

"Might be a good idea," Jess said. "Save Jake from getting grounded for life."

She didn't need any further encouragement. Lilliana edged closer to look at the damage. She surveyed the mashed front end with the intensity of a little girl trying to figure out how to snap together her first Barbie Dream House. She looked under the bumper and smoothed her hand across the sleek hood to the crumpled fender. She trailed her fingers over the wrinkled metal, gliding her palm over chipped, dust-spattered, black paint, caressing the injured car as if it were a suffering animal. As she did, tiny stars poured out of her fingertips, dancing over the dents, gathering and spinning into miniature galaxies that whirled across the damaged front end.

"Whoa." Mark jumped out of the way as dagger-like fragments of glass and plastic flew up from the ditch, whizzed through the air, and melded onto the car.

Jess watched, mesmerized, as the smashed front end unwrinkled. In seconds, it morphed into a gleaming, perfect fender. Steel wires snaked up from the shredded tires and curved around the chrome wheels. The scent of fresh rubber filled the air. New tread flowed over the steel belts, hissing and fizzing as the front end slowly raised and the car balanced on four perfect tires.

"There." Lilliana stepped back next to Jess.

Mark whistled softly.

The corners of Jess's mouth quirked up into the unfamiliar shape of a smile. "Not bad," she conceded. "Not bad at all."

Jake grabbed Lilliana's hand and dragged her with him to survey the repairs. "This is…" He shook his head, struggling for words. "Amazing! Incredible. Thank you." He pulled her fingers up to his lips and kissed them. Not a hot kiss. It was a thank-you kiss.

Jess's Fairy Godmother turned pink all the same.

Directive 16

It is commonplace to develop some fondness for your C.O. However, successful Fairy Godmothers guard against these unproductive emotions. They strive to maintain a professional distance from their subjects.

In addition, susceptible young fairies must be particularly mindful of Council Decree #4, which clearly states: it is forbidden for any fairy to fall in love with a human.

[For an official list of all Council Decrees, refer to Appendix 2.]

Historical note: these disgusting unions between fairies and humans are not only shameful, but have caused centuries of heartache and trouble for fairiekind. Furthermore, nearly all of the cases on record have resulted in death.

– Gryndelyn Myrddin

Good-bye Yellow Brick Road

Lilliana stared at her fingers still clutched in Jake's hand. *Lucky fingers.*

It had been a simple kiss of gratitude, and yet, in the space of one heartbeat she understood exactly why her mother had ignored the Council Decree, why she had risked everything. Her father must have had this same power over her mother. Jake's touch was a force of nature that reduced calculations of shame and equations of death into meaningless quivering fractions. His touch sent vibrant joy pulsing through her, as if their shared strength multiplied their individual power. All this because he held her hand.

Lucky hand.

Her gaze drifted from her own blessed knuckles up to Jake's mouth, to lips that had so eloquently thanked her. He was saying something as he stroked the sleek new black paint with his other hand. *Lucky car.*

Happy. He was so happy. His Cello played jubilantly.

Then he glanced in her direction, and bow abruptly scraped strings. Worry returned to his eyes, a thinly cloaked sadness that too often tainted his expression lately—ever since he'd learned the truth about her. He took a deep breath, and she heard that sad melody again, that horrid fatal resignation. He studied her fingers, brushing his thumb across them with the slow mournfulness of a man who thought he might never hold her hand again.

Lilliana's cheeks burned even hotter than before.

"I'm sorry," he said and let go of her fingers.

No. Don't be sorry. Don't let go.

"I know we can't be, you know, ever..." He sighed. "More than friends."

She wanted to shout. *Stop! Don't say that.* But all she could do was to look away from his face as it filled with regret. She clamped her bottom lip hard between her teeth, and stared at the lonely fields that stretched for miles in every direction, focusing on reedy tufts of wheat struggling up through dark clumps of dry earth.

"I shouldn't have…" he kept on.

Yes, you should've! But next time, no more palm kisses, no more finger kisses. Next time, my lips.

Of course, that would've been all wrong to say. She peeked at him and wished he would stop flexing his jaw and looking so guilty. He'd done nothing wrong. If only he knew what she was thinking.

"It's just that I was so glad you fixed it." Jake nodded toward the car, excusing the kiss that meant so much to her. "Thank you."

"Yeah, it's incredible. Like new." Mark squatted next to the wheel well, closely inspecting a repaired tire. "Can't tell anything happened." He stood up, brushed off his hands, and playfully slugged Jake's shoulder. "Now your dad won't go to jail for murdering you. And we can get home without a tow truck."

"No! Not home." Jess slapped the repaired fender, leaving fingerprints on the shiny new paint. "We're almost to Dreston. Only a few more miles."

Mark's mouth fell open as if he might laugh, but he didn't. "You figure the Radio-Witch will be okay with that?"

Lilliana sighed. She needed her grandmother now more than ever, but she couldn't put them in danger. Not again. "He's right. Gryndelyn is too angry. I can't predict what she might do. I've never seen her this mad."

Jess pressed her lips into a stubborn line. "We're not turning back now."

"What if…" Cai glanced up from fiddling with her camera, probably checking the photos she'd snapped during the car repair. Lilliana made a mental note to erase those later. "What if Lilliana puts a force field over the car?"

Jess snapped her fingers in Cai's direction. "Great idea!"

"But would it work against Gryndelyn?" Cai retracted her enthusiasm and frowned. "I mean, Jake and I couldn't budge it, but Jess walked straight through. And, by the way, I'd really like to know how you did that."

Jess shrugged. "I figured Lilliana opened it for me."

Lilliana shook her head. "No, that wall should've kept everyone back."

Why hadn't it?

She took a harder look at Jess. What was she dealing with here? Something was going on, something much bigger than the mission's simple goal of pacifying one troubled genius.

"That's the problem," Cai said. "If Jess got through your shield, maybe this Gryndelyn can, too."

Maggie, whose thoughtful inner music flowed like rippling chords on a classical guitar, came out of her reverie. "I think Lilliana let Jess through without realizing it. Subconsciously, they're linked because of the whole Fairy Godmother thing. As long as Lilliana blocks Gryndelyn, and if we keep the radio turned off—"

"I see what you're getting at." Jess nodded. "That way Gryndelyn can't penetrate the field via radio frequency."

Lilliana silently inspected the physics behind their idea. "Technically it should work, but it's all conjecture. Too dangerous. Too risky."

Jess planted both hands on the fender and leaned toward Lilliana. "Aren't you the least bit curious why your *guardian* is so set on keeping you away from your grandmother?"

Lilliana considered Jess's question, started to answer, closed her mouth, and tried again. "This has nothing to do with my grandmother." Even as she said it, she sensed the fallacy in her denial. "Gryndelyn is upset because I broke the rules, her directives. She wrote them. She's my mentor, my guardian. It reflects badly on her when I disobey." The certainty in her voice trailed off. "I'm *supposed* to be helping you—not you helping me."

"Oh, I see." Jess nodded as if she understood. "And what's the normal penalty for not following one of her precious directives? *Death?*"

Lilliana glanced fleetingly at Jake, remembering which rule often *did* bear that consequence. "Not usually."

Jess leaned closer. "Then why'd she use extreme force this time?"

Lilliana felt queasy again, momentarily dizzy. Darn this whole indecipherable mess. She scraped her hair back, not caring whether anyone noticed her pointy ears.

Jess was right. This wasn't the first time Lilliana had pushed the boundaries or broken rules. Normally, her busy guardian held back and let Lilliana step into bat droppings deep enough to make a giant stink cake of herself. Gryndelyn's violent reaction this time didn't make sense.

"I don't know," Lilliana answered quietly, etching a line in the dirt with her toe. The line pointed west, toward Dreston, toward secrets, secrets that had everything to do with figuring out her past and maybe her future. She tilted her eyes briefly in Jake's direction and then faced her excessively logical C.O.

One of Jess's singed eyebrows arched triumphantly. "I say it's worth the risk to find out. Let's go."

Lilliana knew it was dangerous. Foolhardy. She'd be dragged in front of the council, brought up on charges. It didn't matter. Jess was right. She had to go. Her instincts screamed that she would find answers down the forbidden road. If she ever wanted to understand her place in this world, there was only one decision she could make.

"You're right. I'm going," Lilliana announced. "But I'm going alone. Just tell me how to find her, Jess. Who do I talk to?"

STEALTH MODE

"**O**h no, I'm going, too!" Jess flipped up her sunglasses so they could all see she meant business. "I'm not staying behind. This is personal. That witch can't bully me. I go *where* I want *when* I want." She balled her fists and rounded on Jake. "Are you coming? Because even if I have to hitchhike, I'm going to Dreston."

Jess knew her brother. No way would he let the woman he loved traipse off to danger alone, and he wouldn't abandon Jess, either. They were going to Dreston. Jess's mind was made up. Just let the Radio-Witch try to stop them. This time Jess would be ready. "The force field will work. We can do this. I'll coach Lilliana. We'll beef up her skirmish tactics."

After ten minutes of pointless arguments, they all piled in and drove off to Dreston with the Lincoln encased in an extrathick Jell-O bubble. Lilliana made the force field so thick that it distorted the landscape, giving them an eerie underwater feeling. Cai sat in the front muttering, "Nice Korean girls shouldn't get mixed up in magical battles."

They hadn't gotten very far down the road when a cardinal, it had to be the same crazy bird from the lake, dive-bombed the force field and bounced off like a red rubber ball. He left behind a small blood-red feather stuck in the barrier. It fluttered outside Cai's window. "An omen," she predicted.

"You're not superstitious." Jess thumped the back of Cai's seat with her boot. "And anyway, this is great practice for when you do a stint as a war correspondent."

168

"I'm thinking of editing my career plans," Cai snarked.

Jake drove really slow. Too slow. They were leaving a slime trail on the highway like a giant snail. "Can't you speed it up?"

"No." Jake answered tersely. "If Gryndelyn does something, I want to be able to control the car."

But Jake picked up the speed anyway. Lilliana clutched the edge of her seat, warily scanning the horizon. The deranged cardinal must've survived his encounter with the force field because he came back and flapped alongside them.

It looked like he was trying to get Lilliana's attention. She shooed him away. "Go away, Napoleon. Hide. I have to con-centrate." She talked as if the bird could hear her outside the bubble.

"Just keep that glitter stuff handy," Jess counseled.

With the radio off, the only sound besides their pounding hearts was Maggie humming to keep calm. Eight miles seemed like a hundred. When Dreston finally came into view, Jess felt like cheering. *Yay! Civilization. Safety.*

She'd seen Dreston dozens of times before, but it had never looked so good. Today the old familiar rundown buildings on Main Street seemed picturesque and strangely reassuring.

"There." Jess pointed. "Pull in by the hair salon."

Directive 17

Remember who you are. In spite of superficial similarities, you are nothing like the humans you are trying to help. Long after they have turned to dust, we will still be here tending nature in both realms.

It is the Fairy Godmother's job to minimize the mess humans make of things. Thus, we serve them in order to preserve the delicate balance in our own world. Earth is, after all, home for both species.

—Gryndelyn Myrddin

Memories

Preston echoed with memories. Lilliana had been here before. She could feel it, hear it in the rhythms of the town.

When she lifted the invisible shield and climbed out of the car, time seemed to fly backward. She was small again, holding her grandmother's hand. Smells unique to the street tickled her nose—old wood, musty sidewalks, hairspray, a lake in the distance. Faint moisture misted her skin, teased at her senses. The thick, rich fragrance of foliage meant a river flowed nearby. She could almost see it winding through a ravine north of town, dense underbrush, tall cottonwood trees and cedar elms.

She knew this place. She'd been right to come. Her fingers trailed over an old streetlamp. Thick green paint covered over years of chips and peels. She stopped in front of a large picture window framed by an ornate black Victorian façade.

Maggie walked up beside her and haltingly read the words painted in a half circle. "The Glass Slipper Hair Salon. Our magic scissors will turn you into a princess." She chuckled. "That's promising."

Lilliana smiled and nodded.

Jess walked up beside her and mumbled, "Let's just hope there aren't any pixies running wild in there."

A joke? Lilliana almost fell over. Jess had made a joke. But the moment skirted past them as swiftly as a mayfly, and Jess started issuing orders again. "Get out the photo. I'll show you what you're looking at."

They all gathered around, pushing close, leaning over Lil-

171

liana's shoulder as she pulled her mother's picture out of her pocket and held it up.

"See there," Jess pointed. "The columns beside the window match. You can only see half of the name on the window. If you could read it all it would say, *Dreston Beauty Shop, Home of the Kut & Kurl.* That's what the place used to be called."

The name had been chopped off by the edge of the photo. The three arching lines actually read, "Dreston Bea—, Home of—, Kut &—" As a child, Lilliana had memorized those odd fragments, imagining them to be mystical puzzle pieces that would one day lead her to her grandmother. Now that Jess had solved the riddle, the fractured phrases seemed silly, mundane, certainly not the mysterious link to her past she'd imagined.

Lilliana tried to focus on what Jess was saying.

"I searched county property records, and the best part is, even though they changed the name, the same family has owned this place since 1968."

They all stared silently at the picture. Lilliana wondered if they were thinking the same thing she was. What if the answers weren't inside this old building? What if The Glass Slipper didn't fit? What if midnight had come and gone too many years ago, and any clues about her family had crumbled to dust and blown away?

Jake seemed to read her mind. He put his arm around her shoulder and led her to the door. "Come on. We won't know unless we go in."

She wished she'd worn a different shirt. The rose petals would compress and change color under the warmth of his arm. The seat belt had obliterated the bottom of it during the accident. She looked a raggedy mess. She couldn't go in there.

He leaned next to her ear and whispered, "I'll be right beside you."

And somehow, that got her through the door.

BEAUTY SHOP WARS

Jess didn't wait around for them. She marched through the green door of The Glass Slipper Beauty Salon and whipped off her aviators, ready to get down to business. The shop didn't look anything like a glass slipper inside. Walls were harvest orange, and the faded linoleum was speckled beige. Shelves and racks were made of curling wrought iron and painted cream, which made the old place look like—.

"Feels like we just walked inside a pumpkin," Cai whispered.

"My thoughts exactly," Jess said. "Except this pumpkin stinks like permanent solution and hairspray."

The women in the shop, hairdressers as well as customers, were having a hen party in one of the styling booths. A customer in huge pink rollers gushed over a photo album. "LaVonda, your daughter is the prettiest bride ever."

A heavyset stylist, presumably LaVonda, grinned broadly. "I can't believe my baby girl is all grown up and married."

A small bell jingled lightly when Lilliana and Jake came through the door.

"Little help." Jess rapped on the reception desk.

LaVonda held up one finger. "Be right with you."

The ladies oohed and ahhed over the next photo, and the client sitting in the chair draped her plastic-caped arm around a small elderly stylist. "Etta Mae, you must be the proudest grandma in all of Texas."

Jess knocked again. "In a hurry here."

LaVonda finally hustled over to the reception desk. "You kids have an appointment? I'm afraid we don't have any openings 'til two thirty."

Jess lost patience. "We need to speak to the owner."

"That's me." LaVonda set down her pencil. "How can I help you?" She did a double take when she noticed Lilliana.

Lilliana pulled the photo out of her pocket. "I'm trying to find my grandmother."

Jess snatched it of Lilliana's hand, slapped the photo down on top of the appointment book, and pointed. "Do you recognize either of these women? Especially this one?" Jess tapped the black-and-white Polaroid, trying to get the woman to focus. "Have you seen her lately?"

LaVonda followed Jess's insistent pointing briefly, but then her wide-eyed gaze snapped back to Lilliana. "Mama!" she shouted over her shoulder. "Better come here. Somethin' you gotta see."

Etta Mae strolled over and stood next to her daughter. She took one look at Lilliana and inhaled sharply.

"You knew them—my mother and my grandmother?" Lilliana practically jumped up and down she was so excited.

The old woman nodded and glanced down, resting her fingertip on the young girl in the photograph, and said softly, "You look just like her."

LaVonda chuckled. "Of course we remember 'em, child. This here was taken right after your grandma Rose helped us buy this place." She wrapped her arm around her mother. "Remember that day, Mama?"

Etta Mae's eyes glistened as she smoothed her knobby fingers over the scalloped borders of the snapshot and smiled. "Oh, yes," she whispered. "I'll never forget Rose. She was my Fair—"

Against the wall, a bank of four antiquated dryer chairs clicked on, blowing full blast. They drowned out Etta Mae's softly spoken words. LaVonda frowned at the row of dryers. At the far end, a blonde sat under one of the hoods, but the rest were empty, blowing for no reason.

"Controls must be on the blink." LaVonda trundled over to the nearest machine and twisted the knob, talking loud enough to be heard above the noise. "Thought I saw Rose at the wedding, didn't you, Mama? Sittin' at the back of the church? Only caught a glimpse of her, but—"

LaVonda switched them off, but the hoods clicked on again, humming even louder than before. She thumped the controls. "What is goin' on with these things?"

Lilliana reached over the desk, clutching Etta Mae's weathered fingers as if they were a lifeline. "Please. Do you know where my grandmother is? I need to find her."

Etta Mae nodded, still gazing in awe at Lilliana. "Sam always swore you'd come back."

Jess wedged them apart. "Sam who? Do you have an address? A phone number?"

Someone screamed.

The tight circle of women at the styling booth burst apart. Women stumbled, yelped, and leapt out of the way of a wildly revolving styling chair. The lady seated in the whirling chair clutched the armrests and braced her feet against the footrest. "Laaaa Vooooonda!"

The footrest smacked a customer in the back of the knees and sent her sprawling to the floor. The downed woman scuttled out of the way like an injured crab.

"Lord A'mighty!" LaVonda came running. Despite her bulk, she couldn't stop the chair. It knocked her aside. Hair trimmings sprayed across the room as it picked up speed and whirled faster. The hapless rider's plastic cape whipped back as if she was flying down the road in a convertible.

"Turn it off!" she screeched.

"Can't." LaVonda's eyes bugged out. She crossed herself. "It ain't electric."

A new scent crept into the air. Sulphur. It reacted badly with the hairspray fumes and ammonia from dyes. Static crackled in the air—ions were changing their polarity the way they do right before a lightning storm.

"Oh, no," Lilliana groaned.

The blonde sitting under the hairdryer flung off the clunky hood and stood up. Ozone filled the room. Lithe and beautiful, with long golden hair, she was certainly in no need of Lavonda's Glass Slipper service. She glided toward the reception desk and seemed to grow taller with every step.

The dryers fell silent.

The chair stopped spinning. Its dizzy occupant slid to the floor.

Commanding complete attention, mesmerizing them all with her languid movements, the golden goddess spoke. Her siren voice resonated through the salon like low hypnotic jazz. And the voice was infuriatingly familiar. Jess wanted to spit the acrid taste out of her mouth.

"Gryndelyn," Maggie murmured.

"My poor, poor, wayward Lilliana." Gryndelyn stared at her ward. "All these years, I've tried to guide you, struggled to keep you on the right path. And yet, here you are in precisely the wrong place." She swept her hand out, encompassing the entire pumpkin and maybe even the town. "You just couldn't leave well enough alone, could you?"

Jess sensed volcanic bile simmering beneath the witch's cool tone.

Jake pulled Lilliana and Etta Mae behind him, trying to back them away from the desk.

"But you wouldn't listen." Gryndelyn kept coming at Lilliana. "You had to stick your nose in where it didn't belong. Had to break the rules, didn't you? You're stubborn and weak—just like your mother."

Her scorn hit the mark. Lilliana's face blanched.

"Look at you, hiding behind a human." Gryndelyn smirked. Then she took a harder look at Jake, and her goddess face turned sour. "Him?" she spit. "One of the offspring!" She stopped, inhaled deeply, and smoothed the hostility out of her voice. "But then, you would pick *him*, wouldn't you?"

"Lay off, witch." Jess bristled forward with her fists clenched.

"Well, well, if it isn't the demon seed." Gryndelyn assessed Jess the way one would a maggot on a piece of rotting meat. "Love the new haircut, Miss Harrison. Very G.I. Jane." She glanced sideways at Lilliana. "Your doing, I suppose. Improving the appearance—how very prosaic." She faked a yawn. "Didn't work, did it? She's still the same little pile of angry madness."

Jess glanced down guiltily at her fists.

"Ah, but no matter. Lilliana was guaranteed to fail with you, wasn't she?" Gryndelyn leaned close to Jess, as if she was sincerely fond of her. "You were the perfect assignment. I knew she'd be no match for you."

Jess stepped back. Freaky dryers and the merry-go-round styling chair didn't scare her. They were circus tricks, kid stuff, nothing. But the witch's syrupy smile, now that unnerved her.

"You and your lovely rage. Such promise." Gryndelyn's silky voice stroked Jess's skin and made her shiver with disgust. "I was positively itching to watch you use all of that marvelous creative energy of yours to rid the earth of so many of its pestilent humans. And the whole thing would be her fault. But now..." Gryndelyn stiffened. Anger blazed in her eyes. "You and your brother are in my way."

"Don't hurt them!" Lilliana tried to wriggle out from behind Jake, but he held her back. "I'll come with you. I'll do whatever you want, just leave them alone."

"No!" Jake was fighting to stay calm. He didn't yell. He used Jess's dad's master and commander tone, which meant he was plenty mad. "You're staying with us."

Blow-dryers at the styling stations clicked on and flew up into the air. One stylist shrieked and tried to grab her runaway equipment. It eluded her faltering fingers. The blow-dryer flew higher, jerked the plug out of the socket, and lashed the stylist with thc cord. Four more joined it in the air, snaking beside Gryndelyn, undulating and hissing like dancing cobras.

The stylist and three frantic customers ran for the front door, but Gryndelyn and the dryer snakes blocked their escape. The screaming women scampered back and ran to hide in the bathroom.

Etta Mae tugged Lilliana toward the door. "Go find Sam! Hurry. We need your Grandma. He knows where she—"

"No." Gryndelyn raised her hands like a symphony conductor. "Do you really think I'd let you ruin everything?" The hyperactive dryers ramped up to super speed, blasting hot blue jet exhaust streams of air straight at Etta Mae and Lilliana.

Jess swore.

Jake spun around to shield them. The hot blast singed the cloth on his shoulder. He wasn't quick enough. Etta Mae cried out and fell to the floor, covering her face from the searing heat.

LaVonda let out a primal howl. "You leave my mama alone!" Like a lineman sacking a quarterback, LaVonda charged Gryndelyn and slammed her against the wall. Stunned, the Radio–Witch tuned out. She slid senseless to the floor, where LaVonda promptly sat on her.

The mechanical cobras' flames flickered out and clattered to the tile, lifeless.

Jess wanted to cheer. She would have, except the flattened fairy puffed up again. Stark white rage blazing in her eyes, Gryndelyn flung LaVonda off as if the big woman weighed no more than a kindergartener.

"Mama, get outta here!" LaVonda went from gutsy linebacker to frightened fifty-year-old in a split second. Without taking her eyes off Gryndelyn, she scrambled up and backed away. "You hear me? Go! Get help."

Help? From who? Jess seriously doubted a local sheriff would be able to rescue them. All the same, Etta Mae bravely ran to the front door, but it didn't open. She rattled the handle futilely.

Mark and Jake tried to help her, but the old wooden door wouldn't move. Mark hit his palm against the crash bar. "Trapped."

Outside, the crazy red cardinal was pecking wildly against the window. His loud tapping made Lilliana turn. "Napoleon?"

With a sharp snap, the roller shades on the door and windows zipped down, concealing the interior from passersby, darkening the room.

Reenergized, the blow-dryers shimmied up beside Gryndelyn, undulating around her shoulders, aiming deadly blue tongues of heat straight at LaVonda.

"Gryndelyn!" Lilliana stood with both hands stretched out. Glitter swirled unsteadily from her fingertips. "Stop!" There was wobbly courage in her voice.

The Radio-Witch whipped around. "You don't seriously think you can take me on?"

"Do it!" Jess yelled.

But Lilliana's mouth drooped into a sad thin curve.

Reluctance? Why? What was going on with her? Why did Lilliana care about this creature who was about to cremate them?

"Do something!" Jess ordered.

Glitter kept building around Lilliana's hands like miniature nebulas, two amazing little galaxies ready to do her bidding. But instead of flinging the magic stars at her enemy, she pleaded with the witch. "Please, don't make me do this. Don't make me fight you."

"Crap." Jess growled, raking back her short curls. "Can't you see? She's trying to roast us."

But Lilliana didn't hear. She was focused entirely on Gryndelyn. "You're my teacher. My mentor. My..." Each word trembled with uncertainty until she blurted, "I can't fight you. You're all I have."

"No!" Jake looked gut punched. "You've got us. Me."

Maggie stood up from where she'd been hiding behind the

couch. "All of us."

"I'm not *making* you do anything, Lilliana." Gryndelyn laughed once and picked stray clumps of human hairs off her white dress. "We're here because of you, you reeking little Halfling." She said the last under her breath and glowered at Lilliana. "You've been nothing but trouble since the day I took you in."

Quick as a match strikes, Gryndelyn snapped her wrist. Dozens of scissors and razors sprang to life, their blades snapping like hungry mouths. Click, click, click. Airborne, they twisted and gyrated, awkwardly changing shape, until each one sprouted a pair of silver bat wings to go with their lethal scissor beaks.

Lilliana's face crumpled. "Why are you doing this?"

"To teach you a lesson. You should've done as you were told." She shrugged and with a smile said, "These little darlings will amuse your friends while I give you the instruction you so richly deserve." As she spoke, her electric cobras revved up like blowtorches spewing blue flames.

"Someone could get hurt."

Gryndelyn smiled wryly at a scissor bat snapping eagerly in the air beside her. "I believe that's the point, my dear."

Lilliana couldn't hold the whirling stars steady. Her hands shook. "I'll follow the rules." She dashed away tears on the mashed rose petals on her shoulder. "I promise."

"*Rules* are no longer the issue." Her guardian rolled her eyes, "Haven't you figured that out yet?" Tendrils of smoke undulated up from the floor near Gryndelyn's feet, writhing around her like cloying worshipers. "What is that odd expression humans use? Oh, yes. *You* are the *fly* in my soup." She grinned. "A delightful euphemism, don't you think?"

"Fly? How? It doesn't make sense." Lilliana shook her head, blinking. The nebulas twirling in her palms slowed down. Shrank. "What did I do?"

"No!" Jess shouted. "Don't listen to her. Stay strong. Hit her with that stuff. Now!"

No one listened to Jess.

Gryndelyn clucked her tongue at Lilliana in a motherly fashion. "Now, now, Lilliana. Chin up. It's not your fault. It's simply a consequence of your unfortunate birth." For a moment, she actually appeared to be sorry for Lilliana. But then her bosom heaved with resignation. "Nevertheless, you are the wee little worm—" She squeezed her thumb and forefinger together demonstrating exactly how tiny a worm. "—in *my* PEACH."

She laughed, genuinely this time, as if she'd cracked a clever joke, and then signaled her cobras to advance."FYI, my dear, you couldn't stop me if you wanted to." She held up her fingers again. "Worm."

Flying scissors and razors swarmed above Gryndelyn, awaiting her command to dive-bomb the occupants of the room. She waved them into action.

Maggie yanked Cai down behind the couch in the waiting area.

"Lilliana. Do something," Jess ordered. "Now!"

"Jess, get back!" Mark tried to grab Jess, but she wrenched free.

Jess screeched at Lilliana. "What's wrong with you? Throw stars!"

But Lilliana glanced despondently around the room, the sparkles in her hands diminishing to nothing more than two wimpy puffs of glitter.

Mark kept trying to haul Jess toward cover. Flailing stubbornly, she snatched a bottle of shampoo from a product rack and heaved it like a grenade at Gryndelyn. Without waiting to see where it landed, Jess threw another bottle. Her first shot thudded ineffectually to the floor. The second shampoo burst open on impact and splattered on Gryndelyn's gown. All it did was elicit a hostile sneer from the enemy.

But Jake followed her lead. He put his quarterback skills to use, hurled an aluminum can of hairspray across the room, and nailed one of the cobras. Dryer and hairspray slammed against the wall, exploding in a burst of flame and acrid smoke. Remains of the dryer crashed to the floor, splintered and reeking of burnt plastic.

"Nice shot!" Mark let go of Jess, grabbed a can, and threw it, hitting one of the dryer handles, sending it into a spiral.

"Humans." Gryndelyn spat the word. "*Pond scum.*"

A winged razor streaked toward Jake. The blade flicked out and cut his forehead. Blood streamed over his left eye. He wiped it off on his sleeve and grabbed a supersize can of mousse. Dripping blood, Jake hit a line drive and sent that razor back to its creator.

Gryndelyn looked royally pissed when it hit her in the shoulder. She spread her arms, and her fists pulsated with orbs of bright blue and white flames.

Jake swung again and smashed another flying scissor. It spiraled toward the back wall. Home run.

With a battle cry of "Batting practice!" Mark grabbed a tall red aluminum can and stepped up to the plate.

The vicious winged scalpels darted through the room hunting for targets. With rolled up magazines in both hands, LaVonda swatted at them furiously. She yelped in pain as one of the wicked pests bit into her backside. Maggie yanked a small shelf off a manicure cart and swung away at an attacking scissor. Cai was cornered with only a flat iron to fight off a trio of snapping razors. She wouldn't last long.

Jess shouted for Lilliana, but she was in some kind of weird trance, like she'd been in the day of the ghost frogs. Only today, they didn't need singing frogs. They needed help. Jess darted through the melee to grab Lilliana's arm. "Snap out of it!" She shook her. Lilliana still wasn't quite with them. Jess got an idea "Hey, Fairy Godmother! Snap out of it. I need you to turn these—" Jess swatted a razor bat away. "—into something else. Something less deadly. Quick!"

Lilliana blinked.

She'd heard.

Instantly, she threw a cloud of glitter swirling into the air. The clicking and snapping stopped. Bats froze midair. Their silver wings and shiny blades suddenly changed to dull brown clay. They dropped like rocks, shattering against the linoleum.

"Stones, Lilliana. Really?" Gryndelyn chuckled as if it was all nothing more than a game. "You'd have done better to turn your *friends* into stone so they wouldn't get scorched." She hefted blazing fireballs in each of her hands as if trying to decide which one to fling first. "This is pointless, you know. Fire has always been stronger than water."

"No!" Maggie shouted from under the couch where she and Cai had crawled to hide. "Water is stronger. You're stronger."

Fire? Water? What did that have to do with anything? Jess was just about to nail a dryer snake with a bottle of cream rinse. But she stopped. Her mouth fell open. It all made sense. Lilliana's green eyes—the color of a stormy sea. Pale watery complexion. Dark wavy hair as if she'd risen from a lake. And Gryndelyn— eyes blazing like the hot blue center of a flame. Yellow hair. Smoke coiling around her.

Elements.

"Maggie's right!" Jess whooped. "Water quenches fire."

Jake understood it, too. His gaze raced back and forth between Lilliana and Gryndelyn. "Lilliana, you're stronger!" Except his face suddenly filled with alarm. He dove for Jess.

But Mark jerked her to the ground before Jake landed on them both. Jess hadn't noticed the fireball streaking straight for her. She peeked out from under the shelter of her boyfriend and her big brother.

Water spouted up to meet the flames.

Gryndelyn's fireball evaporated into a fizzle of steam. Lilliana's nebulas were back. Only now, they were huge rushing whirlpools, glistening like silver-scaled fish. A shower of glittering droplets twirled around Lilliana in a jubilant sparkling dance.

Jake, Jess, and Mark lay in a tangled heap on the slippery floor.

Jake leaned up, gazing at Lilliana as light and water bathed her. Color blanched out of his face. Jess couldn't tell if he was frightened or astonished. "Wow," he mouthed reverently.

Then he turned sad. Jess saw his amazement drain away and grief sag his bloody features. She understood. Even though Lilliana had saved them, she'd just transformed into something Jake could never possess. Clearly they were not the same species. Not even close.

She was incredible.

"About time." Jess sat up, brushing grime off her hands. "If you ask me—"

"Incoming!" Mark yanked her down again, shielding her underneath him as another of Gryndelyn's flaming missiles headed straight for them.

Fairy Godmother Training Manual

Directive 18

You've heard it said that "Things are not always what they seem." This statement is deceptive and panders to the feeble minded.

The truth is: things are *never* what they seem.

Every act cloaks an ulterior motive. A flower does not bloom simply to please us with her beauty. Her colorful petals are merely a lure by which she fulfills her ambition to propagate. As soon as a flower has been sufficiently pollinated, her enticing petals drop away, revealing an ugly, swollen seedpod.

If you wish to be successful, don't be naïve. Ferret out the motives of those around you.

—Gryndelyn Myrddin

I am Water Hear Me Roar

Lilliana stepped between Gryndelyn's ruthless attack on Jake, Jess, and Mark and blasted the fireball out of existence. Then she commanded the hoses on the shampoo sinks to rise up and douse Gryndelyn.

I am the worm in her peach.

Her guardian squawked when the cold spray hit her. Lilliana increased the water pressure from the nozzles. A microburst of terror flitted across Gryndelyn's perfect features.

She deserved it. She'd attacked innocent humans. And a C.O.! She could've killed them. What chance did humans have against Gryndelyn? None.

Lilliana took a quick backward glance at her friends. Jake's shirt and the side of his face were crimson with *blood!* She dared not look away from Gryndelyn more than an instant. Clamping her teeth together, she turned back to her so-called mentor. Why had she never admitted to herself how merciless and cruel Gryndelyn was?

Because she'd been naïve.

Blind.

Foolish.

A foolish little worm.

The more she thought about it, the more water whooshed inside her. Until finally, a flashflood burst from her palms. A mighty waterfall arced up and splashed over Gryndelyn. Wet fists thundered down on her head, beating out the fire. Drenching her mentor with sheets of water. Smothering the flames. Extinguishing evil.

Amid the torrent Lilliana vaguely heard rustling behind her. Jake and Jess clambered up. The others came out of hiding and gathered around her. *Friends.* She registered the thought in the deep recesses of her mind but couldn't find the meaning of it.

There was only water.

Water quenching fire.

Beneath the thrashing waterfall Gryndelyn's hunched figure collapsed in a shivering fetal lump. All of her sparks and embers, all of her smoke and flames sputtered out. So much water poured over her that she might be screaming or even drowning. It was impossible to tell. The last of the blow-dryers fell into the flood around its master and expired with a short synaptic zap.

Jake reached through the curtain of droplets swirling around Lilliana and put his hand on her shoulder. "Lilliana, you can stop. We're safe."

Lilliana shuddered, unable to catch her breath. Dizzy and cold, she started to shake uncontrollably. The water wouldn't stop.

Jake called to her again. "She's drowning. You don't want to kill her."

No, she didn't. Jake's words finally penetrated her blind torrent. Lilliana might be a fly in Gryndelyn's soup. *A worm.* But she wasn't a murderer.

Trembling with spent fury, Lilliana calmed the flood. She took a jagged breath and closed her eyes. Everything had changed. Reality had pivoted. She was different now. She could see an entire universe she hadn't been aware of. Her universe. Water waited for her command. She called it, letting the element rush back inside her where it belonged, transfusing her with its energy. When she opened her eyes, the floor was nearly dry. Nozzles lay flaccid in the sinks, barely dripping.

Gryndelyn hunkered at Lilliana's feet, a shivering, gasping lump. Her wet blonde hair, now sooty and gray like her charred gown, fizzled and steamed. The molten lava in her core had cooled to nothing more than blackened sludge. Only the acrid smell of damp ashes remained.

Yet, when the vanquished fairy finally looked up, her eyes smoldered with hate, and somehow she summoned the strength to vanish.

Escaped.

Lilliana stared at the scorch marks on the floor where Gryndelyn had been kneeling. Jake's hand on her shoulder was her only tether to reality.

In the ensuing silence, Lilliana felt inextricably connected to every molecule of water in the universe. The same way a mother's hearing is amplified and attuned to her child's slightest whimper, even the tiniest drop of moisture falling from the faucet into the sink echoed in Lilliana's ears like thunder in a canyon. Water sluicing through the plumbing in the walls rumbled as noisily as a freight train. The river, miles away, flowed so loudly it may as well have cut through the center of the shop. Miniscule droplets in the atmosphere pattered like mice on a tin roof.

And every glorious particle seemed to belong to her.

Or did she belong to it?

"It's over," Jake whispered. The warm moisture of his breath beside her ear teased her senses, coaxing her once again into the world, his world.

As much as she wanted to believe him, Jake was wrong. This wasn't over. She could no longer afford to be naïve. Everything had changed. His world. *And* her world.

She turned to look at him. "You're bleeding." She reached up to examine his wound.

"I'm fine." But he wasn't. A new agony marred his strong beautiful features. More sad music tolled in his soul. She guessed it had little to do with the gash on his forehead, but she would do what she could for him. Stars flittered from her fingertips to heal the cut.

He clasped her shoulders and tried to convince her. "I'm okay.

188

Really."

For how long, she wondered, letting her hand trail down his blood-smeared cheek. If anything else happened to him…

Waves crashed violently against the rocky shores of her sanity. Deep in the unsettled seas of her soul, she knew that if anything ever happened to him, the power inside her would become a roaring wall of water, a tsunami of such destructive force that Jess's prophesied explosions would seem tame in comparison. She shuddered and backed away.

His lips were moving, but she couldn't hear him for the roaring in her ears. He gave her shoulders a gentle tug and pulled her closer. "Lilliana, look at me. I'm fine. Stop worrying."

He called her name again and smoothed away a tear from her cheek. At least, she thought it was a tear. Maybe it was the tidal wave leaking out. For both their sakes, she had to keep him safe. To do that, she needed the truth.

What peach of Gryndelyn's was Lilliana spoiling?

She broke away from Jake and spun around to search for Etta Mae—Etta Mae who'd been keeping secrets.

Instead she found herself face to face with Jess, something odd in her expression, not the familiar hostility.

"Not bad, Tinkerbell. Not bad at all." Jess nodded with something strangely akin to admiration in her eyes. "Waited till the last minute. But then you pulled it out."

SURVIVORS

"**W**e won." Jess stood next to Maggie surveying the aftermath of battle.

"Round two goes to us," Maggie agreed. "I just hope–"

"Yeah, I know. She'll be back. Wonder what's eatin' her?"

Armed with a soggy magazine in each hand, LaVonda crawled out from under her styling station. She stumbled over to the restroom door and rapped. "Ya'll can come out now. It's safe."

A customer with dangling pink rollers cracked the door open. "You're sure?" She took a hesitant step out of the bathroom. The others emerged behind her, shaken and pale. "What on earth happened here?"

LaVonda grabbed a broom and began the daunting task of sweeping up the hundreds of pebbly bat bodies and mumbled, "Don't know how in blue blazes I'm gonna explain this to the insurance company. Won't do me no good to file a police report..."

The window shades suddenly snapped up, bathing the room in sunlight, and the previously inoperative front door swung open wide, allowing a spring breeze to waft in before drifting shut again. A light shower of glitter whirled over LaVonda and the distraught customers and stylists. Their expressions changed from shell-shocked terror to dreamy confusion.

Etta Mae tiptoed out from behind the couch and whispered to Lilliana, "Was that *elin-gíl*?"

Lilliana nodded.

LaVonda stared in stunned confusion at the broom in her hand

and the mess in her shop. "What in the world happened here?"

Etta Mae carefully circumnavigated a pile of broken stone razors, sidestepped a charred magazine, kicked aside a dead blow-dryer, and cleared her throat. "A big dust devil blew the door open. It was full of these here pebbles." She shoved one of the scissor bat bodies toward LaVonda's broom.

"But there's smoke damage." LaVonda shook her head.

Etta Mae righted a toppled wastebasket, retrieved a drippy half-melted bottle of shampoo and deposited it in the trash. "One of those faulty dryers threw a spark. Caught fire on that pile of magazines. Lucky for us, I sprayed it out before the sprinklers came on."

The women gaped at her. She avoided looking at them as she rescued curlers and combs from the debris on the floor. "Y'all musta been so busy talkin' in the bathroom you didn't notice."

The bedraggled women looked from one to another, trying to reconcile their haggard appearances with her explanation. A gray-haired client plunked down in a stylist's chair. "I musta been asleep on the john." She adjusted her plastic cape and swiveled to face the mirror. "Come on over here, Vicki." She signaled one of the stylists. "You can do better'n this with my hair. Looks like I was the main feature at a haunted house."

Vicki popped her gum and checked the mirror, straightening a few of her drooping punk-rock spikes. "Yes, ma'am. Bad hair day, for sure."

Jess noticed Etta Mae and Lilliana had slipped off to the corner. Their heads were bent together in earnest conversation. "Sam's at the pharmacy." Etta Mae glanced up at the clock. "No, wait. It's almost twelve. He'll be at the café."

"I can't leave you with this awful mess."

Etta Mae dismissed the demolished shop with wave of her hand. "If it weren't for your grandma, I wouldn't have none of this stuff. I owe her. You gotta get to her pronto, cause that she devil ain't gonna give up."

While Etta Mae talked, Lilliana sent a low flying cloud of glitter floating stealthily along the checkered tile, breezing along the walls and whisking across shelves, straightening, polishing, replacing missing scissors and broken dryers. The women of The Glass Slipper seemed blind to the fact that sparkly stuff was silently turning their smashed pumpkin back into a gleaming salon.

"The sooner you find your grandma, the better for all of us." Etta Mae glanced meaningfully at Jake and Jess. "You kids gotta hurry." She herded Jess and the others to the door. "Anyway, Sam's been waiting half a lifetime for you to come back."

As they left the shop and headed up the sidewalk, Etta Mae pointed across the street at the Destiny Café and hollered after them, "He named the café after you."

Lilliana whirled around. "Sam did?"

"No. Your father."

Directive 19

Unusual events occur in the human world for which it is simply impossible to be adequately prepared. Humans are, after all, bizarre and impulsive creatures. On these occasions a successful Fairy Godmother must rely on her instincts.

—Gryndelyn Myrddin

Women's Chorus

Father?

It took Lilliana a minute to comprehend. She wasn't used to thinking in terms of a father. Her earliest memories were entirely of women, her grandmother and Gryndelyn. Fairies were a predominately female culture, just as their counterpart, Elves, were a predominantly male culture.

But, of course, she had to have had a father.

The idea bubbled up, warm and healing, a hot spring filling her with hope.

⌐RENDEZVOUS

AT DESTINY'S CAFE

Jess stared at her Fairy Godmother. Was Lilliana going to fade away entirely? She was normally pale, but she stood there on the sidewalk and turned almost as transparent as an ice sculpture. "Come on," Jess urged. "Let's go find him."

"Father," Lilliana mumbled. Color flooded back into her cheeks, and she took off running. For such a skinny, fragile-looking girl, she ran blazin' fast. Jake sprinted all out to stay up with her. The rest of them double-timed it up the sidewalk behind them and burst through the doors of the cafe.

Destiny's Café smelled like bean sprouts and vegetable soup. It was one of those healthy places, full of organic cucumbers and tofu paste on whole wheat bread. Definitely not Jess's kind of food.

Lilliana stood next to a booth occupied by a man wearing a white pharmacist's coat. He peered at Lilliana over the top of his newspaper. The pharmacist reminded Jess of the guy who played the Professor in *X-Men*, Patrick Stewart, only this guy wasn't quite as bald, and he had really intense eyes.

"Samuel Clayton?" Lilliana asked.

His newspaper drooped to the table, and he squinted at her, tilting his head to escape the glare glinting in through the big picture windows. His coffee cup clunked against the saucer as he set it down and yanked off his reading glasses. "Gilly?" he asked in a trembling rasp.

Without answering, Lilliana slid into the booth and sat across

195

from him.

He shook his head and pinched the bridge of his nose. "No. No, of course not. You couldn't be her. I'm sorry. You are?"

"Gilly was my mother."

Directive 20

Humans are forever getting themselves into predicaments. Consequently, in the Godmothering business there are more downs than ups. Therefore, one must take pleasure in the rare happy moments.

—Gryndelyn Myrddin

Her Father's Eyes

The river inside Lilliana could have carved the Grand Canyon in the time it took Samuel Clayton to gather his thoughts.

"Your mother?" He blinked studiously. "Then you're…" A slow unconscious smile widened his open mouth. "Of course," he breathed. "You're our Lilliana."

Our Lilliana?

She belonged to him in some way. He knew her name. Lilliana sat back and folded her arms around her middle, holding in the white-water rapids churning in her belly.

He leaned forward, filling the space she'd evacuated. "Oh, yes, I see it. You look so much like her! Like Gilly. But I see my brother, too. Your eyes. The way you angle your head. Inquisitive. Quiet. Just like him." He grinned full on. "Welcome home!" And spread his arms wide, welcoming her even though the table was between them.

My father's brother. Here. Real. Uncle. She had family.

Dizzying blood throbbed against Lilliana's temples. Human blood. She was not all water. Her heart pounded against her ribs, pumping humanness through her cells. She was bone. She was earth. She was human. "My father," she whispered and gripped the edge of the table. "Is he here?"

Sam's sudden shift in expression gave her the answer. Newspaper rustled as he folded his hands atop it and nervously rubbed his thumbs against one another. He shook his head and glanced up at her, his face lined with sadness. "Not a day goes by that I don't miss him."

He waited for her reaction. Perhaps he'd expected a flood of grief for having lost a father she never knew, but she was still drowning in shock, overwhelmed with the newness of it all. Everything inside her came to a sudden stop.

For a moment she had no inner music. No music at all.

Her human emotions, the ones she'd inherited from her father, pumped her full of neurotransmitters, chemicals that made her want to cry or fly away. They clashed with her calm, orderly Fairy nature, neutralizing her. The duality of her nature held her in a stalemate, just as it had when Gryndelyn attacked. She recognized the problem now, and with a deep breath she forced herself to harmonize, choosing to be fairy, calm and in control.

During her prolonged silence, Sam produced oboe tones of curiosity. Lilliana guessed he was searching her face for traces of his dead brother, remembrances, just as she was searching his for clues to her humanity.

"What happened to my father?"

"Your mother died," he blurted, as if the simple explanation was all encompassing. It wasn't. It couldn't be.

Lilliana nodded, accepting her part in the tragedy. "Yes, she died giving birth to me, but what happened to him?"

"It's difficult to explain." He shrugged, pinning his lips together, hesitating, holding back. In the face of her probing silence, he finally surrendered. "He and I were twins, did you know?"

She shook her head.

"Yes. Very close, he and I, peas in a pod until Shaun met your mother. The two of them became..." He trailed off, tracing imaginary circles on the newsprint with his finger. "Theirs was an unusual relationship."

Did he know exactly how strange? *Fairy mating with human.* Lilliana shifted uncomfortably. The booth suddenly felt cramped and confining.

199

"I'd never seen anything like it. They were incredibly drawn to one another." His smooth brow furrowed, and he closed his eyes, remembering. Then he asked a strange question. "Have you studied chemistry?"

The corner of her mouth twitched. *Chemistry.* Elements and particles. How odd he should ask. She was very nearly an element herself. And ever since she could toddle over to a sandbox and change sand into glass, she'd loved the science.

As a pharmacist, Samuel Clayton combined chemicals. She, on the other hand, played with the sparks of light hidden inside electrons and neutrons. Despite the fact that he was her uncle, she doubted he'd appreciate the way *her kind* routinely violated his understanding of the laws of physics. So she urged him on with a cursory nod.

"Excellent, then you'll understand. From the moment your mother and father met, they couldn't bear to be apart. Much like the way hydrogen bonds with oxygen, they became inseparable." He explained in the language of a chemist, hooking his fingers together in illustration. "Like free-floating molecules they attached. Instantly. Permanently. Once bonded, they seemed to form an entirely new element." His eyes blinked open, suddenly intense. "Do you see?"

Lilliana nodded.

Oh yes, she understood her parent's compulsion. All of her life she'd heard about her mother's obsession with her human lover. It had been publicly condemned. Scoffed at. Tittered about. But now she understood that compulsion too well. A sidelong glance at Jake and her throat tightened.

He'd been listening intently to Sam. His accepting smile broke her heart. Did he know? Did he know what it meant to them? Her parents' compulsion hadn't just hurt her and her mother, it had destroyed her father. Lilliana's heart fluttered like a panicked sparrow caught in a net.

"I wish you could've known your mother." Sam gazed across

the room as if he could still see Gilly standing there. "She was just a little mite of a thing. So vibrant and intelligent. Exquisite, really. She could've had her pick of the men in town, including me, but she never had an interest in anyone except Shaun."

Just as I have no interest in anyone but Jake.

Hot wind raced through her, prickling her scalp, drying her soul, leaving parched crackled mud in her stomach. She struggled to catch her breath, turned and found Jake's gaze riveted on her, unmistakable devotion in his eyes. God help her, she was doing the very thing she vowed she'd never do—repeating her mother's mistake.

Sam paused his story and followed her gaze. "Oh, I see. You and him?"

Blood raced to her cheeks, scalding her face with shame, but there was no point denying it. It was true. She was already caught in her mother's fatal trap. "Yes."

And Jake—Jake was following in her father's footsteps. To where? She grabbed Sam's hands and begged. "Tell me exactly what happened to my father. I need to know. He needs to know."

Sam's face pruned up with sorrow. He shook his head and lowered his eyes. "Two days after you were born..." His jaw tightened, and he stared helplessly at their hands clasped atop the newspaper. "His heart, it—" A jolt of anger wrung out his features, or maybe it was frustration. He let go of her. "Look, it was all very disturbing. How much of this do you want to hear?"

"Everything."

"Very well." He sighed and continued on in a clinical voice, a pharmacist's voice, detached, informative, as though explaining the death of a stranger. Not his twin brother. Not her father.

"I found him on the floor next to your cradle, lying in a puddle of water. His fingertips had been badly burned. At first we thought he must've been electrocuted or struck by lightning. It was all so strange."

Sam coughed and cleared his throat, rinsing away a slight

quiver. "The autopsy found charring on his internal organs consistent with electrocution. But they also found water in Shaun's stomach and lungs as if he'd drowned. Of course, that was impossible. He died in your bedroom, not in a bathtub. And his heart had burst. It was torn to shreds."

Her own heart nearly thudded to a stop.

"They said he died of heart failure." Sam's jaw tightened. He shook his head. "I knew better." He took a deep breath, allowing the crashing waves of his anguish to subside, to wash back into his ocean of grief. Calm again, Sam pressed his index finger against the newspaper, pointing, not at the news, but at an invisible solution he had settled on years earlier. "Do you see? Shaun couldn't exist apart from her. Without your mother, his heart burst. Literally. He died because she died. I know it sounds strange, but it's the only explanation that fits."

Lilliana's mouth turned to dust.

She and her uncle sat blanketed in woolen sorrow until at last Sam raised his chin. With a fresh dose of resolve and steadiness, he met her gaze. It was as though, once again, her uncle bravely hefted the painful loss of her father onto his shoulders. A huge boulder of sadness, his to carry for the rest of his life.

Too heavy. She crumpled.

Jake slid into the booth beside her. Without a word, he gathered her into the comfort of his shoulder. Did he know it was not for her father she wept? Did he know these stinging tears were for him? For Jake. For their doomed future.

Their friends gathered around the table. It was good of them to so willingly share her grief, to murmur kindness. She'd never known friends like these. What boulders of sadness would they be forced to carry because of her and Jake?

Jess! How much had she heard? How much had she understood?

Lilliana tore away from Jake and swiped away her selfish tears. Jess was staring at her, fierce blue eyes searing Lilliana with a look made of equal parts anguish and comprehension. She knew.

Even Gryndelyn, with her scythe-like scrutiny and condemning barbs, had never made Lilliana feel as guilty as Jess did in that brief moment.

Lilliana could not rob Jess of another brother.

Would not.

She reached across the table for her uncle. "I need to find my grandmother. It's a matter of life and death."

PEACE NEGOTIATIONS

Enough with the reunion. It was time to go. "We need directions," Jess demanded.

Sam gave his answer to Lilliana. "Take River Road north. Follow it through the hills until you come to a sign that says "Grandma Nature's Nursery." Your grandma Rose runs an organic greenhouse. It's where we get all the fresh vegetables for this place. You'll see a gravel turnoff." He slipped off his white lab coat. "Wait, I'll take you. Give me a minute to go next door and tell my assistant I'll be gone from the pharmacy for the rest of the afternoon."

"No. It's okay." Lilliana practically dove over Jake as she scrambled out of the booth. "You don't need to come."

"Nonsense. You're my niece. If you're in trouble, I'm going with you."

"It's not like that. I didn't mean it was *actually* life or death. Not exactly."

Yeah, she did. Jess rolled her eyes and headed for the door. That was *exactly* what she'd meant. Because it was true.

"I can't lose you again," her uncle argued. "I won't."

"I'll come back. I promise."

He squinted at her skeptically.

Then Lilliana, Superfairy, Master of Magic and Water, did what any other teenager would do. She reassured him with empty platitudes that had to be as satisfying as one of his tofu burgers.

"It's not dangerous."

Couldn't he tell that was a lie? He didn't say anything.

204

"I'll be fine. Really."

Not buying it, her uncle crossed his arms. "Uh-huh."

"This is just something between me and my grandmother. I need to take care of it on my own." That much rang true. Her uncle sighed.

Lilliana backed toward the door. "I _will_ come back."

He closed the distance between them and hugged her. "Soon," he said, half command, half plea. Then, with a worried parental frown, he watched as they all bolted out the door.

Once they were far enough away from the Destiny's Café's big picture windows, Lilliana stopped. Jess and the others gathered around her.

"Thank you for bringing me," she started what sounded like a farewell speech. "I'll never forget what you've done. You've all been wonderful. I don't think you'll have any trouble with Gryndelyn on the way home. She won't—"

"Wait a minute!" Jake grabbed her arm. "We're coming with you."

"No." She turned away from his bruised expression and studied the old flag waving in the breeze in front of the courthouse. "I don't want you to."

Jake let go. Crushed rose petals from her sleeve gave way and floated to the ground, scenting the air, leaving her pale skin showing through tattered holes on her shoulders.

"We've been over this." He raked his hand through his hair. "I can't let you go alone."

"Nope. We can't." Mark nodded in agreement. "Your _demented mentor_ might be there."

No one laughed at his word play. They all knew exactly how badly the Psycho-Fairy-Witch wanted to cremate Lilliana.

"Tell him." Lilliana stared straight at Jess. "Tell Jake why he can't come."

Thoughts raced through Jess's mind so fast she couldn't catch them.

Jake didn't wait for her answer. "It's already settled," he said with an end-of-discussion tone. "We're going."

"He can't." Lilliana said flatly, not looking at him, staring straight at Jess, her features torqued by worry. Clearly, she expected Jess to step in and keep Jake from risking his life.

Yeah, and there were a hundred good reasons to do exactly that.

Except now, Jess had hold of something else, something bigger, something more important.

She met Lilliana's piercing stare. "Jake has to choose for himself." And there it was, the truth.

Lilliana turned paler than ever. "No."

"Yeah, he does." Jess felt calm, strong, sure. "Yes, I get it. It's a risk. And I don't know how this relationship thing works with fairies and humans. But I do know this—Jake has a right to choose."

Just then, a hawk wheeled in the open blue sky above them, announcing his joy of the hunt with a triumphant high-pitched skree.

Jess hated words. Words were too feeble to explain what she finally understood. "Ever since Ryan died, the only thing I cared about was keeping Jake safe. I didn't ever want to get hurt like that again. At first, I thought you were like her, like Cheryl. But now everything is different. Now I get it. I see what really matters."

Maggie shifted closer, lending Jess silent backup.

"Now I'm wondering what good it is to be safe if you can't live your life. If you can't be with the people you love." She tossed an apologetic glance at her brother.

He nodded forgiveness, and Jess felt a weight lift from her shoulders.

"And hey! That fight in the beauty shop—wow!" She grinned, looking around their circle. "That was amazing. I haven't felt that alive since—"

"Since before Ryan died," Jake quietly finished for her.

"Yeah." Jess nodded and kicked the toe of her boot against the sidewalk. "His death was pointless. Girls. Partying. Drinking. Stupid stuff. Not like this. Not like trying to do something important, something good, like protecting people you care about. Some things are worth the risk. Jake has to decide."

"I already have."

Jess knew that'd be his answer.

Mark put his arm around her, and Jess didn't shrug away. She shivered. Not because of the cool breeze, but because for the first time in a long time, she'd unbuckled her stifling protective armor.

Maybe her F.G. really had performed a miracle.

In the last few days, lots of supernatural stuff had happened. *Magic*. But this, this was the most amazing thing of all. Here they were in the middle of complete and total weirdness, and Jess hadn't felt *this* sane, this relaxed... Heck! She hadn't smiled this much in over a year.

"I thought we'd lost you forever," Cai mumbled.

Maggie gave Jess a sideways hug. "It's good to have you back,"

Miracle.

She felt alive again. And that was way better than if her F.G. had prissied her up in a big white Cinderella dress and sent her twirling around some fairytale ballroom.

Suddenly, a freezing chill whooshed through the group, sucking away the oxygen. Just as swiftly, the air returned to normal, warm and breathable. Jess caught her breath. Only now, their tight circle had a gap in it.

Jake yelled, "No!" and spun around scanning the horizon.

Lilliana had disappeared.

Directive 21

Maintain your anonymity. Resist the urge to take credit for your good deeds. In point of fact, as discussed in prior directives, it is of the utmost importance that you hide your true identity. It's one thing to let your C.O. know you are a Fairy Godmother. It's quite another to reveal your true nature.

Do not let anyone know who and what you really are.

— Gryndelyn Myrddin

Phantom of the Riddle

Lilliana skated through the atmosphere, invisible. *Water. Wind. Disaster.* That's what she was. That's who she was. *A half-human, half-fairy freak of nature.*

Her mother was dead because of her. They'd found her father lying in water. Perhaps Lilliana was responsible for his death, too. And now, if she wasn't extremely cautious, she might be the angel of death for Jake.

She flashed through the air, zipping over water molecules in the wispy clouds above the river. Just as the water below her rushed over rocks and boulders, she rushed over rippling air currents, except Lilliana did it with lightning speed and materialized beside a small billboard.

Grandma Nature's Organic Farm and Nursery
Providing a loving home for plants.
Nurturing them with the Earth's magical goodness.

The sign depicted a fairy's wand sprinkling *elin-gil* onto the upturned face of a smiling sunflower. Her grandmother didn't seem very concerned about her anonymity.

Grandmother. Naneth. What did Lilliana really know of her? She had vague memories. Wistful longings. But would Rose be glad to see her?

Ahead of her stretched a rutted gravel road lined with red clover and bluebonnets in full flower. Peppery red and pink wildflowers brightened the uncultivated fields. Here and there dragonflies flitted among tall stalks of purple larkspur. Slowly

Lilliana walked toward her destination.

It all smelled achingly familiar.

Flowers. Grasses. Cottonwood trees. And so much water. Scents swirled through the air: the sulfuric tang of algae in the swampy edges along the river, the odor of frogs burrowing under rich mud to hide from the afternoon sun, the faint hint of dragonflies skirting the misty banks, sunfish splashing out of the waves to snag gnats for lunch.

She knew this place.

Sunlight glinted off a tall copper spire in the distance. The closer she got, the more she remembered. Lilliana started to run. Then she unfurled her wings and flew.

She was home.

Home.

The copper spire rose from atop an enormous domed greenhouse that looked more like a glass Taj Mahal than a nursery. At the tip of the spire a copper ball slowly turned, sending thin shrieks of colored lightning arcing into the cloudless blue sky. Lilliana guessed the streaks of white-hot yellow, deep violet and orange-red were beyond the color spectrum visible to most humans. Each colorful bolt was filled with sonic whispers. Elf magic. But for what purpose?

Down the road from the greenhouse stood her grandmother's cottage, a strange hodgepodge house with odd-shaped sections springing out of the original wattle-and-daub structure as if they were afterthoughts. Gingerbread shutters hung beside mullioned windows. A medieval turret bulged out of the northwest corner, while a boxy pink addition done in Tudor style timberwork jutted out over the front porch. Lilliana tucked her wings and stooped under the sagging cantilever to reach the front door.

The minute she pulled the chain on the brass boatman's bell, the door swung open and a green parrot flew out. "Who's there? Who's there?" he demanded in a shrill voice.

A young ram galloped from the side yard followed by a bevy

of cackling hens. He lowered his nubby horns, ready to charge her.

The parrot's red crown flipped up as he fluttered past her face. "Oh, it's you! Where've you been? Where've you been?" he squawked. "You're late! Late. She's gone. All gone."

"No! She can't be gone." Lilliana knocked loudly on the open door. "Hello? Naneth?"

The ram gave her leg a halfhearted bump, and the silly chickens pecked her tennis shoes in the hope of finding bugs.

"Yarwk. She's not here." The parrot bobbled crazily in the air, screeching. "Not here!"

Lilliana thumped her hand against the door. "Then where is she?"

"This way! Come on! This way."

The lamb capered after her as Lilliana followed the green parrot. Jabbering loudly, he darted and zigzagged all the way back to the greenhouse. At his approach, the glass doors creaked open. The noisy bird perched on one and preened his leg feathers. "Hurry up. Go in. Go in," he squawked. "You know the way."

"Thank you." She was not at all certain that she did know the way, but she certainly didn't want to tax her ears further by asking him for directions.

"Stay out!" The parrot swooped at the ram. "Stay out. You'll eat the flowers. You'll eat the flowers."

The ram seemed determined to follow Lilliana, but she patted his curly top knot and pointed at the door. "He's right. You'd best go out and play." The ram bleated his displeasure but turned and gamboled after the parrot.

Naneth's greenhouse was the size of a gymnasium, filled with rows and rows of wooden tables, and the tables were covered with thousands and thousands of potted flowers. Every flower was happy. Ecstatic. Their roots vibrated with contentment. They sounded exactly like children humming.

"Naneth?" she called. There was no answer. She looked in every direction, hurried to the end of the row and then headed to the other side of the hothouse.

Butterflies meandered through the aisles, so heavily laden with nectar they could scarcely fly. Mist dispensers flipped on and filled the air with a gentle spray that sent the butterflies skirting toward the ceiling singing joyful feasting songs. They were almost too deliriously sated to notice her arrival until a beautiful blue swallowtail flitted past Lilliana's nose and yodeled the news to the others. Soon, a bright fluttering chorus followed her.

In high, breathy voices they trilled a ballad about a princess returning home and how much all the butterflies adored her. The exquisite harmony nearly made Lilliana cry. They so perfectly captured the loneliness of a child lost from home. But this was no time for sentimentality. She blocked out the sound. Besides, their blatant flattery quickly became annoying. She was no princess. She was here on urgent business. "I'm busy." She quickened her steps. "Go on. You must feed. Seize the day."

They tittered and swooped, bringing their airy song to a final crescendo with "Hail! Hail! Our princess returns." At least they finally stopped embarrassing her and went back to sipping their lunch and singing praises to the flowers for producing such delectable nectar.

Still no sign of her grandmother.

Did the parrot mean something bad had happened to Naneth? Lilliana called her grandmother again and hurried down each aisle searching under tables, behind piles of potting soil, around wheelbarrows and gardening trolleys.

As she rushed past the tables, flowers bowed their heads and changed their song into a solemn worshipful hum. Mimicking the butterflies, no doubt. Even the snapdragons leaned over. Which was completely ludicrous because everyone knows how notoriously cheeky snapdragons are.

"Enough of this!" She put her foot down beside a row of particularly effusive ruby red gerbera daisies. "Stop it. All of you. You've had your fun. Now, if you please, where is my grandmother?"

In unison the daisies tipped their petals toward the back of the greenhouse, to the east wall. A stream of butterflies corkscrewed through the air, spiraling in the same direction. She rushed to follow. They alighted on the glass and formed a living arch over a small bronze door set in the east wall. Moss clung to the moist glass beside it, but in front of the door the floor was bare where it had swept open. The door had been used. Her grandmother had to be on the other side.

It had no handle to pull it open with, and yet, the aged metal had remained untouched for so long that it had oxidized to a whitish green. There had to be a way to open it without pulling or tugging.

Lilliana stooped to study the ornate design. She considered simply materializing on the other side. But it wouldn't do any good. Just to prove it to herself she peeked through the glass wall and saw nothing but a broad flat field of Texas wildflowers on the other side. No grandmother in sight.

No, this door had to be a portal of some kind, a door to another world, which might explain the cosmic signal on top of the spire. Lilliana brushed cobwebs and white dust from the eroding bronze surface and traced her fingers over the intricate patterns of twining roots and leafy vines curling around rows of symbols. It looked to be one of the old Elvish languages, not Quenya, probably early Sindarin. But it seemed to be an archaic form. She stumbled through sounding out the first phrase and discovered the cadence was vaguely familiar—fragments of an ancient poem.

> *These roots from which I sprout*
> *Wend through stone*
> *Split up rock*
> *Lap dry brooks*
> *Wander out*
> *Lost.*
> *Hasten back*

213

To home soil,
Turn north twice
Speak the word thrice
Enter in, ye child of Ayre.

"Ayre." Lilliana clutched the panel. *Ancient Elf Lands.*

Could it be? She'd never been there. None of the younger fairies had. A few of the elders on the council recounted adventures through the legendary land from their journeys long, long ago. Of course, Gryndelyn claimed she'd been in Ayre. But no one else had reported seeing it for centuries. Most of Lilliana's peers thought the ancient lands were simply myth, a fabled place of dreams, wishful thinking. Could this really be a door to Ayre?

She reread the inscription and chewed the corner of her lip, considering the possibilities. There was only one way to find out. Lilliana stood up and rubbed her hands against her jeans. First, she pivoted to true north, stopped, turned back to face the door and turned north once more.

Speak the word.

"What word?" she whispered. Neither the butterflies nor the flowers offered any ideas. It would have to be a Sindarin word, but what? Perhaps the obvious, *open.*

"*Edro!*" She commanded the portal to open three times. "*Edro. Edro.*"

But the door remained closed. Perhaps she'd been too rude, except Sindarin had no word for please. She tried *díheno*, which was like saying excuse me. Nothing happened. Home, *amar*, she repeated thrice.

She tried *cofn*, which meant lost.

Child.

Homeland.

Nothing budged the door. It didn't even creak. Then she demanded entrance as a daughter of Ayre. "*Híneva-Ayre. Híneva-Ayre. Híneva-Ayre.*" The bronze barricade remained as unyielding as ever.

Lilliana pushed her hair back behind her ears and massaged her forehead, trying to recall the many elves of her acquaintance. What word would they have chosen to protect a passageway to the sacred land of their ancestors? Elves were clever, shrewd, tricky. That much everyone knew.

Too clever! She stamped her foot, frustrated.

"*Nanethdaer!*" she shouted, knowing full well the Sindarin version of Grandmother wouldn't be right either. But just for good measure, she called it out two more times. The bronze gate remained solid and impassive to her pleas.

Lilliana dropped to her knees and studied the verse again. Elves always thought themselves so much smarter than everyone else. *Arrogant buggers.* Ornery, that's what they were, feisty and stubborn. And they'd be especially bullheaded if they were protecting something as precious as this.

Lilliana sighed. She had to admit the wisdom of carefully guarding Ayre. "Fine," she admitted aloud. Yes, okay, elves were wise. Cautious. Prudent. And elegant—

Abruptly, she stopped her litany of elf virtues and fixated on the key phrase in the riddle. She groaned and shook her head. How had she missed it?

Lilliana jumped up and started over. She turned north twice and then faced the door. In clear confident Sindarin, she spoke the word "*neled,*" which meant "Thrice."

Once.

The bronze gate swung open.

IN PURSUIT

"Dad's suspension is going to be totally trashed," Jess warned. Jake was driving like a bat out of hell. Having just been fighting bats from that locale, Jess knew exactly what she was talking about. He tore down River Road, squealing around sharp turns and flying over bumps.

Jake didn't say anything in reply. He didn't ease up either. They hit another pothole and rebounded like a basketball.

"Seriously. Slow down a little."

"Can't. She's gonna get herself killed."

Cai had a death grip on the armrest. "Yeah, well, let's not beat her to it."

"She'll be okay," Maggie tried to reassure him. "Her grandma is there."

"Unknown," Jess countered in a flat military tone. She could feel Maggie glare at her but shrugged it off. "Face it. There's no guarantee the grandmother is an ally. If she is, why hasn't she been around for the last ten years?"

Mark leaned forward and clapped Jake on the shoulder. "Don't worry about it, man. We'll be there soon. Besides, she can take care of herself. Don't forget, the girl is armed with some awesome fairy gear. Fire-hose fingers."

"Not when she's scared." Jake didn't take his eyes off the road, and he didn't let up on the gas. "Not when something catches her off guard."

Directive 22

A successful Fairy Godmother does not give way to weakness or self-doubt. Remember, our failures are often more illuminating than our successes. You must simply unlock the secret truths hidden behind your mistakes.

For each of us there exists a secret well of strength. Every Fairy Godmother must find the source of her strength and inspiration. This is the emotional well to which we must return and drink whenever we feel defeated or fragile.

—Gryndelyn Myrddin

Songs of Ayre

It was dark as night on the other side of the door. A thick canopy of branches blocked most of the sunlight. Lilliana cautiously felt her way into a dense forest, running her palm over the rough bark of a pine tree, reading like braille its girth and antiquity. Yet even in the nightmarish gloom, her heart thundered with excitement. She was in Ayre! And soon, very soon, she would find her grandmother.

Lilliana wove through the giant pines, listening to the wind's eerie tune as it blew ancient songs through the boughs. Her shoe crunched against a patch of snow melting atop pine needles. Was it winter here? No, it couldn't be. The trees breathed with the warmth of spring. Memories of a nursery song came back to her. She hummed the tune softly as she walked.

> *Ayre is trapped in the folds of time*
> *Caught mid jealous seasons.*
> *Winter splashes her frozen tears*
> *Across Ayre's mountain faces.*
> *Autumn scatters golden embers*
> *Upon Ayre's leafy places.*
> *Summer blows her softest winds*
> *Through Ayre's emerald grasses.*
> *Springtime dances 'cross every clime*
> *And drapes the world with blooms.*
> *For Ayre lies tucked in the folds of time*
> *Nursed by zealous seasons.*

218

As if attesting to the truth of the song, she spotted one of springtime's children, a small white crocus pushing up through a clump of snow, bravely struggling to survive in the gloomy light.

If the songs and stories were true, Lilliana didn't want to stay in these dark woods long. She sensed she was being watched. Something padded quietly among the trees, barely crackling the pine needles. The air carried the scent of sweat, blood, and saliva caked in thick unwashed fur. She didn't recognize the creature's musk. Whatever it was, it tracked her from less than a furlong away.

According to legend, Ayre was sanctuary for all the earth's lost creatures, beasts forgotten from modern memory. Good and bad. That meant huge boars roamed these woods, manticores prowled in the shadows, and primeval wolves as tall as a man hunted here. And then, there were the wyverns. Small dragons with razor sharp—

A screech broke the cushioned stillness.

A flash of red.

"Napoleon?"

The little cardinal zipped under a pine bow and swooped over Lilliana's head, twittering like crazy.

"What are you doing here?" She tried to sound stern, but part of her was relieved to see a familiar face, even the pesky scarlet bandit who must be Gryndelyn's spy.

He fluttered to a branch, checking nervously in every direction, chattering so fast Lilliana couldn't catch everything he was saying.

"Naneth sent you? Why? You're Gryndelyn's servant." She frowned at him. Had Gryndelyn gotten here first and brought him with her? Was he trying to trick her?

Napoleon didn't answer. He clicked, whistled, and bobbed apprehensively on the thin pine branch.

"I heard it too. Come along." She waved him forward.

In the distance she spotted the faint golden glimmer of sunlight at the base of the trees. It meant there was a clearing of some kind. Lilliana hurried in that direction, keeping a wary eye on Gryndelyn's cardinal. "How did you get in here, anyway?"

Trilling smugly, he fluttered ahead of her.

"An entrance for birds?" She glanced up as she scrambled over a boulder covered with lichen. She could scarcely see the sky beyond the thick boughs, much less pinpoint a bird door in the heavens.

Napoleon landed on a branch directly in front of her and barked shrill demands.

"No. I left the portal open." Yet another infraction he'd undoubtedly report to his master. "I had to in case I needed a way out."

His feathers ruffled out indignantly.

"Oh, don't be a grump. You're here. Obviously, it isn't that difficult to get in." She pushed past his branch. "You still haven't told me what you're doing here?"

He flew off without answering.

"Wait!" She dashed after him.

The rascal didn't stop. He shot straight out of the woods, and Lilliana sprinted after him.

ℒPORTAL TO THE WAR ZONE

"There it is! That's the sign," Jess shouted as they blew past Grandma Nature's billboard showing a sunflower grinning as it got sprinkled with fairy dust.

Jake slammed on the brakes. The Lincoln fishtailed to a halt. He threw it into reverse, backed up to the turnoff, slammed the car into drive, and they sped down the dirt road with a tornado of dust rising behind them. But the road suddenly dead-ended.

Jake skidded to a stop. At the same time, they almost smacked into a bright green parrot. Its beak was wide open in a terrified screech as the bird's feathers swished against the windshield in a narrow escape.

"Jeez! What's a parrot doing out here?" Jake raked back his hair as the dazed bird fluttered unsteadily past his window.

Mark whistled and pointed at the mammoth greenhouse in front of them. "Whoa! That's some hothouse." They all piled out of the car.

The parrot landed on the roof right beside Jake and mimicked the piercing squeal of a police siren. "Yarwk! In trouble now, mister. Where's the fire! What's your hurry?"

Jake frowned at the squawky bird as if he didn't know whether to answer him or shoo him away.

"Ask him if he's seen her," Maggie advised from the other side of the car.

The parrot flapped wildly and landed on Jake's head. "Seen

221

who? Seen who?"

"Hey, little guy, watch the claws." Jake gently lifted the noisy bird off his head. "We're looking for someone. A girl." He held his hand just below his chin indicating Lilliana's height. "Dark hair."

"Funny man. Ha. Ha. Funny man." The crazy parrot jumped onto the roof of the Lincoln again and let loose with a goofy neck-stretching chortle and marched in a drunken circle. "Better get glasses, chump. That's not a girl. Not a girl. Ha, ha, ha."

Jake's jaw muscles were flexing impatiently. Jess figured he wasn't loving the parrot.

"Fairy," Jess corrected. "We're looking for a fairy."

"Fine," Jake said through gritted teeth, obviously trying to stay cool. "What about a fairy?" Momentarily, his lips pressed together hard, like it pained him to admit Lilliana wasn't human. But he continued on, speaking clearly and distinctly the way a teacher talks to a slow-witted child. "Have you seen a fairy?"

The parrot stopped bobbing in circles. He flipped up his red topnotch, tilted his head sideways, and blinked quizzically at Jake.

"Uh-oh," Cai warned and pointed to their right. "Looks like more welcoming committee."

A lamb galloped full speed toward them. He lowered his nubby little horns and charged at Jake. Jake neatly sidestepped the ram at the last minute. All those years of dodging linebackers came in handy.

"Oh! Look." Maggie grinned and went into vet's daughter overdrive. "Instead of a watch dog they have a watch ram—a little Rambo." With a series of half whistles she called the confused lamb over and started scratching the curls behind his ears.

"Yeah, so we've met the animal sentries." Mark scanned the surroundings. "But the place seems deserted. Where is everybody?"

"Ywark! Nobody's home. Nobody's home." The parrot pecked at Jake's shoulder. "Go away, Jay. Beat it, Bub."

"Right! What am I doing wasting my time talking to a dumb

bird?" Jake slammed his car door and startled the parrot into flight. "Where is she? Lilliana!" Jake shouted for her and headed for the open doors of the greenhouse, still calling. "Lilliana! Where are you?"

"Okay. Okay. Come on." The parrot fluttered in front of him. "This way. Come on. Follow me. Don't touch anything. Follow me."

Their green-feathered guide whooshed in the open doors of the hothouse. Jake dashed after him, running past tables full of flowerpots, squeezing between gaps in the rows, crossing the maze-like room to the far wall where a cloud of butterflies hovered.

Jess and the rest of them were right behind him.

"Look at this place," Maggie half whispered as she hurried inside with the ram trotting behind her. "It's incredible."

Cai turned a quick circle. "It smells amazing. Did you see those hummingbirds drinking out of the gigantic pink lilies back there?"

There was a lot to take in, but they were on a mission. "Come on," Jess urged.

But Maggie stopped and stared up at the ceiling. A canopy of butterflies floated above their heads. "So many," she muttered. "Do you hear something?" Her eyes were wide open, and she held a finger up beside her ear. "Singing? Except it sounds really far off."

"No time, Maggs. Come on." Jess tugged her forward.

"Yrawk! This is it. Enter at your own risk." Jake and the noisy parrot came to an abrupt halt in front of a small brass door hanging open. "Enter at your own risk!"

That side of the greenhouse faced a broad sunny field. Weird thing was, inside the doorway it looked as murky and dark as a cave, and yet, Jess saw the sun was shining through all the windows along that same wall.

"The fairy girl went in there?" Jake frowned at the dark passage.

The parrot mimicked a train whistle, fluttered in a loop, and made an awkward landing on Jake's shoulder. "Yesiree! All aboard. Enter at your own risk."

"You're sure?" Jake dislodged his raucous tour guide and stooped over to look inside. "She went in there?

But the parrot was off, flapping at Mark. "Don't touch! Don't touch. Keep your hands inside the cockpit."

"Shhh." Mark waved him away. He was leaning over a nearby table, nose to nose with a huge blue swallowtail. "Maggs, that sound—it's the butterflies. I think maybe they're humming or something."

"Not important," Jess interrupted. "Unless they're singing the coordinates to Lilliana's location." She peeked into the dark doorway beside Jake and pointed. "Those are tree trunks." She scooted in a little more. "And we're not in Kansas anymore, Dorothy. Looks like a forest of some kind. You know, the deep, dark, fairytale kind."

"Yeah." Jake ducked all the way under. Instantly thick shadows enveloped him and then he quickly disappeared into the darkness. "Here's a footprint," he called back. "Another one! Has to be hers."

"Come on." Jess motioned for the others as she followed Jake through the door.

"Right behind you." Mark dipped through the portal and caught up to Jess.

Cai trailed in after him, but Maggie hedged by the door. "Rambo is following me. Maybe I should leave him out here."

"Can't. How you going to make him stay? *No pets allowed.*" Cai imitated their boisterous host. "Besides, a lamb might come in handy there. You know, like Toto did in *Wizard of Oz*. Or like the white rabbit in—"

"I get it." Maggie took a deep breath, squared her shoulders, and reached for Cai's hand. "Come on, Alice. Let's find out if we get ten feet tall."

"Yrawk! Watch your step," the parrot warned. "Adios. Bon voyage. Bye-bye."

As soon as Maggie and the lamb crossed the threshold into Wonderland, the metal door banged shut, cutting off the parrot's blathering. The metal reverberated with finality as their doorway home vanished.

Directive 23

At present, humans are blissfully ignorant of the fey world surrounding them. Our dimension is, of course, invisible to them. Regrettably, some of our less cautious sisters have enjoyed teasing mortals and cavorting openly in their realm. Consequently, fairies have been spotted dancing in forests, frolicking through gardens, splashing in creeks, and, in short, behaving irresponsibly. Fortunately, humans have written off these incidents as hoaxes or hallucinations.

As a Fairy Godmother, you will have prolonged interaction with mortals. You may be tempted to relax the rules of secrecy you were taught at the academy. That would be a grave error.

It is your solemn duty to protect fairiekind by preventing the discovery of our world. Given the strides humans have made in science during the last century, we must be especially vigilant. Consider the destruction that might befall us if mankind were to develop fairy detection devices or weaponry to use against us. Such a course would end in disaster for both realms.

– Gryndelyn Myrddin

Queen of Hearts

Lilliana burst out of the dark woods of Ayre into blinding sunlight and raced down a steep slope. Her wings unfurled of their own volition, lifting her off the ground slightly to prevent a fall. She quickly steadied herself and peered downhill. A plain stretched as far east as the eye could see. To the west a vast sea lapped at the base of the mountains, shimmering like blue diamonds under the sun's brilliant white rays. Lilliana's wings arced forward to shade her eyes. She spotted a woman kneeling over a small tide pool, stirring the water. It had to be—

Naneth!

Lilliana opened her mouth to shout a greeting. But what should she say?

Hey, remember me? I'm in big trouble, and I need your help. No, no, that didn't sound right. *Hello. Hi. How've you been? Oh, by the way, my teacher has gone off her nut and is about to roast me and my friends alive. Any ideas about how to stop her?*

Before she could figure out the right words, her wings had whisked her nearly there. She hovered in the air just above her grandmother, hesitating, nervous.

The white-haired fairy beside the water seemed so much grander than the plump nondescript woman from the photo. Naneth waved her hand over the water, authoritatively dismissing whomever she'd been speaking with. She stood up and sent a trio of messenger pixies streaming off in different directions.

Then Naneth glanced up, and a slow, sure smile crinkled her

face with joy. Wordlessly, she held out her arms. Lilliana's wings stopped beating.

"Naneth!" she cried out like a pitiful lost child and collapsed into her grandmother's embrace, nearly tumbling them both to the ground. Except her grandmother felt surprisingly solid. Like a rock.

"Oh, my dear one. My sweet, sweet, Lilly." Naneth stroked Lilliana's hair and kissed her cheek. "I've waited so long for this moment."

At her grandmother's words, Lilliana felt as if she'd been punched. She let go and staggered back, suddenly drowning in anguish.

Yes, it had been too long.

Way too long.

Suddenly, years of loneliness and grief, all of the unuttered wails she'd held in for so long, hundreds of uncomforted nightmares frothed up and spilled over into one gnashing word.

"Why?"

Why had her grandmother abandoned her for so many long, gray, aching years? The sea responded to her anguish, and like her heart it rocked violently in its cradle. Lilliana was too upset to stop it. Waves crashed against the shore, spraying them with salt water.

"Why?"

The cruel weight of the question pulled the joy from Naneth's face and dimmed her radiance. Her arms dropped empty to her sides. She nodded slowly, silently. When she finally spoke there was no artifice in her voice, no hint of defense.

"By the time you were two years old, I knew you were more fairy than human. There were..." She caught her lip in her teeth exactly the way Lilliana did when struggling for the right words. "Accidents. When you reached six, I was forced to admit to myself you needed training. More than that, you needed to understand what you were, and who you were. You needed to be around your own kind."

"You're my kind! Why couldn't *you* have trained me?"

"I did train you, child," Naneth firmly corrected. "As much as I could. Surely, you can tell I'm not a water fairy." The corner of her mouth twitched with the inkling of a smile. "Oh my dear, you should have seen the messes we made together." Another wave crashed against them. When it ebbed, Naneth glanced down at the mud building around her bare feet. "I'm earth. Can't you tell?"

Lilliana recognized it then, the differences in their structure. Her grandmother's once dark hair had turned white with age, but not crisp white like crystalline snow. Her hair was milky, like quartz embedded in granite. And her skin wasn't pale like Lilliana's. Naneth had the rich warm tones of fertile soil. She was shorter than Lilliana, thicker boned, with large feet. Naneth's connection with the earth was incredibly strong. If Lilliana closed her eyes, she could sense her grandmother's force radiating out, touching every root, every worm, every pebble, every—

"It doesn't matter!" Lilliana's eyes flew open and she shouted loud enough that it should've bowed the grasses on the plain. "Don't you see? They never taught us any of that stuff. The academy was all about worthless flight tests and stupid council bylaws, and *elin-gíl* etiquette." She stomped her foot hard against her grandmother's precious earth. "I didn't even know about my connection to water until today! I could've stayed with you. It would've been better. A hundred times better. You could've kept me with you, or we could've lived in Erinfae."

"You don't understand, little one." Naneth shook her head. "I was trapped. I couldn't go to Erinfae. The only world I could offer you was the human one. And this." She held her hands out to Ayre and sighed. "Which isn't really a world at all, just a pocket in time, an elvish zoo for forgotten creatures."

As if to prove Naneth's point, a small green warthog-shaped creature with wings dropped out of a nearby tree and thudded awkwardly onto its neck. The poor thing squealed like an injured pig-let. Lilliana hurried over to see if it needed help, but immediately jumped back when the scaly hog lunged at her. Its tusked mouth opened wide in a crocodile-like hiss.

Naneth hurriedly pulled Lilliana back even further. "Don't worry. It's just a baby peccaveryn learning to fly."

Baby or not, it waddled angrily toward Lilliana with its shiny scales bristled up and its stubby green wings fanned out in a menacing dragon-like show.

Lilliana was about to fling a handful of *elin-gíl* into its hissing face when Naneth tapped her foot. Instantly, vibrations rippled through the ground, sending shivers up Lilliana's legs. The peccaveryn jumped and squealed in fright. He retracted his barbed wings and scampered away into the underbrush.

"Don't mind him. Poor thing was just afraid, that's all." Naneth held out her arm in invitation for Lilliana to be comforted. "Come."

Lilliana held back and frowned. She resisted, even though her grandmother smelled incredibly welcoming, like warm baked bread and fresh fruit. It was probably just the orange blossoms Naneth had so cleverly laced into her dress. Or the strawberry vines winding through her hair, laden with red berries and delicious-smelling blossoms. Or it could have been the rich scent of honeycomb oil she must've rubbed on her skin. Soothing. Almost hypnotic. As if one hug from her might melt away all the troubles of the world.

But it wouldn't!

Lilliana fought the urge to lay her head on Naneth's shoulder. She didn't want her anger soothed. She needed answers.

Naneth finally gave up and lowered her arms. Lilliana couldn't help but notice the sorrow bruising the elderly woman's brown eyes. Her grandmother seemed to overflow with the nurturing power of earth, but she understood sadness, too.

Lilliana loosened her grip on anger. The waves behind her settled into a rhythmic lapping.

"I had to do something so you wouldn't end up like your mother." Naneth bowed her head and spoke in low confessional murmurs. "I couldn't hide you away like I had her. I kept her too isolated. It was wrong. Selfish of me. Overprotective. But Gilly was such a delicate child. Air. Sky. The older she got the more fragile she became. I didn't know how to help her."

Naneth bowed her head and pressed her palms together, touching them to her chin like a pilgrim in prayer. "How could I, earth and heaviness, teach my daughter about the lightness of air, the expansiveness of the sky? I had no idea how to teach her to control her gifts. I'd hoped when she fell in love with Shaun she would get stronger. I thought love would help her find her way, just as it had me. Instead, it overwhelmed her even more. She became a wisp tossed in the wind. Until, in the end, she finally broke."

"Because of me." Lilliana could barely speak.

"No! No." Naneth grasped Lilliana's shoulders and forced her to look at her squarely. "It wasn't your fault. Gilly simply couldn't contain the enormous forces within her. Once you were born, it was as if she had nothing tethering her to earth any longer." Naneth's face crumpled at the memory.

With a strength that seemed as solid and eternal as the mountain behind her, she regained control. "I failed your mother. That's why I thought you should go to the academy. Gryndelyn made me promise I wouldn't interfere with your training. But she agreed we could be reunited after you successfully completed your first assignment."

Naneth glanced down at her feet, nestling her bare toes into the loose soil. "I'm sure my sister has explained the arrangement."

Lilliana tilted her head, trying to grasp the meaning in Naneth's strange words. "Sister?"

"Gryndelyn."

Lilliana's legs felt weak. She staggered to a large boulder near the water and sat down with her head clasped in her hands. All those years, Gryndelyn had never said a thing about any arrangement, not a word about being her aunt. It couldn't be. Lilliana must've heard wrong. "Your sister?"

"Yes." Naneth nodded. "Half sisters. There were seven of us. Same mother. Different fathers."

"But..." Lilliana could only shake her head, confused and shocked. "What arrangement?"

A thick-necked raven hopped around the side of the boulder. From the top of a tall pine, Napoleon dive-bombed straight at them, whistled a shrill alarm and attacked the raven.

"Napoleon, stop!"

The small red bird kept pecking fiercely, his bright yellow beak tattooing the black raven in a flurry of feathers, squawks and shrieks. The raven knocked the cardinal aside with a vicious stab of his beak and cursed them all with a rude guttural caw before flapping awkwardly up and soaring away over the lake.

Napoleon fluttered limply onto Naneth's shoulder and rubbed his scarlet crest against her cheek. "Thank you, my friend." Naneth stroked the little red bird. "That was very brave."

"What was he doing?" Lilliana suspected nothing was as she'd thought, not even Napoleon.

"The raven is one of Gryndelyn's spies." Naneth soothed the cardinal's heaving chest. "Peace *verya ohtar*." Brave soldier, she called him, and then instructed, "There is no way to avoid this day. Go. Tell her to meet us here, on the plains of Ayre. Tell her Lilliana is with me and knows everything."

"You're sending him to her, to Gryndelyn? No! Don't let him go. If she finds out I'm here, she'll—"

"Lilliana, I'm certain she will have guessed. And if not, she will know very soon. That raven will not waste any time reporting to his master." Naneth shook her head sadly and glanced in the direction of the fleeing spy.

Napoleon shot skyward, a red speck fading into the broad expanse of blue.

"She'll be furious. She hates me. And she certainly didn't want me to find you." Lilliana's shoulders slumped. "Besides, you shouldn't have told Napoleon I know everything. It isn't true. I don't know anything at all." She pounded her fist against her thigh. "Nothing! I don't know why she hates me. Or what I'm supposed to do about Jake. I don't know anything!" She glanced up, making no attempt to hide her frustration from her grandmother.

"I'll explain as much as I can." Naneth sat down beside her on the rock and wrapped her arm around Lilliana's shoulders. She smoothed her hand over the edge of her granddaughter's wings. "They're magnificent! So tall. Blue, like your mother's, but much darker. Sapphire, like the sea, and yet they have some green in them, like mine. Beautiful."

What else would a grandmother say? She was just being nice. Lilliana retracted her too-big wings. "We have to hurry."

"Very well then." She patted Lilliana's shoulder. "For centuries one queen ruled over all the fairy kingdoms. My mother was the last of these queens." Naneth sighed heavily. "When she died, I knew my younger sisters would quickly grow restless and dissatisfied with their lot. I was the eldest, you see. Unfortunately, I hadn't paid much attention to the intrigues and politics among the fey. In my youth, I'd lived with my father, gallivanting among mortals, and later, I was busy with all the Fairy Godmother business. A duty I cherished.

"Unlike my sisters, I like humans. They're fascinating creatures! Capable of so much good, and yet, equally adept at evil. From birth they hold the promise of breathtaking beauty or stunning horrors. Each day they choose—"

"So, if you're queen, then I'm—"

"Then I met Cinderella. From the first moment I adored

Cinders." Naneth's shoulders scrunched up, invisibly hugging the memory. "And that's how the Godmother thing got started."

"*You* were Cinderella's Godmother? The very first one?"

"Yes." She smiled. "Darling girl, Cinders. You know, it's really too bad they never tell the rest of her story. Did you know she turned out to be an extraordinary leader? Kind. Wise. Her people prospered."

"You were *The* Fairy Godmother." Lilliana mouthed the words. "And queen?"

Naneth nodded. Her shoulders bounced up in a happy shrug again. "Yes, but because I was so wrapped up in the human world, I had no idea how to manage all the double dealings and plots among my sisters. So I held a council. Surely you've read about it at the academy."

"Yes, but I didn't know you were her—the queen."

"No matter." She waved away the issue. "Just as the elves did a century earlier, we divided the fairy domain into six kingdoms." She ticked off the kingdoms on her fingers.

Lilliana nodded. She knew the kingdoms by heart, as did every fairy.

Naneth continued. "Each kingdom was to be ruled by a council. One sister to preside over each council. It seemed a good plan. A plan that, so far, has spared us from war."

"Seven sisters. Six kingdoms. Who was left out?"

Naneth caught her lip, pensive again. "I'm afraid that's where the trouble began. At first, no one cared that I chose only to retain stewardship over all the fairy godmothers. They seemed happy with the arrangement. Later, when so many of Cinderella's descendants immigrated to America, naturally I went to watch over them. But this, of course, is Gryndelyn's kingdom. As youngest sister, you see, it was only right that she'd been given the new lands. Unfortunately, she felt slighted, complained not enough forests, not enough antiquities, too few fairies. Mind you, her complaints were all utter nonsense. There are more forests here than in Europe, and one need only speak with the native Americans to ancient places." Naneth sighed. "My little sister can be frustratingly stubborn."

Lilliana nodded mutely, recalling all too well how implacable her mentor could be.

"I blame Gryn's unhappy nature on her father." Naneth grimaced. "Dreadful man. You know who he was, of course. She's always been quite vocal about it."

"Oh, yes, everyone knows about her famous sire." Lilliana grumbled his name as if it were a pruney old curse. "Merlin."

"Mortal poets have been so kind to him. No doubt they were influenced by his mammoth ego. But really." Naneth clucked her tongue. "His father was an incubus. *An incubus.*" She shook her head. "If it weren't for his sainted mother...well, I ask you."

Naneth pressed her lips together in distaste. "Gryn has the absurd notion his celebrity status gives her rights the rest of us don't have. When she found out I'd come to America, she threw a royal tantrum. She was convinced I'd come to steal her kingdom. None of my assurances appeased her. Ornery girl. In one of her rages she set fire to Chicago. Some cow got the blame, but I assure you, she—"

"You don't have to convince me." Lilliana shuddered.

"And then she threatened all kinds of awful disasters on the rest of Cinderella's descendants. Oh, I came so close to burying the little firebug under a mountain..." Naneth clinched her fists for a moment. "But she's my sister. What could I do?" Her hand fluttered helplessly in the air. "So I made a pact with her. A vow."

"Uh-oh." Lilliana's stomach twisted into a horrid, dry knot. Vows among fairiekind were dangerous things, irrevocable and binding, but fairies often used them to trick one another in horrible ways. "What? What did you promise her?" She clutched her grandmother's sleeve.

"I vowed never to set foot in Erinfae. I was allowed in the human realm but not the fairy realm. In return, she promised never to harm Cinder's children. I agreed to leave the fairy dimension here in the Americas entirely to her. And so I have." Naneth patted Lilliana's hand. "For nearly two centuries everything has gone along smoothly. Then, you were born."

There it was. The curse of her birth. She was always messing things up, destroying the lives of everyone she loved. Lilliana groaned.

"No, child. I can see what you are thinking, but it isn't true." She lifted Lilliana's chin. "I adored you. You were a gift. A miracle, really. And such a comfort after..." Her smile wilted. "If only they could have known you."

Naneth meant her parents, but hadn't said their names. Maybe it hurt her as much as it did Lilliana to think of them.

"Those were lovely years with you. Good years." Naneth sighed. "But you grew up too fast. You were an amazingly precocious child, my dear. Flying before you could walk. Toddling across the yard, changing the grass into rainbow colors." She chuckled. "And long before you learned to talk, squirrels and birds flocked around you, listening to you babble."

"I was happy back then," Lilliana remembered wistfully.

"Yes, but I couldn't ignore the fact that you desperately needed training. *And* exposure to other fairies. With your heritage, it was essential that you become familiar with the fairy world. So Gryndelyn and I struck a bargain."

"You let her raise me at the school." Lilliana sagged against Naneth's shoulder. "I wish you hadn't."

"I had to." Naneth's tone turned brittle. "I made a fatal error when I kept your mother away from the fairy world. I certainly wasn't going to repeat my mistake."

Ah, so both she and Naneth were trying to escape those fatal mistakes of the past. And yet, here they were, repeating history. Her grandmother's well-laid plans falling to ruins, and Lilliana trying to do her duty, but caught in her mother's trap—falling in love with a human and bringing disaster to everyone around her.

Was it death or destiny that swung his wicked scythe so unerringly from the past to the present? It would seem that in one curling stroke he would cut down both their good intentions.

"Gryndelyn's academy had been so successful she wanted to add a training program for fairies destined to become Godmothers. To be honest I think she enjoyed infringing on my territory." Naneth shrugged. "But, it made her happy, and it provided you with the opportunities you needed. So I agreed to her plan with one caveat. I retained the right to choose the Godmothers' assignments."

"*You* sent me to Texas! I thought the council sent me."

Naneth gave her a sly wink. "I agreed not to interfere until after you completed your first mission, but no one said I couldn't assign you nearby. Grynie-poo wasn't happy; I can tell you that. She sent me letters that nearly scorched my fingertips when I opened them."

Lilliana crossed her arms indignantly. "You should never have agreed to her rules."

"What else could I have done?" She patted Lilliana's knee. "It worked out fairly well. It doesn't take me long to retrain her students. The worst part was being away from you. As amicable as our arrangement was, bound by the original vow, I still was not allowed to step foot in Erinfae."

"Well, *she* has certainly broken her side of the vow. She tried to harm my C.O."

Naneth rocked slightly and nodded. "Napoleon told me."

"How can she get away with breaking her vow?"

"I don't know. She will have paid a price—a reduction in her power perhaps, or..." Naneth shook her head. "I don't know."

"She seemed plenty strong to me." Lilliana ticked off Gryndelyn's infractions. "She exploded Jake's tires and nearly roasted us alive at the beauty shop."

"I know." Naneth massaged her temple. "I'm privy to most everything in the human world, especially if it involves one of Cinderella's offspring."

"She must know that."

"Of course she does."

"Then *why*? Why would she risk it? Why would she break the vow?"

"Ah, that's where you come in. You see, there was one more thing I kept from the old kingdom. One small trump card to keep all of my sisters in line."

Lilliana grew wary of the unexpected shrewdness in her grandmother's voice and eyes.

"This." Naneth tapped her foot. The ground mounted up like an instant anthill and kept growing until something glowing and shiny poked out of the top. Dirt and sand sprinkled away from it like sugar pouring from a canister. Naneth took hold of it and raised it up.

"A wand!" Lilliana exclaimed.

It wasn't like any wand she'd had ever seen. Sculpted primarily of gold and silver; carvings of vines, flowers and dancing fairies twined around a long rosewood handle. At the tip, fairy arms held a glowing pearlescent sphere. More than a wand, it looked like a magic scepter.

"Is this…" Lilliana whispered reverently. "It's a queen's wand, isn't it?"

"Exactly." Naneth smiled conspiratorially. "My mother's."

Lilliana itched to touch it. Her finger traced the air above the beautiful gold and silver metalwork, feeling the power in it, the resonance, the harmony.

Naneth held it out to her. "And now it belongs to you."

SCOUTING ENEMY TERRITORY

Jess's eyes adjusted to the dim light. The doorway had disappeared. "No retreating now," she said under her breath and pressed forward.

Maggie ducked around a pine and quickly caught up to Jess, whispering, "I think there's something else in these woods. Something not so friendly."

Rambo echoed her sentiments with a subdued, "Baa-ah—"

Maggie clamped her hand over his mouth, muffling the rest of his commentary. Wise choice, considering wolves in this part of Alice's rabbit hole might consider lamb a tasty entrée.

Cai hung behind Jess as close as a shadow. "I heard something. This is starting to feel like a horror movie, Jess. I hate scary flicks."

Jess heard it, too. She picked up a fallen branch and checked the weight in her hand. There was only one way to deal with unseen threats. "Keep moving," she ordered. "Maggie, you and that bear bait go ahead of us. If we're attacked, it'll probably come from behind."

Maggie tugged her sheep around a pine and moved in front Jess.

"You too, Cai. Get in front of me."

Jess stepped back, letting Cai slip in front of her. She took up the rear guard position with her makeshift club at the ready. She didn't notice she'd been holding her breath until Mark dropped back beside her. She inhaled deeply and nodded her appreciation as he picked up a baseball-sized rock.

Whatever was out there already knew they were here. So she stopped trying to move quietly through the trees. Instead Jess stomped noisily. Their best defense was to act like they weren't afraid. They needed to sound big, bad, and dangerous.

Jake was up ahead in the lead, tracking Lilliana. He started moving faster. "There's a clearing."

"I see it." A flicker of light at the base of the trees, Jess estimated it was only a hundred yards away.

Then she heard a stick crack right behind her. Jess pivoted, her stick poised to strike, expecting to confront huge clawed feet and drooling fangs.

Her shoulders relaxed. "It's just a bunny."

A very big, very weird, yellow bunny.

Jess tensed up again and kept her club in position. The overgrown rabbit had a sharp unicorn horn, and she didn't like the way it stared at them—very unbunny-like.

"I bet he's never seen people before. Look, he's not afraid of us." Cai started to reach out to pet it.

"No!" Maggs jerked Cai's arm back. "It's not frien—"

The bunny growled. His mouth flashed open, baring a row of dagger-like teeth a man-eating shark would envy.

"Run!"

Directive 24

Our chief duty to the progeny of Cinderella is protection. Why her offspring are so prone to getting themselves into trouble remains one of life's unfathomable mysteries. Nevertheless, we are obliged to protect them.

—Gryndelyn Myrddin

This That Go Bump in The Forest

unlight glinted off the silver filigree on the wand. Lilliana blinked at Naneth. "You want me to have it?"

Naneth nodded.

A shiver of warm delight ran through Lilliana, followed by a knotting sensation in her stomach. She shook her head and backed away. "No. It wouldn't be right. I can't."

"Nonsense. You're the natural heir."

As if her grandmother was brandishing a red-hot poker instead of a dazzling wand, Lilliana edged back until she was trapped against the banks of the lake. Waves splashed up and grasped at her ankles.

"Now that you've completed your mission, it's yours."

"My mission isn't complete. Jess still needs me. " Lilliana shook her head. "And I can't be queen. I'm a Halfling. The other fairies would never—"

"I'm not asking you to rule. I'm only asking you to accept the wand."

Even so, she couldn't. To do one meant she might have to do the other.

"You must take it. I'm getting old." Naneth thrust it forward. "There's no time for this, Lilliana. Your friends will be here any minute."

"My friends? No. I left them in Dreston."

Naneth glanced over her shoulder toward the woods. "They've followed you into Ayre."

"They found the door?"

"Yes. Wellington will have shown them the way."

242

"Wellington? Oh, your parrot. Then, you knew they'd come." Lilliana jumped up and pushed past her grandmother. Jake and the others had followed her straight into danger. "There are *things* in that forest. Things that could kill them."

"The creatures in those woods are considerably less harmful than what's coming with *her*." Her grandmother shaded her eyes and pointed at a dark cloud rising over the eastern horizon.

Lilliana didn't look east. Instead, she whirled around and flew back to the forest, shooting through air currents, speeding straight into the trees. Darting between trunks. Dodging branches. Swatting boughs out of her way. She whipped through the forest so fast she could hardly see.

Then she froze.

She heard Cai screaming. Jess shouted as if they were in a battle.

Lilliana zigzagged toward the sound, frantic to get to them. Through the trees she caught glimpses of them.

"Behind you!" Jess warned.

She saw Jake spin around, axing through the air with a thick pine branch. His stick banged into a tree. A large Persian hare leapt at him. Jake whipped around, swinging the branch with him. He caught the hare flush in the mouth. The rabbit chomped down on the branch in a bite that would have crushed Jake's arm.

Jake finished his swing and smashed the hare against a large redwood tree. On impact, Jake's branch splintered apart, leaving him weaponless. The hare slid to the ground, dazed.

Lilliana burst into their circle.

Jake whirled around, ready for an attack. "Lilliana?" His eyes opened wide with astonishment. Just then the Persian hare righted itself, growling and snapping, lowering its horn to charge. "Toss me your stick!" Jake shouted to Mark. "Get the girls out of here!"

Instead, Mark thumped the ground beside the rabbit with a stout piece of redwood. "Hey, Easter Bunny! Over here. That's right, big guy. I taste just as good as he does."

The confused hare turned in his direction.

Jess was sneaking up to the side, ready to clobber it. Before either Mark or Jess could do anything, Lilliana flung *elin-gíl* at the hare. It toppled sideways and fell asleep.

"You all have to go back," she urged them in hushed tones. "Now!" she pleaded and tugged on Jake's arm. "It's too dangerous for you here." She glanced one by one at their faces, hoping they'd see reason. "That was only a Persian hare. There's much worse—"

"We can't go back," Cai interrupted. "The door slammed shut and disappeared."

Lilliana groaned and slumped against Jake's shoulder.

He put his arm around her. "You okay?"

How was she supposed to be okay? If anything happened to them...

Lilliana pulled away from him. "I'm not the one in danger." She clamped her lips together and walked as fast as she could. The sooner they got out of the woods, the better. "This way."

Jake caught up to her and grabbed her arm. "We had to come."

She said nothing, just kept walking. Crumbling rose petals fell away from her sleeves, dripping an ominous crimson trail across the pine needles. He slid his hand over her arm and found her fingers. She should be happy, but the tenderness of his touch, each thrilling sensation that tingled through her, reminded her of his mortality, his vulnerability. Finally, as they neared the clearing, she couldn't hold back her fears anymore.

She let go of his hand. "Persian hares are extremely fast. Excellent hunters. You could've been killed."

"Phfft." Jess came up behind them and kicked a pinecone. "Done in by a rabbit. I don't think so."

Lilliana took a deep breath and tried to control her temper. "You are lucky there was only one. Persian hares normally hunt in pairs. Fortunately for you, something must've killed its mate, probably a manticore or a griffin." She glared at Jess. "Of course, that probably doesn't scare you. You'd probably consider a griffin just a birdie, wouldn't you? A seven-foot-tall birdie with razor sharp talons." She had their attention now. "If that doesn't frighten you, maybe a Cerberus would—a three-headed wolf with a mane of poisonous snakes."

"I was scared," Cai blurted. Lilliana heard the truth of it in Cai's racing flute heart music.

Maggie's lamb echoed the sentiment, bleating to Lilliana about the yellow monster that almost tore them to shreds, telling her of how the tall boy saved them but had nearly gotten eaten himself.

Maggie patted the ram's head, quieting him down as they walked. "What about you, Lilliana, aren't you scared?"

"It's different for me. This is something I have to do." Yes, she was scared. Lilliana didn't look at Maggie. The girl might read too much from her eyes. There was something else she might see. Maggie might be able to tell how glad she was that they'd come. Lilliana pushed the thought away. It was wrong. Selfish. But true. She felt stronger because of them. Stronger, yes. And yet, their presence here gave her five more reasons to be terrified.

Jake stepped around a tree and matched her stride for stride. "What was I supposed to do? Let you face Gryndelyn alone?"

"Yes."

Jake didn't say anything. Lilliana glanced sideways at him. Light filtered through the trees and caught on his features. The muscles at the corner of his jaw had hardened into a stubborn knot.

"Come on, Jake. Did you really think it was a good idea for you, a human, to walk through an Elf-made portal into another dimension? For all you knew," she struggled to think of a bigger threat other than the one they were about to face, "this place could've been filled with poisonous gases. Deadly insects. Or what if you could never cross back to your world?"

He didn't answer.

Cai stumbled on a tree root. "Will we be able to? Get back home, I mean?"

"Yes." Lilliana said firmly. They were finally out of the forest, standing on a rise overlooking the huge low plain and the sea. "At least, I hope so," she added under her breath.

"Wow!" Mark gazed at the broad vale below. "Is this really an Elf-made dimension?"

"Yes." Lilliana nodded, only half listening to the rest of his questions. She concentrated on a less scenic part of the view—the darkness swirling up from the southeast horizon.

"Does that mean Elves live here?" Cai asked, checking her camera settings. "Will we get to see any?"

"No. Ayre is like a zoo for fairytale creatures and mythical beasts like the Persian hare you saw. And other things," she added, feeling sick to her stomach at the thought. She desperately hoped Naneth would be able to send Jess, Jake, and the others back to Texas before Gryndelyn got any closer.

"Is that your grandma?" Jess pointed at Naneth, who was climbing the hill toward them.

"Yes."

Jess leaned close and quietly asked, "Did she give you a reason?"

For abandoning you.

The unspoken words hung in the air. Lilliana nodded, glad Jess hadn't said it aloud.

"Better've been good." Jess folded her arms across her chest.

"It was."

"That isn't a storm, is it?" Maggie pointed at the churning blackness rising on the far side of the valley.

If only it was a storm, but storm clouds didn't usually buzz. The sound was so faint Lilliana knew the humans couldn't hear it yet. Soon, she guessed, it would become an intolerable roar.

"Trouble. Hurry!" She grabbed Jake's hand and they ran down the slope.

MUSTERING THE TROOPS

Jess ran all out. Tall grass slapped against her legs, but she loved it. They were running straight for that dark cloud. Straight into danger, and yet she wasn't afraid. She felt like a Celtic warrior running into battle. Everything inside her rejoiced. Her heritage burned in her veins. Even this place, strange as it was, felt connected to her somehow. This was what she was made for. Jess was made for battle.

"Wait up!" Maggie shouted.

Jess glanced over her shoulder.

Maggie was pulling on the ram. "It's like all of a sudden he's gained weight."

Jess couldn't believe it. Rambo looked twice as big as he had a minute ago. She stopped in her tracks. He was actually taller than Maggie's waist. Full grown. He bleated in alarm, not his usual high-pitched baa, a low rumble that surprised even him.

"What's happening to him?" Maggie demanded.

"Maybe it's this place." Cai jogged up beside Jess. "Look at his horns!" They were growing longer and sharper, curling outward like a bull's.

Jess glanced at the cloud on the horizon. It was growing as fast as Rambo. "I don't know, but we'd better get going."

Rambo bucked. His newly sprouted muscles boosted him too far forward and he tumbled past them and was partway down the hill before finding his balance and galloping off.

"Get back here!" Maggie shouted in a worried mother's voice. "Who knows what's hiding in that grass."

She took off after him. Except then, the crazy ram did a U-turn and bolted back uphill to Maggie, bucking and lunging like a clumsy colt. He was even bigger now. Much bigger. Taller than Maggie. Buffalo bigger! He galloped toward them, weaving unsteadily from side to side and tossing his head. His horns had grown into deadly curved spikes.

"Look out!" Jess hollered.

Cai dove out of his way into the grass. A flock of birds with peacock-like tails burst into flight, fleeing the rambunctious wooly mammoth.

Jess lunged right. Rambo thundered past her, trampling the exact spot where she'd been standing. He tossed his head and bellowed, sounding like a cross between a revving motorcycle and an off-key tuba.

"Calm down, boy. Slow down." Maggie grabbed a handful of grass and held it out to him. "It's okay," she soothed. He circled and trotted back to her. "Here you go. Growing so much, you've gotta be hungry."

He eyed her offering suspiciously.

"Go ahead. Eat up, big fella." Rambo greedily chomped down the grass and gave her a grateful slurp on the cheek. She patted his neck and handed him more grass. "Poor little guy, doesn't know what happened to him."

Jess rolled her eyes at the gargantuan *little guy*. "Let's go." She signaled Maggie to move. "We'll ask Lilliana's grandmother what's going on."

Jess ran ahead while Maggie lured her white buffalo downhill with big handfuls of grass. When she got there, Lilliana, her grandmother, Mark, and Jake were already huddled in a heated discussion.

"You've got to send them home, Naneth," Lilliana insisted. "Somehow."

"I suppose." Naneth didn't look convinced. "There is another portal just across the valley."

"I won't leave you to face *that*—" Jake pointed at the storm. "—alone."

"I'm not alone."

"Face it, Lilliana," Jess barged in and crossed her arms. "You're stuck with us."

Mark glanced at Cai and Maggie coming toward them. His mouth fell open. "Is that Rambo?"

Rambo stopped munching grass and rumbled in answer. Not waiting for an introduction to Lilliana's grandmother, Maggie pushed into the circle. "What's happened to the lamb?" Rambo's big head bobbed inquisitively over her shoulder.

Naneth didn't seem surprised by Maggie's presence nor disturbed by the question. "He changed for you, dear. He became what you imagined you needed. That's how this world works." She frowned. "At least, it works sometimes. Other times it's entirely unpredict—"

"Then why isn't there a portal right here? Right now?" Lilliana shoved Rambo back out of the group. "They're humans. They need to go back to their world where it's safe."

"I can only guess, my dear." Naneth smiled patiently. "Our hearts do not see through duty-colored lenses. Evidently, you need your friends here with you more than you need them to be safe."

Lilliana paled.

Maggie stroked Rambo's wooly neck. "So, if he's as big as a horse, does that mean—"

"Bigger," Cai corrected.

"Does that mean I can ride him?"

Naneth's eyebrows cocked quizzically. "Isn't that why you've imagined a saddle on his back?"

Sure enough, on Rambo's back there was now a tooled western saddle that looked a lot like Maggie's barrel racing saddle at home. She grinned, and instantly the reins to Rambo's halter appeared in her hand.

"Well done," Naneth congratulated her.

Maggie backed Rambo into a squatting position and climbed on.

"Hey, look!" Cai pointed at the camera hanging around her neck. A swirl of glitter dissipated, and the camera was bigger, way more advanced looking. It had been a very cool top-of-the-line Minolta. Now it was bigger with a detachable flash and an oversized lens. She held it up, speechless.

"Guessin' you need to take pictures?" Jess rubbed her neck. "How's that gonna help?"

"I have no idea." Cai framed Maggie riding the sheep-buffalo-horse, whatever it was, and snapped the shot.

"Interesting choice of weapons," Naneth said and smiled fondly at Cai. "But then, my dear, you've always been an extraordinary child."

Jess studied Naneth. There hadn't been any introductions, and yet it seemed like the elderly fairy knew each of them like she'd known them all of their lives. Then Jess seized on something she'd said. "*Weapon*? These are weapons?"

"Yes, in a way." Naneth glanced briefly at the cloud moving toward them from the east. "Maggie and Cai have dreamed up something to help them with—"

"I know what I want!" Jess excitedly rattled off her request. She couldn't keep from bouncing up and down like a kid at her first birthday party. "A Lightweight Ground Assault Vehicle armed with a Microburst Sonic Cannon! I call it an SAV, a Sonic Assault Vehicle. I've been working on the specs for months."

"Yeah, and it makes people deaf," Cai grumbled.

"No, it doesn't." Jess didn't even look at Cai. She kept her eyes focused on Naneth expectantly. "It shuts down the nervous system. The perfect weapon." Jess couldn't wait to see it. *Wouldn't it be cool if—*

The SAV suddenly materialized. Four oversized tires, all-terrain chassis, and her cannon mounted on top of a rotating turret—for real! She ran to it. "Oh, man! Check out the sonic dish," she shouted. It was rigged with the same exact focusing mechanism she'd been working on earlier this week. Jess smoothed her hands over the side of the vehicle. Gorgeous lightweight titanium painted in perfect green and gray camouflage. "I can't believe it!"

"That's just the point. You do believe it. You imagined it into being." Naneth patted the angular front end as if it was a friend's ugly child. She politely added, "Good job."

Jess didn't care if anyone else appreciated her baby. It looked beautiful to her. She squatted down to look under the wheel wells. "Independent suspension. Roll guard stabilizers. "Yep, it even has my traction maximizers." She ran around to the passenger side where the sonic cannon was mounted on a rotating deck. "Do you think it's functional? I was still ironing out some of the kinks."

Naneth's brow knit together as she glanced again at the darkness swirling toward them. Under her breath she muttered, "We'll find out soon enough."

Mark jumped into the driver's seat. "Whoa! Check it out." He pointed to a knob on the dash in front of the stick shift. "Jess, baby, does this thing have nitro boosters?"

Jess grinned big time. "Yeah, and that's not all. But…" She stopped grinning. "Don't you want your own weapon?"

"You kidding?" He cranked up the engine. "Man the cannon, Army Girl. I'll drive."

Jake turned to Naneth and glanced down at his empty hands. "I've never invented anything like that."

"I don't imagine many people have." Naneth smiled and shook her head. "That's okay. It can be anything, even something you've daydreamed about."

Jake nodded, deep in thought. "Well, um, there was this—" Before he could say another word, glitter swirled around him.

His shirt transformed into a ribbed padded tunic with a high stiff collar and no sleeves. Leather straps crisscrossed his chest, buckling armored moldings onto his shoulders. Metal armbands, etched with strange symbols appeared on his forearms. Steel bands coiled over his thighs forming shields in the shape of runes or symbols of some kind. Metal shin guards above heavy black boots appeared, and a thick belt with a scabbard angled across his hips.

In his gloved hand, he held up a sword. Jake lifted it, staring at the glistening blade with as much amazement as the rest of them.

They all stared at Jake in shock. There was something so familiar about the way he looked, but Jess couldn't place it.

Mark leaned over the SAV's steering wheel and with a wink at Jess said, "Someone's been playing Final Fantasy."

"That's it," Jess chuckled. "In seventh grade he spent his whole Christmas break playing Final Fantasy XII. Beat it three times."

Jake glared Jess and Mark into silence and then turned back to Naneth, all business. "Great sword. But I can't protect her if she's up there," he glanced skyward and then sheathed the blade. "I've got to be able to fly." He looked wistfully at Lilliana, whose wings were still extended.

She retracted them. "It isn't your job to protect me."

The dark army coming at them hummed like a plague of locusts. They wouldn't be locusts. Jess knew Gryndelyn wouldn't bring anything so benign as grasshoppers.

Jake turned to Naneth. "What if you made me taller or something? Like a giant."

"No!" Jess stood up in the SAV and exhaled her exasperation. "That'll just make you a bigger target."

"I know just the thing." Naneth smiled

Naneth tucked back her lips and pressed two fingers against her teeth, letting loose with a deafening whistle. Then she patted Jake's arm, just as if she hadn't just gone off like a wacky whistling teapot. "So, you want to fly, eh?"

He nodded suspiciously.

A bloodcurdling screech startled them all. Jess whipped around and spotted a huge griffin soaring down from the mountains.

She turned to Lilliana. "I thought you said they were only

seven feet tall."

Lilliana's eyes were fixed on the incoming griffin. "I've never actually seen one before."

"This is a *giant* griffin, my dear," Naneth explained in a teacherly tone, not sounding the least bit concerned.

"Just so it isn't hunting dinner." Jess fingered the controls on her sonic cannon just in case.

"Tavari is an old friend," Naneth assured them.

Friend or not, they all backed up as the huge half lion, half eagle glided in for a landing. Even though it towered over them, the griffin seemed as wary of them as they were of it. It fanned the air with enormous wings and clawed skittishly at the ground with talons the size of butchers' knives. Lions were impressive enough. This one was gigantic. Thick bulging muscles flexed on its hindquarters, and a long tail lashed impatiently back and forth. Jess swallowed hard when she sized up the huge eagle's beak. It could easily nip off a man's head—any of their heads.

As dangerous as the griffin looked, it was also majestic. Its head feathers were stark white except for the dark ones shooting up over her brows like a warrior's headdress. Those were blood red like its predatory eyes. The rest of her feathers were shades of liquid chocolate. As she moved they glinted with red, purple, and even blue.

Naneth nodded in greeting. "Tavari."

The gigantic bird/lion bowed her head to Lilliana's grandmother.

"Thought you said they were dangerous." Jess glanced sideways at Lilliana.

"They are," she said quietly.

Naneth patted the side of the griffin's neck. "I have an understanding with this one. Don't I, Tavari?" She glanced over her shoulder at the swirling black horde approaching and sped up her introduction. "Suffice it to say, one of her kits was in trouble once, and I rescued it."

Naneth stepped back and waved Jake forward. "Tavari, meet your rider."

The giant griffin whipped her attention to Jake. She thrust her massive hooked beak only inches from his face. Jake held perfectly still, scarcely breathing under her menacing scrutiny. Tavari's dark raptor eyes were so cold and merciless that she seemed blind, and yet so shrewd and ancient it was if she saw past Jake's blanched features straight into his soul.

In a startlingly fast movement, the griffin's beak darted to his thigh. She tipped sideways, as if inspecting the metal designs on his leg armor. She pecked it lightly. Still, Jake did not move. Tavari abruptly raised her head. Face-to-face with him, she let loose with a deafening "Skree!"

"Ah, she recognizes the symbols on your leg armor." Naneth nodded. "You've pleased her. She'll allow you to ride her."

Jake swallowed hard. "What do the symbols mean?"

"You created them. Don't you know?"

He shook his head.

"They're the emblems of the fifth ele—"

Suddenly, a noisy flock of birds sprang out of the grass and took flight. Another group shot out of the trees by the lake and headed north toward the mountain. The temperature shifted, and the air around them grew close and humid.

Tavari clawed the ground, uprooting grass and dirt. She tossed her head in the direction of the gathering darkness in the south.

"Yes, old friend. I see her." Naneth sighed heavily.

Emblems forgotten, Jake hurried to Tavari's back. "How do I ride her?"

"Don't worry. You'll like riding a griffin much better than riding a dragon." She said it as if Jake was an old hand at riding a dragon.

"This will help." Vines shot out from Naneth's hands, winding and weaving into a saddle on Tavari's back. "We haven't much time, so listen carefully. A griffin senses the rider's desire. Be careful. You've only to think about a place and Tavari will instantly change course. Control your thoughts. I've ridden her a time or two myself. It's not as easy as one might think."

Jess was pretty darn sure none of them thought it looked easy. She watched in awed silence as the monstrous lion-eagle knelt down so that her brother could climb on. He swung onto the griffin's back and sat in the saddle as if he'd been born to it. He looked magnificent.

Mark leaned on the steering wheel and stared at Jake. "Now that is way cool."

Pride filled Jess's throat, and she felt the uncomfortable sensation of tears. Instead, she choked them back and thrust her fist into the air in tribute to her brother.

Lilliana approached the griffin and brushed her hand lightly over Tavari's snowy white neck feathers. She said something in a flowing musical language. Strange thing was—Jess thought she understood. In fact she knew what Lilliana had said. "Wise and mighty lioness, fly strong, fly true, and guard your rider. For this service I will owe you a great debt."

Tavari turned sharply and appraised the young fairy. With arrogant reserve she nodded her acquiescence. Then the mighty griffin turned away, fanned her wings, and shrieked at the coming horde.

Maggie trotted Rambo up on the other side of Jake and stopped. Rambo eyed the griffin and pawed the ground like a stallion wanting to race.

Maggie called to Jake. "Better give it a try before..." She frowned at the enemy coming toward them.

Tavari leapt to the challenge. Her powerful lion's hind legs boosted them several yards in one bound. Her wings stroked the air the way a swimmer glided through water while her thick eagle forelegs served as perfectly balanced pistons over which they vaulted into an incredibly fast gallop. Maggie and her giant ram couldn't possibly keep pace. She kept trying though, galloping after the griffin at breakneck speed.

Jake didn't become airborne. He galloped along the valley floor until it became clear he and Tavari had outstripped Maggie and the ram. Then he wheeled sharply and headed back to Lilliana.

Directive 25

Secondly, it is our duty to help Cinderella's offspring rise to their full potentials.

We must gently guide them. They have a tendency to wander off course. Frankly, without our help it is doubtful any of them would find their ways. Admittedly, when properly directed, their unique gifts benefit both mankind and fairiekind. Astray, however, Cinderella's prodigal progeny have been responsible for some of earth's greatest calamities.

– Gryndelyn Myrddin

Aria

Lilliana pressed her hand against her chest, trying to control her pride. She could scarcely believe it. Jake was riding a griffin, one of the fiercest beasts from any world.

Naneth put her arm around Lilliana's shoulders and gave her a gentle hug. "Sweetheart, you must teach him to fly."

Lilliana shook her head. "Why? He's doing quite well, don't you think?"

"On the ground, yes. Unfortunately our time is short. He needs to be confident in the air."

Lilliana shook her head. "I've never ridden a griffin. You should teach him."

"No, my dear, his ability to ride isn't the problem. He's a natural, and Tavari likes him. As I feared, his thoughts do not stray far from you. The griffin is conceding to his desires. You must lure him into the sky."

Lilliana saw it then, the fierceness on Jake's face as he rode toward her. It wasn't the conquering brutality of a soldier lusting for the blood of his enemies. Jake's expression was the terrifying ferocity of love. She saw it in the steady serenity of his eyes, in the determined set of his mouth—a warrior who would lay down his life to save hers.

Her breath caught.

Her heart forgot its steady rhythm.

And she rose without using her wings, drifted up and up, never looking away from the intensity of his gaze. He flew to meet her high above the trees. The nurturing moisture whispering around her faded in importance. She saw nothing but Jake and the fierce adoration in his eyes. Nothing else mattered. Not even the shrieking hordes coming ever closer.

She unfurled her wings and used them to hover beside him. She wanted to say, "Do not die today, Jake Harrison." She wished more than anything she could make him promise it. A futile wish. There were no guarantees of forever. Not with a human. Not with anyone. Even she could not make him that promise.

Did it really matter? Yes, it mattered. She wanted forever with him, and yet…

She had now.

That was something.

Something magnificent.

Moisture in the air above the lake bathed her. In that moment, she felt completely full, overflowing, bursting with more happiness than she'd ever felt in her whole life. She might live a hundred lifetimes and never feel this much joy.

She no longer cared about time.

Or death.

All that mattered was the all-consuming goodness of this one moment.

There was only one thing worthy of being said, but words would not do the feeling justice. So Lilliana slipped between Tavari's neck and wings. floating there, she faced Jake and pressed her lips against his.

Jake wrapped his free arm around her, pulling her closer. Time seemed to close its eyes. The world around them faded into a forgotten dream as their lips spoke wordlessly, eloquently, of sweetness, joy, and longing.

She could not pull away until she realized they were dropping through the air. Their mesmerizing kisses had confused the griffin. Jake had stopped thinking about where they were, so Tavari had stopped flying. Lilliana broke away from him and spiraled upward, knowing Jake would follow.

Spreading her wings and arms wide, Lilliana soared up, grinning at the sky. Air currents rippled around her as Jake and the giant griffin followed. She laughed and arced backward. Letting them chase her. Teaching him to soar. Death could not steal anything from her now. Today, *she* was the eagle. Today, she had captured divine happiness. No matter what, it would be hers forever.

She slowed down and let them catch up to her. Jake smiled. The peace she felt was written on his face. He understood.

Softly, she spoke, letting the words drift on the eternal breeze. "I love you, Jake."

It was enough.

Together they flew down near the others and turned to face the threat.

BOGEY ON YOUR SIX

Jess wriggled out from under the dashboard of her SAV after making a few last minute adjustments to the sonic cannon. "Done," she announced. Mark nodded absently. He sat at the steering wheel with his gaze riveted on the approaching horde. Gryndelyn flew in front of the buzzing cloud like a blazing archangel.

Jess's blood began to pound as if ancient war drums throbbed in her veins, stirring her up for battle. She grabbed the cannon controls eager to test out her invention.

Cai and Naneth stood beside the SAV. Cai looked a little pale. She covered her ears for a moment. "That awful howling is driving me crazy."

"Yeah, what *are* those things?" Jess focused the cannon on the approaching swarm. Whatever they were, they were close enough now that Jess could tell they weren't flying so much as undulating through the air.

Naneth sighed heavily. "She calls them firebugs."

Cai squeezed her thumb and forefinger together and asked wishfully, "Like little fireflies?"

"Sadly, no, my dear." Naneth shook her head. "Nothing so tiny or endearing. More like fat moray eels. I call them *fire snakes*." She stretched her arms wide. "Only instead of scales they have metal segments. And don't let the lacy wings or the pink fur on their heads deceive you. Those are childish decorations used to hide their all-seeing spider eyes and poisonous fangs."

"Oh," Cai mouthed, fiddling with her camera. "I don't know what good this will be against a creature like that." She glanced sideways at Jess, looking nervous.

Jess patted her cannon. "Don't worry. Got it covered."

"Gryndelyn dreamed them up when she was just a little girl." Naneth's hand went to her pocket where she gripped what looked like the end of a wand. "The wretched things are almost helpless on the ground because of their heavy metal shells. Shameful, really. She didn't give them legs because she liked to watch them squirm. But don't be fooled. Fire snakes are lethal on both ends. When they begin to glow orange, watch out. Their scorpion-like tails can whip around and shoot fire."

"Great," Mark said softly and clutched the steering wheel. "Fire-spitting, armor-coated, poisonous flying eels."

"That shriek you hear," Naneth explained. "is because they have to fly with their mouths open; otherwise, their bodies are too heavy. Wind vibrates through their curved fangs and tubular bodies making that shrill sound. With their mouths open, the airborne snakes are always ready to strike."

"*Nice*," Jess said.

"Yeah, I'm real comfortable now." Mark leaned over to Jess and patted the cannon. "You a good shot with that thing?"

Jess raised an eyebrow. "They won't know what hit 'em."

He grinned. "My beautiful little warrior."

Warrior. Jess felt her cheeks heat up under his praise.

Cai aimed her camera and tried to take a picture of Gryndelyn and her horde. "Hey! It's not working." She shook it and tried again. Nothing happened. The flash didn't even go off. "Great." She sighed.

All of a sudden Naneth planted both hands on the front of the SAV and stared intently at Jess. "I have a favor to ask you." She paused. "Please don't harm Gryndelyn."

"What!" Jess practically jumped out of her seat. "Are you crazy? She's been trying to kill us all day." The cannon in her hands veered dangerously in Naneth's direction.

Mark pushed it aside.

"You can't ask that." Wind swept through Jess's short hair, but it didn't cool her down. Its sticky humid fingers only riled her up more. "We're putting our lives on the line here."

For a moment, no one said anything. Grasses bent in the breeze, and a family of scaly green warthogs with wings scampered past, fleeing the battlefield.

"I *can* ask," Naneth said softly. "I've watched over your family for centuries." She stared down at the camouflage paint on the SAV as if she was embarrassed. "Gryndelyn is my sister."

"Your sister?" Jess dropped into her seat with a thud.

"My youngest sister." Naneth bore down on her. "Yes, I know she's misguided, spoiled, and—"

"Dangerous!"

"Yes, I know. But she's..." Naneth threw up her hands. "Family."

Jess gritted her teeth and glanced at her brother riding the giant griffin high above the trees. *Family.* She understood, even though it made her shoulders knot up and her blood boil. "Unbelievable." She slammed her fist against the dash. How could she promise? She couldn't. "Sister or not, I can't promise. I won't." She sank deeper into the seat and glared at the problem fairy in the sky. "But I will give you my word that I won't hurt her unless there's no other alternative."

"Thank you. That's all I ask." Naneth nodded. "I knew you'd understand." With that she turned and strode out to meet Gryndelyn. "Grynnie, dear!" Amazingly, her voice boomed over the noise of the howling fire snakes as if she had a 1500-watt amplifier. "How nice of you to drop by."

Gryndelyn inclined her head as if she were a queen irritated at having to acknowledge a peasant.

Cai snapped a picture. The flash worked this time, so maybe she'd actually captured the spectacular panorama—white smoke writhing around Gryndelyn as she floated in the air in front of thousands of undulating pink-headed snakes with glowing red tails.

Gryndelyn jerked in Cai's direction and shaded her eyes from the flash. "What are human brats doing in Ayre?" She waved her hand at Cai, Jess, and the others as if they were annoying gnats. "See, this is the problem with you, Rose. You never do anything by the book."

"From what I hear, you've been breaking a few rules yourself."

"Fine! Let's stop beating around the bush, shall we? I've come for what's mine." Gryndelyn flared up like a pulsating star about to go supernova. Thousands of firebug tails suddenly turned a bright electric orange. Like hot air balloons, the added heat in their bellies lifted the pink-haired demons higher. Their howls changed into whooshing furnace sounds. "Are you going to hand it over or not?"

"Don't be absurd. If I ever give up the wand, six others stand in line to inherit it before you."

Gryndelyn fumed. *Literally.* Dark smoke seeped out of her pores and steamed upward. "It's MY birthright."

Jess caught a glimpse of Lilliana overhead. Her hands glittered with starry whirlpools ready to drown her combustible aunt. Tavari screeched a warning, and Jake unsheathed his sword. Jess aimed the sonic cannon at the nearest section of fire snakes.

Naneth didn't seem bothered by Gryndelyn's show of power. She just crossed her arms and shifted her weight to one hip, clucking her tongue the way a mother scolds a naughty child. "Oh, please. You're not going to bring up that Merlin rubbish again, are you? You know perfectly well Lilliana is the heir."

"That abomination!" Gryndelyn spit embers as she screamed and pointed at Lilliana. "A Halfling on the throne? Over my dead body."

"Don't be silly. There is no throne. You know perfectly well we abolished the old ways."

"*You* abolished them. A foolish blunder I plan to correct."

"That *foolish blunder* has kept peace for seven hundred years." Naneth sounded irritated now.

"At what price? Do you have any idea what turmoil the fairy

realm is in?" Gryndelyn shouted. "No, you don't. Face it, Rose. You're out of touch. Past your prime. Look at you! Gray as death. And vines? For pity's sake, you look like a gnome. So passé you're almost primordial."

"Thanks, Gryn, darling. Complimentary as ever." Naneth planted one fist on her hip. "You look lovely, too. Like something out of the pit of—"

"You've had your way long enough!"

Naneth patted the wand in her pocket. "I'll be having it a while longer, I think."

Gryndelyn's hand filled with white-hot fire to heave it at her sister.

"Naneth, look out!" Lilliana raced down to save her grandmother.

"Pest!" Gryndelyn turned sharply and jolted the fireball at Lilliana.

Lilliana tumbled sideways through the air, narrowly escaping.

Fire snakes swooped in to attack.

Cai took another picture of the witch who would be queen. This time the flash went off. Big time! Lightning exploded out of the camera. Gryndelyn screeched as the bolt zigzagged and hit her, burning a hole through the lower half of her white gown. She blasted a stream of fire at Cai.

Naneth stomped the ground. A slab of stone jutted up, shielding Cai from the inferno. Flames roared on either side of her as she huddled behind the rock staring at the confusing camera in her hands.

Jess fired the sonic cannon at a swarm of fire snakes. One earsplitting boom and dozens of the buggers fell out of the sky, sizzling like mosquitoes in a bug zapper. She fired again. Aftershocks from the sonic boom made everything quiver, even the air. More stunned fire snakes dropped out of the sky, shattering against the ground, clattering and exploding like stainless-steel popcorn. Gryndelyn roared with anger.

265

"Cai!" Maggie yelled as she and Rambo galloped past. "Above you!" A fire snake undulated right above Cai's rock hiding place.

Jess wheeled the cannon around but there was no way to shoot the bug without hitting Cai, too. Cai held the camera over her head and squeezed the button. White light burst all around her. Thousands of tiny dots of light bounced across the snake's enormous compound eyes. It screeched and reeled backward, flailing through the air. Fire burst out of its tail. A patch of grass in front of Cai lit up like a Texas grass fire.

Jake seemed to come from nowhere. He dipped Tavari low and slashed the snake in two. The writhing halves crashed to the ground. Its hollow segments burst apart and rolled across the dirt. What was left of its body hissed and snapped like a downed power line. Jake and Tavari wheeled skyward, cutting down another firebug.

Lilliana flew low, splashing water over the fires igniting on the field. Then she whooshed up and extinguished an airborne swarm of fire snakes with a torrent of water.

"We've gotta get Cai." Jess pointed at her friend hunkered down behind a rock slab. Mark hit the gas, and they raced across the scorched grass toward her, swerving to avoid falling snakes.

Just then, Jess heard a trumpet. She whipped around to see what it was. Salt spray from the sea dampened her skin as huge waves crashed against the shore. Suddenly, a massive dragon burst out of the water like a golden freight train. Its long neck rose up and up, and in one arcing motion the monster snagged a firebug in its teeth, crushed it, and gulped it down the way a trout swallows a mosquito. It shook its frilled head, trumpeted steam out of its bassoon nostrils, and disappeared under the waves.

It was killing fire snakes. That meant the sea serpent didn't take orders from Gryndelyn. Good thing, Jess thought. They needed an ally or two. The SAV roared up beside Cai. "Get in!" Jess yelled.

Cai pointed at the churning sea. "Di-Did you see that?"

"Yeah. Hurry!" Jess commanded.

Cai ran toward them but stumbled when the ground shook. Not the cannon this time. Jess glanced at the field and couldn't believe what she saw charging toward them. Creatures bigger than gorillas but way uglier. Toad ugly. Flinging mud and slime as they galumphed across the plains.

"Um, you go ahead." Cai patted the SAV door and saluted. "Go fight those things. I'm fine here."

Jess and Mark didn't wait around. They peeled out, bouncing across the field to deal with King Kong's ugly brothers. Naneth was ahead of them, busy fending off Gryndelyn's raging inferno. When she saw the big gorillatoads galloping across the plain, she gave the wand a hard thrust.

"Swamp trolls?" Naneth bellowed and thrust the wand again. An invisible hammer slammed into Gryndelyn, knocking her backward. As she fell, fire jetted out of Gryndelyn's palms and accidentally toasted a line of fire snakes. A dozen pink-fringed eels turned into crispy black ash.

"I can't believe you brought swamp trolls!" Naneth sounded royally pissed off. "How could you? Poor ignorant creatures—this isn't their fight. They could get hurt."

"They wanted to come. Besides…" Gryndelyn jabbed a finger in Jess and Mark's direction. "It isn't their fight, either."

Naneth shook her head. "Shame on you! Involving helpless beasts."

The swamp trolls were swinging clubs the size of tree trunks and loping at them like crazed apes. They smelled worse than wet, filthy dogs. Their putrid stench nauseated Jess as it mixed with the acrid smoke on the battlefield. She aimed her sonic cannon.

"Don't hurt them!" Naneth shouted.

Jess groaned. How was she supposed to fight this war if Naneth kept expecting her to use kid gloves on the enemy?

Not everyone heard Naneth's entreaty. Downfield, Rambo butted one of the stinky toad gorillas with his horns. The troll flew up and smashed into three of its comrades, knocking them down like bowling pins. High above them, Jake had his sword drawn, and Tavari was diving toward the trolls, claws out, as if she'd just spotted dinner.

"No. No! NO!" Naneth aimed her wand at the beasts. "Stop!" she thundered. The ground beneath them heaved. Trees swayed. All of Ayre quaked and rumbled. The SAV swayed. A fissure ripped across the plain, tearing open in front of the charging swamp trolls. Most of them froze in their tracks, but six or seven trolls tumbled into the crevice.

With a loud frustrated skree, Tavari swerved and abandoned her prey.

"Enough!" Naneth aimed her wand at Gryndelyn.

Too late.

Gryndelyn had already sent a fireball screaming toward Naneth. It exploded, hurtling dirt and rock in every direction. Naneth stumbled sideways, flinging her arm up to guard her eyes from chunks of flying debris. Before the dust even cleared, Naneth stomped out and jabbed her wand skyward. Suddenly, Gryndelyn scudded side to side in the air as if an unseen hand was shaking her. Then she plunged from the sky, flopping like a rag doll as she fell. She slammed against the grass in front of Naneth, who held the wand at her sister's throat. Roots sprang from the ground, shooting up in hyperspeed. Hundreds of tentacles twined around Gryndelyn's arms and legs, handcuffing her to the earth.

Gryndelyn wheezed for air. Naneth was breathing hard, too. The flowers in her hair drooped. Wilted petals fluttered down, mixing with the dust in the air. Her crown of vines withered, shriveling back into her hair. Neither of them said anything. They just stared at each other with pure anger. A look Jess knew by heart.

The field echoed with battle noises. Lilliana was splashing water. Tavari and Jake were battling a swamp troll. The sea serpent snatched another firebug out of the air, and Jess blasted a flock of fire snakes out of the sky. The creepy worms littered the field, their metal bits twitching and sputtering as they cooled. Yet the silence between Naneth and Gryndelyn was more alarming.

Naneth glared at her sister and finally spoke. "Your toys are getting ruined. Why don't you take them and go home?"

Wisps of smoke leached out from under Gryndelyn, wafting up and coiling around the wand at her throat, caressing it, mimicking Gryndelyn's desires. Her arms strained at the roots binding her. She clawed the ground, clenching her teeth as if mustering every ounce of energy she had.

"You don't really think I'd give up this easily?" Gryndelyn twisted her right hand over and opened it wide. A vortex of fire and light shot out of her palm and split open the sky. Then she relaxed against the grass and laughed mirthlessly.

The fiery tornado picked up speed, whirling faster, blazing brighter, getting bigger and more dense, hotter and redder. Volcanic heat radiated from the burning mass turning ocean spray into steam and searing nearby trees.

Naneth stared at the morphing cyclone. "Not your—"

"Yes." Gryndelyn broke free of some of the roots. "The new and improved version."

The red pulsating mass slowed down and got darker. When it finally stopped spinning, Jess gasped. She could see what it was going to be. Pure lava.

"Run!" Jess shouted and waved at Maggie and Jake. "Get out of its way" But where could they hide that wouldn't melt like a soft wax candle?

Globs of molten lava separated into body parts, feet, legs, arms and a head. Black patches appeared where it cooled and formed a skin that crackled apart, exposing churning red and yellow lava inside as it took a step. Dripping molten fire, the creature crushed a spruce tree under its massive foot. Green needles burst into flame. The Christmasy smell turned into a nightmare. The creature took another step, leaving behind a burnt blackened footprint with orange flames flickering at the edges.

Naneth moaned and doubled over as if the creature wounded her with each scorching footstep.

Swamp trolls grunted and squealed like frightened monkeys, stumbling over each other as they hurriedly retreated. The SAV bounced across the plain and skidded to a halt in front of the molten monster. Jess detonated her sonic blaster at it. Dead center hit. Nothing happened.

"Back up!" Jess warned Mark. She fired again. No affect. Lava man didn't have ears or a nervous system for the sonic cannon to short circuit.

Naneth slumped, stumbled, and righted herself.

Lilliana flew toward her grandmother. "Naneth!"

Naneth turned to Gryndelyn. "Your big, hot boyfriend didn't work last time. What made you think he'd work now?" Her voice sounded strained, weak. She was barely able to aim the wand at the earth in front of him. But she did. A tidal wave of dirt and sand shot up and collapsed over lava boy. At the same time, Lilliana let loose with a river the size of the Mississippi, drowning him under a flood. Naneth thumped her foot and aimed the wand, hurling another layer of earth over the monster. Dust and heavy smoke from burning trees and baked earth bit into Jess's nostrils.

Lilliana's shoulders sagged. She wavered midair, as if the effort of drowning lava boy cost her too much energy. She floated down to them. At last, Gryndelyn's lava boyfriend was buried under a Mount Everest of mud and hissing steam.

"Nicely done, brat." Gryndelyn broke free of the last few shriveling roots and got to her feet. She proffered three sarcastic claps in Lilliana's direction. "I was counting on it." She smirked and dusted root fragments off her gown before turning to Naneth. "Unlike you, I learn from my mistakes. You'll like the improvements I've made on him since last time we played this game."

A crackling noise interrupted her. Suddenly, the mountain of mud burst apart, spewing dirt, charcoal, and bits of rock. Globules of mud and cinders rained down from the sky.

Lilliana struggled to fly up above the thick haze. "It's moving!" she cried.

"How?" Jess shielded her eyes, squinting to see through the hailing muck. One heavy thud followed another. What she saw made perfect sense. The intense heat, the sand, carbon and massive weight of the earth had changed lava man. Now he was a gargantuan soldier made of huge gleaming chunks of obsidian and dazzling daggers of quartz. He was as stunning as he was terrifying.

Quartz! Quartz would respond to vibrations.

Jess fired the sonic cannon. The enormous creature shivered, and a smattering of crystals fell off his arms and shoulders. She fired again. He shook slightly but then lurched at the SAV and swung down his massive fist.

Mark gunned the engine. He must have punched the nitro button because they sped forward, shooting across the field on a stream of blue flame. The monster's spiky fist plunged into the ground. It left a jagged crater when he pulled it out.

Jess and Mark skidded to a stop in front of Gryndelyn. Jess aimed the sonic cannon at her. "I'm through playing nice. Call off your crystal creep."

Gryndelyn shrugged. "Can't. He doesn't answer to me." She held up her hands in mock surrender, but sparks fizzled from her fingertips like Fourth of July sparklers. She grinned. "He's his own man."

Jess growled. Her fingers itched to pull the trigger.

Lucky for the witch, Naneth stepped in front of the cannon, her wand poised at Gryndelyn. "I'll handle this."

Jess nudged Mark. "Get me someplace safe. I need to adjust the cannon's frequency to shatter quartz."

"Right." Mark glanced around the battlefield. There was smoke everywhere. Fire snakes buzzed through the sky, and the sea dragon shot out of the water and crunched another metal bug. *Safe* was a relative term.

"What about those trees?" As Jess pointed, Cai ran up and jumped into the back of the SAV.

"Decided I'd rather not die alone," she said, trying to catch her breath.

"This isn't over yet." Jess scooted to the floor, ready to twist under the control panel to recalibrate the cannon, delicate work in ideal circumstances. Today their lives depended on it, and she was going to have to adjust it using her fingernails, a shard of metal she found on the floorboards, and not enough light. "Try not to hit any bumps," she said, sliding under. "Oh, and there's a fire snake on your six."

"Cai, camera!" Mark hollered and stomped on the gas as the fire snake zipped after them.

Cai took its picture. A bright flash of light crackled out and zapped the snake. It nose-dived to the ground, howling. Lucky

Jess had to fix the cannon. Fast.

Directive 26

Lastly, let me remind you to **always** be on your guard. It is a common mistake to focus too much on one aspect of your duty and neglect another. In doing so, it is easy for disaster to sneak up on our blind side and catch us unprepared.

– Gryndelyn Myrddin

Hit Me With Your Best Shot

The crystalline giant walked awkwardly, swaying like a stiff old man as he moved his heavy legs. Each thundering step crushed plants and trees as he stomped toward Naneth, who was battling with Gryndelyn.

Tavari's attempts to grab the monster with her claws and pull him over merely left scratch marks on the glistening crystal. Jake tried hacking at it, but his blade only clanged against the quartz, making small chips. In slow, heavy movements, the monster tried to swat at them as if Jake and the griffin were nothing more than annoying mosquitoes.

His incredible weight gave Lilliana an idea. Flying ahead of the creature, she flooded the ground, creating a huge mud puddle.

It worked. The slippery mud unsteadied the massive giant and bogged him down. His clumsy gait halted. When he tried to swing his massive foot out of the muck, Lilliana was rewarded with a satisfying sticky slurping sound. He wobbled and slumped to one knee in the glop.

A little more mud, Lilliana thought, and he would sink even deeper. She focused every last bit of her energy on drenching the ground around him.

She barely heard Jake shouting at her. Lilliana glanced up. Flashing light blinded her and refracting off a giant crystal hand as it swung toward her. From the other side she glimpsed the flare of a fireball zooming at her. She tried to swerve.

Rock.

Or fire.

274

Lilliana didn't know which one hit her first. The impact sent her sprawling through the air. Stunned. Burning. The last thing she heard as she fell was Tavari's dizzying shriek.

BREAKING POINT

"**H**urry." Cai jiggled her leg nervously.

"Almost done," Jess said. "Just have to screw on this panel—"

"Forget the panel! We've gotta get back there. Now!"

The panic in Cai's voice made Jess drop her makeshift screwdriver. She left the panel hanging open and slid out from under the dash. "Hit it!" she ordered and pulled herself up behind the cannon.

Mark punched it, and they jetted across the field, tearing over bumps, dodging fire snakes. They whizzed toward Naneth and Gryndelyn, swerved to miss one of the witch's flaming volleys, and bounded over a hill that Naneth had stomped up to block her sister. Seconds later, they closed in on the crystal giant. He was stuck in the middle of the field, struggling to climb out of a deep puddle of muck.

"In range yet?" Mark shouted.

"Yeah, slow down." Jess focused the dish at the monster's nonexistent heart. "Cover your ears," she warned, grabbed the handles, and clamped her thumb down on the red button.

Instead of a sonic boom, the cannon emitted a shrill, ear-splitting vibration. Even though it wasn't terribly loud, it was such a mind-numbingly high pitch that it blocked out all other sounds, like standing under a tornado warning siren.

Jess struggled to hold the cannon steady. The piercing whistle felt like ice picks stabbing her brain. Even Mark relented and covered his ears. If there were any werewolves in the forest, Jess figured they'd be yipping and whimpering like babies. Not

Gryndelyn's crystal Godzilla. He didn't seem to notice, probably because he didn't have ears.

It wasn't his eardrums Jess was counting on. She kept a white-knuckle grip on the red button until even the air started to quiver.

Still stuck in the mud, the giant glanced down at his chest and cocked his head as if he was confused. Sunlight came out and bounced off his massive crystals, sending weird prisms of light shooting across the plains. That's when Jess noticed the first visible effects of the sonic vibrations. Light refracting across the field began to quiver, slightly at first, stuttering on rocks, jittering on the SAV, oscillating on burnt-out firebug hulls.

The crystalline giant stiffened. He started to rattle like a china closet in an earthquake. Clinking. Shaking.

Jess let go of the button. "Duck!" she screamed.

He exploded. Shattered! Pieces of him had to have blown clear into the stratosphere.

Mark slammed the SAV into reverse, backing away as the sky rained crystals. Cai shielded her neck and head with the camera.

Gryndelyn flew at Jess, oblivious of the bombarding quartz fragments pelting her. Screeching, she chased the SAV. It was impossible to distinguish her rants over the tinkling and clinking of hailing crystals. Jess signaled Mark to do a U-turn. It was time to confront the demon fairy once and for all.

Naneth ran toward them, wand aimed at her venomous sister. Just then, a quartz cannonball plummeted into Naneth's back. She yelped and thudded to the ground. Motionless, sprawled out, face down, the wand tumbled out of her hand.

Like a greyhound on a scent, Gryndelyn whipped around.

"Stop!" Jess shouted to Mark. He slammed on the brakes, but they skidded past the wand. Jess dove out of the SAV. She scrambled over the shard-covered grass and lunged for the wand.

She and Gryndelyn grabbed it at the exact same instant.

Directive 27

Congratulations! You have now completed your training course. Best of luck to you as you endeavor to rescue mankind. (Heaven knows, they need it.)

—Gryndelyn Myrddin

Without You

Searing pain jolted Lilliana into consciousness. Her wings and back felt as if they were on fire. She would've screamed except she could hardly breathe because of the weight pressing against her chest. Dragging in a ragged faltering breath, she forced her eyes open.

Jake lay draped across her. Not moving.

"No!" She gasped wildly for air. Panic and bile rose in her throat, choking her senseless. Vulture-like blackness circled as she struggled to lean up.

His eyes were closed. She had the mad, futile thought that maybe he was just sleeping. Hope vanished as she sat up and Jake slid into her lap without a sound. No moan of pain. No breath noises. He was so pale. Horribly pale!

Then she saw the gash in his calf—a gaping mass of mangled flesh and twisted steel from his leg armor. Without thinking she reached out and, with a trembling hand, removed a metal fragment that had cut into his exposed muscle. Blood trickled out of an artery, dripping into the thick red pool on the ground beneath them.

The slow pulsating spurt of blood meant he was still alive. Instantly, she sent *elin-gil* to mend his blood vessels. "Quick!" she urged the star sparks. Or he would bleed to death.

Cautiously, Lilliana traced the jagged edges of his wound with her fingertips. Why was it tinged with an unearthly mustard color? Then she spotted the severed head of a fire snake lying in the grass nearby, its fangs and teeth stained with blood—Jake's blood.

Poison! Even though she'd stopped his bleeding, the fire snake's deadly venom would soon destroy his heart.

Struggling to ignore her pain and stay conscious, she gently rolled him onto his back. His lips were starting to turn the same sickly shade of fungus yellow.

Footsteps pounded toward her, but she had no time to look away. She needed to analyze the poison.

"Jake!" Maggie howled. "Is he—"

"No!" Lilliana shouted.

He can't die. Not now. Not this way. She vowed he wouldn't die on her watch. And he wouldn't, not if she had anything to do with it. But her hands were shaking.

"Lilliana, your wings, they're..." Maggie's voice dropped low, sympathetic.

Lilliana wanted to scream, to shout, *Don't tell me! I can't think about that right now.* She didn't though, she only had enough energy to concentrate on Jake.

"They're almost gone. Burned." Maggie murmured the rest of the pointless news. "Your back, too."

Lilliana ignored her and ran her fingertips over the putrid yellowing edge of Jake's wound.

Maggie cringed. "Don't. You might infect it."

"I have to figure out what the poison is."

"It's from those snakes. Can't you just—"

"Not without the molecular structure." Lilliana's fingertips felt clumsy and dull. The burns had shocked her nerves, leaving her numb. She was losing even more sensory perception with every passing second. She closed her eyes, forcing her nerves to act, ignoring the larger, harsher, pain signals that threatened to overwhelm her senses. She quieted her mind and hunted for small details, infinitesimal observations that would mean life or death for Jake. Suddenly, her eyes flew open. Her hand jerked back.

"What is it?" Maggie's undisguised anguish echoed her own despair.

The poison had a magical construct. Completely unnatural. What could she do against that? Lilliana groaned and stared at Jake's face, touching his white cheek. His skin was cooling. Too fast. Despair shuddered through her. Her shoulders quivered like a sobbing child's. And yet she didn't cry. Couldn't. She was too dry. Horridly dry and empty. Useless.

"Do something," Maggie ordered as if she were Jess, as if she could force Lilliana to do a miracle. "Look at me." Maggie grasped Lilliana's arm and shook it. Her voice cracked, betraying her desperation as it turned into a frantic plea. "You have to do something."

Lilliana didn't look away from Jake.

"Listen to me. You can do this. You fixed the car. At the beauty shop, you…" Tears ran down Maggie's cheeks as she shook Lilliana. "You have to do something. You have to!"

Involuntarily, Lilliana sensed exactly how much sodium and water Maggie's tears contained. She detected the acidic proteins that indicated fear, anxiety, even the tang of anger. Doing that simple analysis jarred Lilliana more than Maggie's shaking. Through the fog and despair darkening Lilliana's mind, a faint beam of hope filtered through. A possibility seeped in and flooded her mind with light. She wondered, briefly, if maybe she was already dead and this was some sort of heavenly illumination showing her truths beyond her normal grasp. It didn't matter. She saw it. A possibility. Hope.

Lilliana quickly unbuckled Jake's metal forearm protector. "Hand me his sword."

She might be able to convert the poison using her own body's ability to heal. Maggie handed her the sword. The heavy blade thunked clumsily against the ground. If only she wasn't so weak.

Lilliana wiped away the sweat and dirt from his wrist, hunting for his pulse. She found a slow, faint dirge. With a cry of hope, she drew the sword across her own wrist and sliced it open.

"What are you doing?" Maggie screamed.

Tavari clawed the ground and shrieked, slapping the air with her enormous wings. Waves crashed on the shore as if she was making a huge mistake. The sea serpent rocketed up from the waves and bellowed.

"It's the only way." Lilliana drew the sword across Jake's wrist, opening a fresh wound, one clean enough to work with. She pressed her bleeding arm against his and sprinkled both wrists with what little *elin-gíl* she had left. Immediately, her veins and arteries began knitting to his, funneling her blood into Jake.

"Bind our wrists." She pulled a leather strap from his shoulder protector and held it out to Maggie, who took it with shaky, hesitant hands.

"Quickly!" Lilliana commanded, squinting at Maggie through an ever-narrowing tunnel of blackness. "I may not—"

She meant to say, "I may not be able to stay conscious," but her words slurred. She gasped as the first of Jake's poison entered her heart, scorching her tissues, dehydrating cells, devouring their oxygen, congealing the ruined cells into a strange sulfur-like mixture. *Of course, that explains the yellow color.* She wondered numbly why she hadn't realized the similarity sooner.

Through a dimming haze, she felt Maggie lift their wrists and tighten the leather thong, binding their arms together. Good, she thought and rested her head on his chest, surrendering to the blackness.

JESS'S LAST STAND

Jess held onto the wand with both hands. Her life depended on it. All their lives depended on it. She had the handle, and Gryndelyn clutched the spherical tip.

"Let go, brat." Gryndelyn flamed up like a gas grill.

Jess held on. In fact, she gave it a sword thrust forward into Gryndelyn's ribs. Only it wasn't a sword, it was a wand. And the wand blasted Gryndelyn clear across the field.

Just like that.

Punted her clear back to the eastern ten yard line.

Her brightly burning body rocketed through the air, past the littered field, past the crevice and flopped onto the grass. When she hit, a thin mushroom cloud puffed up into the atmosphere.

Nobody moved.

Nobody said a thing.

Gryndelyn didn't get up.

Jess stared at the smoking wand in her hand. "Whoa," she whispered. It had felt like a thousand volts of electricity whooshed through her, and yet Jess was fine. There wasn't so much as a scorch mark on her fingertips.

A small shard of leftover quartz fell from the sky and pinged against the SAV. The few remaining fire snakes turned and squirmed through the sky, howling mournfully as they fled after their master.

"Dang, girl," Mark said. "You pack one hell of a punch."

Jess felt a little shaky. "Yeah." She jammed the wand into one of the loops on her army pants and bent to check Naneth for a pulse. "She's barely breathing."

Jess wasn't exactly sure when Cai had gotten out of the SAV, but she was grateful for the comforting hand on her shoulder. "Naneth isn't the only one in trouble, Jess. Before you shattered that monster, he…" Cai pointed at the now-empty mud puddle and took a deep breath. "I couldn't tell you until now," she hesitated.

"Tell me what?" Jess demanded, wary of the *tragic-bad-news* tone in her best friend's voice. She'd heard that tone before, and it had ripped her life apart. "Tell me!"

No time. Maggie screamed for help again. She was across the field near the sea. Jess frantically scoured the skies looking for any sign of her brother.

"I'll go." Mark offered. "You two see what you can do for Lilliana's grandma."

"No!" Cai stopped him. "We all need to go. Naneth, too. I know it's dangerous to move her, but we have to. Let's load her in the backseat. I'll ride on the side rail. And—"

Jess grabbed Cai's arm. "Tell me what's wrong! Now."

"It's Lilliana. She's hurt. And maybe Jake, too. I don't know." Cai swallowed hard, fighting tears. Her tough reporter façade disentegrated. "I'm not sure." Cai just shook her head.

Jess sucked in a quick breath and clamped her lips tight. Images burned into her thoughts—her brother on the ground, his body twisted at odd angles, broken. Jake bleeding. She slugged her fears away.

Act! she ordered herself. Move. Get to them.

Mark sprang to help Jess as she lifted Naneth. Cai grabbed the wounded fairy's legs and kept talking. "The giant hit Lilliana with his hand. Then I couldn't see. There was a big fireball. Jake nose-dived to catch her. And then…" Cai kept apologizing and trying to explain. "I couldn't tell you because the cannon was our only chance. You had to fix it first."

They situated Naneth in the back of the SAV. Mark brushed dirt from Naneth's face. "She's hurt bad."

284

Maggie screamed for help again.

"Coming!" Jess hollered as she jumped into the driver's seat and stomped on the gas. Mark clutched the dash. Jess had no idea how Cai kept her hold on the side rails. She didn't care. They had to get there now. She ripped across the field and skidded to a stop, sending a spray of sand across the beach.

Maggs had gone crazy.

"What're you doing?" Jess yelled as she jumped out of the SAV. "You're going to drown them."

Maggie was dragging Jake and Lilliana across the sand into the sea. "Water. They need to be in the water." Blind with tears, Maggie shuddered, but she didn't stop pulling. "Help me! Lilliana's trying to save Jake. This might make her stronger."

Jess splashed in to help, praying Maggs was right. Mark leapt out of the SAV, too, and grabbed Jake's side. Together they towed the too-still pair into the waves. Maggie haltingly explained what Lilliana had done to their wrists. Carefully, they held Lilliana and Jake afloat in the water next to each other.

Jess stared down at her brother's lifeless body, at the huge gash in his leg, and then back at the dark puddle of blood on shore— Jake's blood soaking into the sand and grass. She shook her head. Jess began to shiver. "He's lost too much blood." She tried to estimate the volume in that blackening pool.

But she couldn't think. Couldn't calculate. Her mind felt numb. She only knew that too much of Jake's blood had seeped onto the beach. He wasn't going to make it.

Jess rocked in the waves, refusing to allow the keening sounds her soul wanted to wail. She would not howl her anguish.

No. That would mean he was dead.

No. Not him.

Why couldn't it be her? Jake was so good. So kind. Everything she wasn't. In broken, jagged breaths, Jess called to him. "Ja-ke. Jake!" She shook his shoulder. "Don't do this. You can't die. You can't."

The wand still hung at Jess's side underwater. She hadn't given it a thought. But now it was fizzing, shooting sparks, sending ribbons of sparkling seltzer into the water around her. Maybe she could use it. It was a wand, after all. She pulled it out and pointed it at Jake.

"Wait!" Cai yanked Jess's arm back. "Remember what happened last time you pointed that at somebody?"

True, *the point-and-shoot* method might just as easily roast Jake as save him. Jess lowered it. Still, she had to try. As she drew the wand back underwater, she waved it underneath Jake and Lilliana and silently wished for them to live.

Nothing happened.

There were no shooting stars, no lightning bolts. The wand just fizzled the same way it had earlier. Salt water was probably shorting it out. It was as useless as she was, and they were a million miles from the nearest paramedic. All she knew how to do was blow things up. "Maggie, can't you do something?"

Maggs shook her head and looked at Jess with an expression so hopeless Jess couldn't bear to see it. Not now. Not ever.

She jammed the wand back into her pants loop. "Listen up, Jake! You can't die," she warned her motionless brother. "Do you hear me? You can't. I won't let you."

Because ordering people around was all Jess had left.

Naneth groaned and struggled to lift her head high enough to peer over the side of the SAV. Her head wobbled, and she was obviously having trouble focusing. When she finally saw what was going on, her face crumpled. "Oh, no," she gasped and hid her trembling mouth behind her hand. "Please, no." Naneth collapsed again.

Jake's Battle

Jake awoke to the sound of his sister shouting at him. "You can't die."

When she took that tone, it usually meant she was about to hit him. He tried to shield himself from her blow, but his arm wouldn't move.

Odd.

Jess didn't hit him.

Was that Cai sobbing?

Why was he floating in water? Nothing made sense. His eyelids fluttered open.

Maggie was leaning over him. Her face looked all puffy and red. Anxious. "Jess," she yelped. "Look! He's awake."

Jess pushed closer. "You're not dead." She sounded surprised.

He wanted to answer, wanted to say something to reassure her. Tease her maybe. But his mouth felt like it had been stuffed with burnt leaves, and his brain seemed unable to mash syllables into words.

"Welcome back, man." That was Mark.

Back from where? Jake struggled to focus. *Water._*They all seemed to be standing in the sea, and Mark was on the other side of...

"Lilliana!" It came out like a garbled croak.

"Don't move," Mark warned.

But he had to. Something was wrong with her.

"Hold still!" Jess ordered, "Or you'll hurt her more."

Maggie's gaze directed him to their wrists. He and Lilliana were holding hands. No, they weren't. Their wrists were strapped together. Why?

He closed his eyes and stilled his wildly racing thoughts. Then he realized exactly what she'd done. In fact, he *felt* her blood coursing through him.

Strange, that he could be so acutely aware of it. No one could actually feel blood flowing through their veins, *could they*? And even if they could, they wouldn't know the difference between their own blood cells and someone else's. And yet, with his eyes closed Jake recognized her blood moving through him, silky, tingling, infusing his tissues with strength.

Incredible.

But she...

His eyes flew open. Water softly lapped against his cheek as he turned his head to look at her. Lilliana's skin looked nearly transparent. An unnatural shade of yellow tinged her lips.

"Is she okay? Is she—" Jake couldn't say the words, didn't even want to think the words.

Mark didn't answer. The strain pulling on his face was answer enough.

Then Jake remembered—a fire snake biting him, its poison suffocating him, paralyzing him. He'd managed to cut off the snake's head just before blacking out. Lilliana must be absorbing the venom.

"Stop her!" He raised their wrists. "Pull us apart. You can't let her do this."

Maggie shook her head and gently pushed their wrists back down. "Half of her blood is inside you. If we separate you now, she'll have no chance at all."

"No!" he yelled in a half growl, half moan—an animal's scream. He wanted to rip their wrists apart and shake her back to life. At the same time, he knew such a deadly stupid act would kill her.

He breathed in and out in frantic rapid blasts. His pulse pounded through his veins. The faster his heart beat, the more aware he became of her life force flowing through him. Intensely aware. She was giving up her energy to save him.

So Jake pumped it back to her in violent, desperate bursts.

He would not allow her to die!

The minute she gave her blood to him, surrendering what little oxygen and vitality she had left, he sent his revitalized blood gushing back to her. He didn't know how he was able to control it. Didn't know how he could see inside himself with such clarity. He only knew that he could feel every artery, every vein, every muscle in his body. If he tried hard enough, he thought he might even be able to feel hers. He forced his strength into her.

But it wasn't working. He had to do more. "Give her to me. Let me stand."

Jess tightened her grip on him. "No. You're wounded. Too weak."

"Jess, I can do this." His jaw knotted up, impatient with his sister's stubbornness. "I *have* to."

It was the truth. Strength was coming from somewhere, flooding into him. He wasn't just stealing it from Lilliana. It seemed to be coming from everywhere. Air. Earth. *Water!*

"But, you can't. Your veins are…" Jess's nose scrunched up. "Connected. What if they tear?"

He didn't have time for this. "I know what I'm doing."

"Trust him, Jess." Good ole Maggs. She was already raising his shoulders, carefully guiding his bound wrist into position. "He knows what he's doing."

Jess's brow pinched up in that argumentative scowl of hers, but she loosened her grip. Cai followed suit and let go of his legs. His feet dropped down until he stood on the silty bottom of the sea.

Mark shifted Lilliana into Jake's free arm. "Got her?"

Jake nodded, ignoring the dizziness threatening to undo his balance. He held her close, carefully floating her atop the water, moving away from the others, farther out, until they were so deep it took almost no effort to hold her up. Waves rocked them gently. Her hair drifted on the surface. The dark silken strands washed around her like a soft funeral wreath.

He hid her from the others, cradling her against his chest, mindful of their wrists but even more mindful of the stillness in her face. "Don't leave me," he whispered next to her ear. "Come back."

He waited, watching her face for a response. A flicker of life. Anything.

Even wounded and with scarcely a breath left in her, she was achingly beautiful. And yet, the part of her he loved most was far, far away, beyond his reach. He pressed his lips against the heartbreaking whiteness of her cheek. "Lilliana," he called and held her tighter.

Out of the corner of his eye, he saw a glimmer of gold under the surface. The sea dragon circled them, gently breathing warmth into the water enveloping them. If only the dragon's heat would warm her back to life.

Her cheek remained cold.

"Stay with me." Jake kissed her. Touching her lips gently at first and then with more fervor, demanding that she live, forcing her to feel how much he loved her.

"Please," he begged, their lips still touching. "Live." His tears trailed onto her lips, adding salt and bitterness to his plea.

A school of minnows, sympathizing with his anguish, churned the water around them. Light caught on their scales, sending streaks of silver radiating through the gently rocking waves. Small fish bumped against his legs, nudged Lilliana's shoulders and arms, pattering the two of them with tiny solemn kisses.

Jake glanced away from Lilliana's face just long enough to see that the water around them bubbled with thousands of tiny sparkling lights. Underwater fireworks.

Beside him, a trio of bright blue fish leapt out of the water, weaving through Lilliana's hair as they swam.

When he looked down again, her eyes fluttered open.

Impossible.

Jake's heart stopped.

He couldn't breathe.

Then he remembered he *had* to breathe. For her. So he did.

He had to clamp his lips between his teeth to keep from shouting and jumping for joy. With an awkward gurgle, he choked back a laugh. Because it was that, or sob. And he sure as heck didn't want to blubber, not now that she was going to live. She *was* going to make it. He could feel her heart beginning to beat stronger.

So he let himself laugh. Except it came out as a shuddering, sort of gagging thing. Totally embarrassing. He shook his head, knowing his eyes were watering. "I'm not crying."

She gave him a weak smile. "No?"

God, it was good to see her smile!

Jake gave up trying to hold back. He kissed her as gently as he could. Her pulse quickened with his. His soft kiss turned urgent, no longer gentle. He never wanted to lose her again. If she hadn't needed to breathe, he might not have stopped kissing her. Ever.

"The others—they're worried," he whispered beside her mouth, relishing the feel of her breath on his cheek. "Waiting."

She nodded. Jake sighed and turned around, carrying her back to them. "She's alive."

They shouted for joy. It seemed like all of Ayre cheered.

Maybe that was his imagination, too many football games. Although, their simple cries of relief were ten thousand times more gratifying than a winning touchdown.

Naneth slogged slowly through the waves, braced by Mark and Cai, valiantly trying to reach her granddaughter, crying and babbling in a strange language.

But when she saw Jess, she stopped short. "The Wand." Naneth looked as surprised at seeing her wand hanging off Jess's pants as she did to seeing her granddaughter alive and plumbed up to a human.

Mark put his arm around Jess. "She took it away from Gryndelyn and used it to…" he hesitated. "To send her to another zip code. She saved us."

Naneth's brows drew together. "How? Humans can't–"

She broke off as Jake and Lilliana neared her. Wincing, she reached out and smoothed a lock of wet hair from Lilliana's pale cheek. "Oh, my dear." Words seemed to fail her then, but the light in Naneth's face brightened and the vines in her hair began to green up.

Maggie pointed at the water and laughed. "You've got fish following you, Jake."

"Not me. Her." Lilliana was a water fairy. Naturally, fish loved her. Thousands of them danced in the water around his legs.

"I'm not so sure." Jess tilted her head sideways, inspecting their underwater entourage.

Jake shrugged, unconcerned about the fish, or even the sea serpent rising out of the water. Although, it *was* strange how, without looking back, Jake knew exactly what the golden serpent was doing. He had no idea how he knew that the low trumpeting call was the serpent's way of saying good-bye before it dove under and headed for deep waters. Not good-bye exactly, it was more like *farewell until later*.

He shook it off. "Help me get her ashore."

JOURNAL
Day 21:

Last night Napoleon brought us a note from the Fairy Council. The Council has heard rumors that Gryndelyn survived Jess blasting her with the wand. Naneth suspected as much, and now she's worried. She wants her sister to be okay, but she doesn't want the fairy realm plunged into war.

Jess doesn't think anyone could survive what the wand did to Gryndelyn. We still haven't figured out how Jess was able to wield the queen's wand. Sometimes Naneth squints at Jess and stares for a really long time as if she's trying to see something or remember something, but she can't quite get it into focus. Jess insists the wand must have some sort of a switch on the handle that she accidentally triggered.

Naneth shakes her head and says, "That's impossible."

Then Jess teases Naneth about how ridiculous it is for a *fairy* to think *anything* is impossible.

As for me, I have my suspicions about Jess. I've discovered humans have a magic all of their own.

They've certainly changed everything in my life. Because of them I'm not alone anymore. I have family. Naneth is here every night. My uncle Samuel comes to visit on Sundays. Maggie, Cai, and Jess usually hang out here after school. Sometimes, on the weekends, Naneth lets them go with her to tend Ayre. Maggie is fascinated by the mythical creatures there, even some of the dangerous ones, and Cai takes pictures of them. If I don't stay on my toes and remember to sprinkle her camera with *elin-gíl* every time she leaves, someday a picture of Jake riding a certain giant griffin might end up in the newspaper.

Yesterday Naneth had to face the Elf Council because of all the damage our battle did in Ayre. Although she'd already patched up the scorch marks, smoothed out the lumpy places on the plains and made the grass grow back. She tried to dry out the gigantic mud hole where I trapped the lava monster, but unfortunately it remains soggy. She convinced the council that a bog would be a good addition to Ayre. Unfortunately, the big crevice won't go away either. It keeps reopening and animals fall in. Just last week she and Maggie had to fish out a very angry family of Persian hares. Not an easy task.

I have to go soon. Any minute, Jake will be here at my cave. My wings haven't grown back completely yet, so he insists on driving me to and from school every day. Yes, I still go to school because even though Jess is not nearly so angry, I'm still on assignment with her. I think Jake and I both know I could simply materialize in front of the school. I don't want to though, because it's my very favorite thing to see him at my door first thing in the morning, all sleepy eyed and mussy haired. What I love most is the way his face changes the minute he sees me. Suddenly, he looks wide awake, his hard features soften, and then he smiles. *Magic.* Jake's smile is like the sun dawning over the ocean. Full of warmth and goodness.

My blood changed him. I can feel it. Jake is no longer completely human, but he's not Fairy, either. I don't know what that means about our future together. I only know three things: I love him. I will always love him. And we have today. That's enough magic for a lifetime. Time to go—

He's here!

We hope you had fun reading *Diary of A Teenage Fairy Godmother*. If you enjoyed this book please **lend** your copy to a friend, or **recommend** it on discussion boards or to your reader group.

We like reading **your reviews!** Reviews help other readers discover your favorite books. If you write one for *Diary Of A Teenage Fairy Godmother* please let us know in an email to: **Kathleen@KathleenBaldwin.com**

We would like to THANK YOU personally and send you a **sneak peak** into the next book.

Contact and info at: **www.kathleenbaldwin.com**

Printed in Great Britain
by Amazon.co.uk, Ltd.,
Marston Gate.